WOLFESHIELD

A MEDIEVAL ROMANCE

BY KATHRYN LE VEQUE

PART OF THE DE WOLFE PACK GENERATIONS SERIES

Sometimes, men are impulsive in life and love. When Ronan de Wolfe, son of James de Wolfe (*A Wolfe Among Dragons*), marries young and impulsively, the consequences will prove to be disastrous when he meets the love of his life.

Will de Wolfe honor stand the test? Or will true love crush a man of good character?

Ronan de Wolfe, the mild-mannered but powerful son of James de Wolfe, married on a whim against the advice of his father and grandfather. He married into the powerful Northumberland de Grey family, a family that rivals the House of de Wolfe in both strength and wealth. Coerced by a cunning de Grey father, Ronan found himself married before he knew what had happened.

The years pass. Ronan is married and miserable. His wife has lovers, shaming both houses. Children are born, but they are not Ronan's. With some measure of peace on the England/Scotland borders, Ronan amuses himself in local tournaments to get away from his horrible home life. Along with his best friend, they enjoy celebrity status of the great tournament champions, but when his friend is mortally wounded and asks Ronan to take care of his pregnant wife, the situation changes drastically.

Ronan meets the woman he should have married.

Isabeth de Brito is a beautiful woman from a minor noble

family. Pregnant with her dead husband's child, she and Ronan form a strong friendship as he tends to her every need. But in Ronan's case, it is much more. Friendship turns to love. When Ronan's petty, foolish wife realizes Ronan is paying attention to another woman, innocent as it is, the claws come out. Her powerful family can ruin Isabeth and her family – permanently.

When Isabeth's father is forced into finding Isabeth another husband, Ronan can only stand by and watch the woman he loves as she is courted by another man.

Will there be a happily ever after for Ronan and Isabeth? Or will Ronan have to watch his love marry another?

It's another wild ride for the de Wolfe Pack Generations.

De Wolfe Pack Generations/ Grandsons of de Wolfe series:

WolfeHeart (Markus de Wolfe)

WolfeStrike (Thomas "Tor" de Wolfe)

WolfeSword (Cassius de Wolfe)

WolfeBlade (Andreas de Wolfe)

WolfeLord (William "Will" de Wolfe)

WolfeShield (Ronan de Wolfe – son of James/Blayth and Rose)

WolfeBorn (Titus de Wolfe – son of Patrick and Bridey – 2023)

WolfeDagger (Gareth de Wolfe – son of Troy and Rhoswyn – 2023)

WolfeFire (Maddock de Wolfe – son of James/Blayth and Asmara – 2023)

De Wolfe Pack Generations

The grandsons of William de Wolfe are referred to as "The de Wolfe Cubs". There are more than forty of them, both biological and adopted, and each young man is sworn to his powerful and rich legacy. When each grandson comes of age and is knighted, he tattoos the de Wolfe standard onto some part of his body. It is a rite of passage and it is that mark that links these young men together more than blood.

More than brotherhood.

It is the de Wolfe birthright.

The de Wolfe Pack standard is meant to be worn with honor, with pride, and with resilience, for there is no more recognizable standard in Medieval England. To shame the Pack is to have the tattoo removed, never to be regained.

This is their world.

Welcome to the Cub Generation.

De Wolfe Motto: *Fortis in arduis*

Strength in times of trouble

AUTHOR'S NOTE

Now, it's Ronan's turn.

We met Ronan in a few of the de Wolfe Pack Generations books, most prominently in WolfeStrike because his younger sister had been wronged. We got a taste of impulsive Ronan, fearless when it comes to defending his family, which I love about him. But, let's be honest – writing a de Wolfe Pack book gives me so much joy!

One of the best things about the de Wolfe Pack Generations books is the fact that I get to set them in a time period when William de Wolfe is still alive. If I'm lucky enough, Paris is around, too. Ronan, however, was still a young man when his grandfather passed away in his mid-90s (at a VERY ripe old age), so although William and Kieran are in the prologue, by the time the bulk of the story comes along, they've long passed away.

Ronan is the first son of James de Wolfe, who later became Blayth (*A Wolfe Among Dragons*), and Blayth's book is one of my favorites of all time. James and his first wife, Rose, were married in *A Joyous de Wolfe Christmas*, so if you haven't read that novella yet, please do so. Ronan is very much like his father, and very much a de Wolfe, but he's got a lot of Kieran Hage in him, too. As you'll recall, Kieran is his maternal grandfather, so he has Kieran's size and strength. He's very much a mix of both grandfathers, his father, and his paternal grandmother, Jordan, so he's got a lot of great traits in him, but I think you'll find he's mostly got Kieran in him. The gentle giant, so to speak. But he also has a tad of his grandmother,

Jemma, in him in his rash decision making (at least he did when he was younger) and that has gotten him into trouble.

There are some fun things in this tale and, as always, I point out a few. One of them is a Medieval version of a Scotch egg. If you don't know what that is, a Scotch egg is a hard-boiled egg surrounded by sausage meat and then coated with breadcrumbs. It's deep fried to produce a yummy delicacy. However, in my research, I came across a Medieval version, which is basically the hard-boiled egg smeared in fish paste and breadcrumbs before being fried. I think I like the sausage version better, personally.

As always, I have a blend of fact and fiction in my novels and this one is no exception. One of the historical "facts" in this novel is the de Grey family, a very prominent Medieval family. There is a mention of Portepool Manor in this book which was, in fact, a real location in London for the de Grey household. Lady Jane Grey, the "Nine Day Queen", was a descendant of this family. And, of course, there's Earl Grey tea.

There are several references to *A Wolfe Among Dragons* in this novel, so if you haven't read it yet, you must do so. Not only to help you in understanding some of the references, but also because I think it's one of the best books I've ever written. It was a book that I had never expected to write because the hero of the book was dead according to de Wolfe history. But… never say never in my world and James de Wolfe rose from the ashes of death in *A Wolfe Among Dragons*. Make sure to grab a copy if you haven't read it.

I've got some Easter eggs in this one, too. For example – a mention of a Dragonblade series knight as a young man. Just a brief mention and nothing more. There are also mentions of scenes in past de Wolfe books. See if you can pick them out.

The usual pronunciation guide:

Isabeth – EEsa-beth

Middlesbrough (for the Americans!): Middles-bruh

And with that, I'll end my notes and introduce you to Ronan and Isabeth, a couple I have become very fond of. I hope you will, too!

Hugs,

*'Tis thee, my dear, that I adore
And will, my darling, forever more.*

PROLOGUE

"I SAW HIM, William. Ramming a sword into the chests of injured Scots and then running off. We need to find him before someone else does."

Kieran Hage was covered in gore and filth from where a band of Scots had pushed him down and tried to beat him to death. But Kieran was strong, and big, and he'd managed to get to his feet and break a couple of necks before the Scots went off to find another victim. In a battle against the English, there were always plenty of targets for their rage.

And apparently, now there was an unexpected target in their midst.

William looked at Kieran with confusion.

"Repeat what you just said to me," he said, keeping an eye out on the fighting around him as he held a conversation. "Say again."

Kieran took a deep breath. He was an old man these days, fighting in wars he should not be fighting in because William was fighting. William de Wolfe never went to battle without his second in command, so no matter how poorly Kieran felt, he was at William's side, always.

He had been for forty years.

But this… this was something different.

"I saw Ronan," he said succinctly. Then, he jabbed a finger towards the field of battle. "James' lad is out there, somewhere, killing off men and then running and hiding. He must have followed us from Castle Questing."

William's jaw dropped as Kieran's news sank in. "He's only eight years of age," he said. "He would never do such a thing."

"I have two eyes, William, and you have only one. I know what I saw."

That was true. William had lost his left eye many years ago in battle. He held up a hand of apology. "I do not dispute your sight," he said. "I'm simply in disbelief that an eight-year-old lad would follow us into battle."

Kieran took another deep breath, a smile flickering across his lips. "He has de Wolfe and Hage blood in him," he said. "He was a knight the day he was born. He is out here, fighting. We must find our grandson before the Scots do."

That was an understatement. They were near Canonbie, Scotland where the large Douglas Clan had pushed through the border and attacked Carlisle Castle because a soldier from Carlisle had killed the son of an important Douglas man. This was an attack of vengeance and the garrison commander at Carlisle had called in reinforcements. Armies as far away as Castle Questing and Northwood Castle, closer to Berwick, answered the call.

And, evidently, one eight-year-old boy.

"Tell Scott and Troy," William said, referring to his older sons and the boy's uncles. "And anyone else in the family that you happen to see. Tell them to keep an eye out for Ronan and hold him for me. I'm going to give that boy a beating he'll not soon forget."

Kieran, who was more of a soft touch with children and grandchildren, put a hand on William's arm. "Nay," he said quietly. "Do not do that. This is the life he was born for and he is eager to fulfill his destiny. You cannot fault him for that."

William was snappish. "Nay, I cannot fault him, but I also cannot lose him," he said, a hint of grief flickering in his face. "He is all I have left of his father. Should he foolishly lose his life out here, then James' legacy is ended. It will be as if he never existed."

Kieran grunted softly. "William," he said softly. "Ronan has a sister. Isabella looks just like James. He will live on through her. But to your point, I cannot lose Ronan, either. We must find him."

William softened, just for a moment, knowing that Kieran's daughter had married his son, James, who had perished in Wales the year before. The de Wolfe and Hage families were so intertwined that William and Kieran shared several grandchildren. But more importantly, their rebel grandson was the eldest offspring of a son William still wasn't over losing. He never would be.

Nor would Kieran.

That pain ran deep.

"I will not beat him," he finally said, forcing himself to calm. "But find him, Kieran. We *must* find him."

Kieran nodded, heading off to find any knights he could to help in the search. William did the same, heading off towards the west where the sun was beginning to set, bathing the battlefield in rays of red and gold light that made it seem as if the entire world were bathed in blood. Men were dying all around them, mostly Scots, and as William walked, he picked up soldiers who naturally gravitated around England's great Wolfe of the Border to both protect him and obey any commands he might have.

But his commands were most confusing at this moment.

Find Ronan!

Men began to spread out, heading towards the outskirts of the battle to search for the errant young lad as William came to a halt. He scratched his chin wearily, trying to think like an eight-year-old boy who was determined to find glory. They were on the north side of Carlisle Castle, between the fortress and the river, and he could see a thicket of trees near the river's edge.

If I was a lad and trying to hide, I might hide there.

He mounted his battle-hardened steed. Spurring his warhorse straight through the battle that was beginning to wane, William had to fight off a couple of Scots who came at him, but they were easily subdued or brushed aside as he went. He headed straight for the trees, now lit up by the brilliant sunset. As he drew close, he could see another horse and rider in the trees, realizing it was Kieran. The man had the same idea he'd had.

He plunged into the brush.

It was cool and damp, moisture from the river heavy in the air. William caught up to Kieran, holding a finger to his lips in a silent gesture as the two of them fanned out, heading southeast. There was movement in that direction that could quite possibly be a young man hiding out from his grandfathers. It was thicker in this area, with plenty of places to hide, and as the two of them created a sweep with the intention of flushing Ronan from the brush, several Scots suddenly appeared instead.

The fight was on.

William took a club to the chest almost immediately. His shield was still slung over his left knee and his broadsword was sheathed on the side of his saddle, so the Scotsman flying out of a tree and clobbering him on the chest took him by surprise. Off-guard, William went toppling off his horse.

Because of the heavy foliage, it was difficult for Kieran to get to William. He could see the Scots attacking him as he lay on the ground and, on horseback, Kieran was at a disadvantage for once. He couldn't maneuver his animal through the saplings and bushes to get to him, which spurred his panic. He began kicking men in the face and using his broadsword to chop through the branches as William finally lurched to his feet.

Without his sword or shield, William was vulnerable. He had daggers and other weapons on his body, so he unsheathed two wicked-looking daggers and began slashing and stabbing at anything that came close. Men were losing eyes or receiving enormous gashes to the arm as The Wolfe cut and chopped and gored. They began falling away only to regroup and make attempts to overwhelm him again. William was in a fight for his life, with Kieran nearly upon him, when another figure rushed forward from the thicket.

The figure was small but as fast as lightning. He had a large dagger with him which, upon closer inspection, was really a small sword. He rammed it into the backs of two Scotsmen before the others, realizing there was some kind of tempest in their midst, turned on the little figure as it darted in and out of the foliage. It was enough of a distraction for William to recover. A couple of limbs were hacked off and one man had his neck broken when Kieran reached down and squeezed, and that was enough for the Scots to take off running.

As William stood in the middle of the carnage, breathing

heavily with exertion, Kieran dismounted his steed and rushed to his side.

"Are you injured?" he asked, concerned.

William shook his head, wiping a bit of blood from his upper lip. "Nay," he said. "I am not. Are you?"

Kieran shook his head. "Nay," he said. Then, he started looking around. "Ronan? Show yourself."

He boomed the words and they echoed off the trees. Both William and Kieran looked around them, looking for that small figure they knew to be around, but no one stepped out of the foliage.

"Ronan," William said loudly. "I promised Kee that I would not beat you, but if you do not show yourself immediately and I am forced to locate you, I could quite possibly change my mind."

"Kee" was what all of Kieran's grandchildren called him. William and Kieran waited a few more seconds with no response before looking at each other, trying to figure out what to do. Either Ronan was ignoring them or he was out of earshot. As William sighed sharply, with frustration, a lone figure emerged from the thicket several feet away.

Ronan de Wolfe appeared, dressed in clothing that blended in with his surroundings. He had a brown tunic and hose on, shoes, and a scarf over his head that covered up his blond hair. His face was smeared with dirt and, as he approached, they could see that the boy was trying not to weep. He was wiping his eyes and smudging dirt all over his neck and hands.

But William was unmoved.

"Well?" he said. "What do you have to say for yourself? You did not have permission to come to Carlisle."

Ronan's lower lip was trembling. "I… I had to come, Poppy," he said. "I had to fight."

"Why?"

"Because my father is not here to fight with you. I must do it in his place."

Those simple words were like daggers through William's heart. They also managed to shred any irritation he had at the young man who was clearly trying to take over where his father had left off. He looked at Kieran, who was gazing back at him with a rather compassionate expression and, in that moment, William knew any anger was futile.

He sighed again. But this time, it was without much force.

"Come here," he said softly, motioning to Ronan. "Come to me."

Ronan did, still wiping his eyes, and William grunted as he took a knee beside the lad. Kneeling wasn't as easy as it used to be with his old body these days and most especially after the beating he had just taken. He was fortunate that he could walk at all.

"Your intentions were honorable," he said, a big hand on the boy's shoulder. "It is noble to want to fill your father's shoes. But right now, it is a little too early for you to do so. You still have much to learn when it comes to battle and I fear you may be hurt or even killed if you try to fight before you are ready. Ronan, it would destroy me if something happened to you. I lost your father. I cannot lose you, too. Do you understand that?"

Ronan's lower lip was still trembling. "Please do not be angry with me."

"I am not angry. But I am concerned."

Ronan looked up at Kieran. "Are you angry?"

Kieran shook his head. "Nay, lad," he said. "But your mother and grandmother and I would be very sad if something happened to you."

Ronan sniffled, trying not to sob, as he returned his attention to William. "I only wanted to do what my father would do," he said. "He taught me to fight. He showed me how to use a sword and I know how."

With that, he lifted the small blade he was carrying and it took William a moment to realize that it was the same blade he'd given his son, James, when he'd been a young lad. Many years ago, his Jamie had learned to fight with that very weapon.

More daggers sliced through William's heart.

"As I said, your intentions were noble," he said, taking the sword from Ronan and holding it up to look at it. He smiled faintly. "I remember when I gave your father this sword. Would you like to hear the story?"

Ronan nodded. "He said he had to fight for it."

William chuckled, standing up wearily, the little sword still in his hand. "Fight, indeed," he said. "Your father has three older brothers in Uncle Scott, Uncle Troy, and Uncle Atty. When your father was about five years of age, he decided that he very much wanted his own sword even though I told him he was too young. Uncle Atty was around eight years of age and your uncles, Scott and Troy, were nearly ten years of age. They already had swords that I had given them and your father decided to steal all of them, which was a mistake. They ganged up on him."

Ronan's lower lip was no longer trembling as he listened. He very much admired his uncles, Scott and Troy and Patrick, the latter who went by the family nickname of Atty.

"What happened?" he asked with concern.

William looked at Kieran, a smile playing on his lips, and

Kieran took the hint. He'd actually been the one to see the situation unfold. "Your father was everyone's favorite child," he said. "He was happy and kind and brilliant and everyone loved him. He was also manipulative when he wanted something. Your three uncles were in the stable yard practicing with their swords when your father ran out to tell them that your grandfather had summoned them. Without question, your uncles went to find your grandfather and when they were gone, your father picked up their three swords where they had left them and ran off with them."

Ronan's eyes widened. "What did they do?"

Kieran grinned, glancing at William as he spoke. "I was in the stables with a lame horse when your father came running in with three small swords clutched against his breast," he said. "He ran into one of the stalls and hid. I did not speak to him or ask him why, but not long after, your uncles came looking for him. Not knowing why, I told them where he was and they ambushed him in the stall."

"Did they hurt my father?"

Kieran scratched his neck, his eyes taking on a distant cast as he remembered the situation. "Your father was, if nothing else, a fighter," he said. "He knew they would come for him, so he was ready. He threw horse dung at them, hitting Atty in the mouth with it, so as Atty is off spitting out horse dung and vomiting, your father whacked Scott on the shins with a piece of kindling, so hard that Scott fell over and lay there, moaning and holding his leg. That left Troy, who wasn't so apt to get close to James now that two of his brothers were down."

Ronan was hanging on every word. "What happened?"

Kieran's grin returned. "Your father was able to negotiate a truce," he said. "He would get to use Troy's sword for an hour every day. Troy agreed, but when James lowered his guard to hand back the swords, Troy grabbed him and hauled him out of the stall. He was preparing to tie your father to a post but I had heard the entire thing. I heard Troy make a deal for peace and I saw him break it. I gathered up all four brothers and made them march into your father's solar and tell them what happened."

Attention shifted to William. "What did you do, Poppy?" Ronan asked.

William, too, was remembering that day long ago. He remembered furious Troy, injured Scott, and pale Patrick. And he remembered James, the littlest, firm and resolute that he'd made a deal his brother had tried to break.

"I listened to each lad's story and I listened to Kieran's version of events," he said. "In the end, I agreed that James had been unfairly treated. But I also sided with his brothers in that James had stolen the swords under deception in the first place, but that did not mitigate the fact that Troy had broken a treaty. I declared that James was to be punished, as were Troy and Scott and Atty, and their penance was to clean out the stables, every stall, for an entire week."

Ronan pointed to the sword. "But how did my father finally get his sword?"

William looked at the little sword still in his hand and chuckled. "Because Scott and Troy and Atty made sure that week was horrible for James," he said. "They made him do the bulk of the work when no one was supervising them and they even rubbed the horse shite into his hair. They tortured him for the entire week and thought I did not know it, so at the end of the week and in full view of your uncles, I presented your father with this sword. He received a new one, whereas your uncles had ones that others had used. They were quite furious. But after that, they did not torture your father again. I think they learned their lesson."

Kieran snorted. "They learned their lesson when James took after them with that sword," he said. "Every time they turned around, there he was, attacking them with the weapon. I think Scott still bears the scars."

William started laughing. "It was no less than they deserved," he said. Then, he handed the sword back to Ronan, hilt-first. "You are very much like your father, Ronan. You are eager and bright and determined to fulfill your destiny as a de Wolfe. But now is not your time, lad. Someday, but not now."

Ronan took the sword back, looking at the blade, now colored with age. "My father is dead," he said quietly. "I must fight in his stead, Poppy. I can fight. I am strong, I swear it. I will stand by your side and I will never leave you."

William put a trencher-sized hand on Ronan's head. "You will never leave me regardless," he said. "You are James' son. I look into your face and I see him. I see that boy who wanted to fight so badly and I see the man who was a brilliant knight, and I miss him every single day. I want you to fight with me, but I also want you to grow up first and learn how to fight like your father did. You are his legacy, Ronan, and it is a great legacy you carry. You do him justice by following the army and fighting the Scots, but you will do him greater justice by learning to be smart in battle. You cannot always outfight an enemy, but you can outwit him. That is what you must learn."

Ronan was back to trembling lips as he realized his grandfather wasn't going to let him fight at his young age. He wiped at his eyes furiously with the back of his hand.

"But you will let me fight at your side, someday?" he asked.

William smiled faintly. "I would have no other," he said.

"You will be my shield, Ronan. A protector of this great empire that you are part of. But you must have time to earn that right. Does that make sense?"

Ronan understood, sort of. As William headed off to find his horse, Ronan looked at Kieran, who smiled and put his hand on the boy's shoulder.

"I told Poppy that you were a knight the moment you were born," he said. "You have the blood of two of England's greatest knights flowing through your veins. You were never meant to be anything else. But Poppy is right – you must give yourself time to earn that right."

Ronan cocked his head. "But what does that mean? Aren't I not earning that right by killing Scots?"

Kieran's dark eyes glimmered. "In a sense," he said. "But it is more than killing Scots. It is learning how to bear your legacy with excellence. Having the rare distinction of de Wolfe and Hage blood, you are already more elite than most. You must learn and grow so you can become the knight we all know you are born to be. And you must not rush things."

Ronan was not exactly sure what Kieran meant, but his grandfather was a wise man. He always knew everything. Ronan let him lead him out of the foliage, back towards Carlisle Castle as the battle around them waned. The sun had nearly set by the time they reached the gatehouse of the great, red-stoned castle, but Ronan was still lingering on what his grandfathers had told him.

It is learning how to bear your legacy with excellence.

God help him, he hoped he knew what that meant.

What he didn't know was how many years it would take him to find out.

PART ONE
MIDDLESBROUGH

CHAPTER ONE

The month of May
Year of Our Lord 1312
Middlesbrough Tournament

T HE SNAP OF a broken lance reverberated throughout the lists and shards of wood, like little knives, went flying.

The roar of the crowd was deafening.

Ronan was reeling from a very hard hit by his opponent, who was an old knight who didn't much care for things like manners or rules. He was an old salt who simply wanted to win any possible way he could, and that included using an illegal move that nearly sent his lance through Ronan's neck. Had Ronan been any slower, it would have. Instead, he was able to lift his left arm, which raised the *ecranche,* or strapped-on shield, at the last moment and deflect the blow.

But the concussion nearly blew the top of his head off.

It was difficult to know where the roaring of the crowd began and the ringing in his ears ended. It all seemed to blend together. He could hear the crowd mingled with the voices of his own men, who were now steadying his horse and pushing him back up into a seated position. He didn't even realize that he'd been listing dangerously to the left.

But someone shoved him right back into an upright position on the saddle.

"You're going to have to destroy him or he will destroy you first," the man next to him was saying. "Ronan, do you hear me?"

Someone grabbed him by the arm and gave him a shake. Ronan blinked away the stars that were still dancing before his eyes. He could see his cousins all around him; Edward Hage, his brothers Axel and Christian, plus Titus de Wolfe and Gareth de Wolfe. All seasoned men, all competing in the Middlesbrough games like a bunch of bloodthirsty knaves on their first kill. Now that Ronan had been knocked silly by the old knight, there was fire in their eyes.

"I hear you, Eddie," Ronan muttered, shaking off the bells and rubbing his eyes. "You lot smell the blood, but it will not be mine. I will do what needs to be done now that my opponent has shown me his true colors."

"Ronan?" A shout came from behind and they all turned to see a knight riding up on horseback. "Did he hurt you, lad?"

Ronan grinned weakly at the heavy-set knight dressed in expensive armor. "I am afraid he did not knock me out of the competition, Dyce," he said. "You'll have to do that yourself if you want your path to the prize made clear."

Sir Dyce de Brito grinned at the man who had been his best friend for the past several years. Big, white teeth parted his dark beard. "If we end up going against each other later today, that can be arranged," he said. "Meanwhile, stop behaving like a weak woman. De Whinfell tried to take your head off. Answer the man and show him what you're made of."

Ronan shook his head one last time to rid himself of his buzzing head and took a deep breath. Grasping the reins with one hand, he held out the other.

"Lance!" he bellowed.

Someone slapped a lance into his gloved hand and he shifted his grip, taking hold. He could feel the weight of the perfectly balanced joust pole, one that was twelve feet long with a great wolf's head on the tip, and put it into the "sling", which was in a tucked position on his right side. The field marshals, seeing that he was upright and armed, dropped the flag.

The opposing knights dug their spurs into the barrel-round flanks of their steeds and the crowd roared. The thunder that filled the arena as the horses charged towards each other was deafening, mingling with the screams of the crowd, building to a piercing proportion as the knights finally came within range of one another. Ronan, a man of considerable power and control, maintained the position of his lance even as his opponent tried to unseat him again. As he dodged the lance aiming for his head, he brought his around and caught his opponent in the throat.

De Whinfell toppled.

The crowd was on their feet, screaming and cheering for the knight who wore the de Wolfe tunic and flew de Wolfe standards over his encampment. Ronan de Wolfe, grandson of the great Wolfe of the Border, William de Wolfe, was a tournament favorite in the north. Muscular, blond, and brilliantly handsome, women threw favors and flowers at him as he made a sweeping pass in front of the stands. Maidens standing down by the barriers wept at the sight of him. One even fainted. Ronan brought all manner of reaction from eager women of all ages, but he ignored them all.

He had a wife.

Unfortunately.

"Well done, Roe," Edward said, grabbing hold of Ronan's horse as the man came out of the arena. "You showed the man your worth. He'll not doubt it again, nor will anyone else."

Ronan pulled his helm off, handing it to his squire, as he dismounted his horse with a good deal of effort. Truth be told, his ears were still ringing a little.

"If de Whinfell survives his fall and I see him anywhere around the encampment, I shall beat the man within an inch of his life," he muttered, loosening his heavy gauntlets. "The man tried to seriously disable me or worse. I intend to express my displeasure."

"Knocking him from his horse isn't enough?"

"It is not."

Edward smirked as Ronan cocked an eyebrow to prove how serious he was. His silent squire was in front of him, taking off his gauntlets and other pieces efficiently. Ronan handed over a few other things he could manage to remove, sending the big, blond young man off towards the encampment as his cousins gathered around to express their mutual opinions about de Whinfell's behavior and Ronan's reaction to it.

"De Whinfell came with some soldiers," Titus de Wolfe said. He was exceedingly tall, with a crown of dark hair and his grandfather's golden eyes. "If we are going to do it, I suggest we do it now while he's walking off your victory."

Ronan glanced at him. "He walked from the field? I hadn't noticed."

Titus smirked. "Aye, he walked from the field," he said. "He only has a couple of men with him. If we intend to send him a message, now would be the time."

Ronan scratched his damp head, looking at the men around him. Men he'd grown up with, men who were like brothers to him. Titus was the son of his Uncle Patrick, the Earl of Berwick, while Edward, Axel, and Christian were the sons of his Aunt Katheryn, twin of his own father, James. He knew, just by looking at that motley gang, that de Whinfell was in for a heaping of punishment.

He grinned.

"Ah," he murmured with satisfaction. "The de Wolfe Pack is determined to help me punish a fool. Well and good, I say. Let's do it now while my temper is still hot."

But Titus stopped him. "You'd better let us go alone," he said. "If you are identified as having roughed the man up, you could lose your place in the lists."

That was very true and Ronan didn't want to be eliminated, not when he was performing well and the purse was substantial. "Very well," he said reluctantly. "I shall remain behind while you take care of business."

Titus turned him in the direction of the encampment. "Go back to camp and let St. Hever strip you out of your protection," he said. "The little squire will be your alibi."

They were starting to walk away in a group and Ronan snorted. "That little squire is as good a knight as I've ever seen and he's only twelve years of age," he said pointedly. "Mark my words, lads – Kenneth St. Hever will be a great knight someday. Better than all of us, I am certain."

"Not better than me," Edward said, frowning. "Get out of here, Roe. Go back to the encampment and we shall tend to the vermin. When we are finished with him, he'll not do to another man what he tried to do to you."

Ronan just stood there and chuckled, watching his cousins

head back towards the arena, fanning out through the crowd as they went in search of their target. It was a large crowd and a large tournament, full of people milling about around the stands, the food vendors, and any number of other vendors that tended to follow the tournament circuit. This tournament was part of the usual northern circuit, but it was also sponsored by the Earl of Teesside because he fancied himself an avid tournament competitor.

Nothing like sponsoring one's own tournament to nearly guarantee a victory.

At least, that's what the old earl thought. That's what his son thought, also, but the son received a rude awakening that morning when he went up against a le Bec knight who promptly knocked him on his arse. After that debacle, the earl himself withdrew, pleading illness. The field was already narrowing down to the serious and skilled competitors, Ronan included.

His friend, Dyce, was competing next.

As the de Wolfe Pack went on the hunt, Ronan remained at the arena in spite of Titus' recommendation that he return to the encampment to the west. It was a sunny day, with a brisk breeze blowing in off the sea, whistling along the River Tees and snapping the standards that were flying over the tournament field, and he wanted to see the rest of the bouts. It was nearing the end of the day's competition and, tomorrow, the winners from today's rounds would compete against each other.

He wanted to see who he would be up against.

As Ronan watched, Dyce managed to do away with his opponent in three passes, barely eking by, in truth. Dyce was a great man, wise and intelligent, but he didn't have the physical prowess or skill that Ronan had. In fact, the truth was that Dyce didn't have much of anything other than a big heart and a big smile. But as he came off the field, Ronan congratulated him as if the man had just won the Olympic games. It was a very good day.

And a night that was about to get better.

CHAPTER TWO

"He's going to expect me to attend and I cannot disappoint him. He actually won his round today, so I must be at his side to show my support."

The little maid, who had asked her lady why she intended to attend the evening's feast when she was obviously not feeling well, simply shrugged to her lady's explanation. There was no use arguing with her when she'd set her mind to something. Gathering her combs and other tools of the trade, she headed off to pack them away.

Lady Isabeth de Brito watched her maid go, fighting off a smile at the woman's reaction of puzzlement and disapproval. The problem was that the maid had known her most of her life and theirs was a relationship that went beyond the usual maid/master boundaries. Old Gerta sometimes thought she was Isabeth's mother. She tried to push her around enough.

But this time, Isabeth would not be pushed.

Standing in the tent her husband's men had pitched for her, one that was comfortable and warm, with several layers of hides on the ground to keep the cold away, she stood in front of a polished bronze mirror, one her husband had purchased for her when they had visited London a few years back. It had come from lands far to the east, borne on the backs of donkeys and brought all the way to England. At least, the merchant from whom they'd purchased the item had made it sound most dramatic.

It *was* a rather nice mirror.

Isabeth inspected her reflection in the weak light. There were banks of candles lit, spitting dark smoke towards the ceiling, but Dyce wouldn't let her have an excess of candles lit because he was terrified she was going to knock one over and set the tent ablaze. Dyce had always been protective of her, even when she was a girl and he was a young knight who had served her father. Even back then, he'd watched out for her in what she'd considered a brotherly way until she came of age and he'd asked her father for her hand on that very birthday. Her father had been so thrilled at the offer that Isabeth had found herself betrothed before she'd ever been courted.

They'd married immediately.

Isabeth inspected the dress she was wearing, one Dyce had commissioned for her. He commissioned everything for her. He took care of every single thing. She'd never had to lift a finger the entire time she'd been married to the man. He was so deeply in love with her that he'd very nearly reduced her to a pretty little wife, sitting in a chair, not moving a muscle. He didn't want her exerting herself, thinking for herself, or even speaking for herself. He did it all for her, not because he was trying to control her, but because he simply wanted to please her.

Ten years of simply wanting to please her.

And what had she done for him? Not very much. She'd married him, she'd let the man bed her whenever he wanted to, surrendering to an act that she'd never taken much pleasure from. But she was his wife and she was dutiful. She loved Dyce like a brother – that had never changed – so intimacy with the man wasn't something she looked forward to. She'd lay beneath him, legs parted, as he thrust into her and told her how much he loved her.

She just tried not to fall asleep.

It was sad, really, and for as much as he liked to bed his lovely young wife, conception had been difficult for them. Almost ten years of marriage, four pregnancies, three of which had ended in miscarriages. Now, she was carrying her fourth child and not yet three months into a pregnancy that had left her feeling weak and weary. Dyce hadn't wanted her to come to Middlesbrough at all, but she had insisted. He asked for so very little and the tournament was important to him.

So, she came to support him.

Old Gerta was just going to have to understand that.

"There has never been a woman more beautiful than you."

Distracted from her thoughts, Isabeth looked over her shoulder to see Dyce standing just inside the tent flap. He was out of his armor at this point, having been bathed by his squire and manservant, and dressed in his finest de Brito tunic. He smiled at her when their eyes met, his big, white teeth surrounded by his black beard. The hair on his head, and his beard, were black and coarse, his eyes of the darkest brown. He wasn't an unhandsome man in the least, but age had not been kind to him. What had been muscle in his younger years was now somewhat flabby and he became tired easily. Still, he was one of the kindest men Isabeth had ever known and she was fond of him.

She smiled in return.

"You are supposed to say that," she said, turning back to the mirror and inspecting her belly in her reflection. "But the truth is that I'm growing larger."

It wasn't the truth, merely wishful thinking. "It only makes you more beautiful," he said, coming over to the mirror and putting his arms around her, kissing her cheek. "How is my son today?"

Isabeth put a hand on her belly, which was hardly noticeable at this early stage. "Fine, I hope," she said. "He is growing steadily."

That pleased Dyce immensely. "Good," he said, dropping his arms from her and turning for the pitcher of wine set upon a traveling table. "He will inherit a great legacy and he will make me very proud as one of the greatest knights in the north."

Isabeth grinned. "The poor child is not yet born and already you have expectations."

Dyce poured himself a measure of wine. "Of course I do," he said. "That is what fathers do – my father had expectations for me. I have expectations for my son. He will be strong and brilliant and I will be the proudest father in England."

This was the usual conversation when it came to the child. Dyce already had the child's entire life planned out for him. But he seemed to ignore the fact that three previous pregnancies had ended abruptly and that troubled Isabeth a great deal.

The smile faded from her lips.

"I know," she said quietly. "But I do not want to become too excited about the babe. Something can still go wrong."

Dyce looked at her. "It will not," he said confidently. "The other children were lost well before now. You will carry this child until he is ready to be born. This is our time, Beth. This will be our son's time. You must have faith."

Isabeth turned away from the mirror, looking around for

her shawl against the coming evening. "I do have faith," she said. "But I also know the pain when that faith is broken, so it is difficult to be completely trusting. Mayhap my faith will be restored fully when I hold our child in my arms."

"His name is Maxwell, after my father. We shall call him Max."

Isabeth wanted to consider other names, but she wouldn't argue with him. "When I hold *Max* in my arms, mayhap my faith will be restored," she said. "But until then… you will forgive me if I am cautious."

She averted her gaze and Dyce did what he always did when he thought she was displeased – he went to her, quickly, taking her hand in his and kissing it gently. Anything to appease the woman who was his entire world.

"I know, my sweet," he said softly. "I do not mean to make light of it, of course. But I prefer to look forward to Max and my life as his father. Next to you, it is all I have ever wanted. I cannot stomach the alternative."

She'd never heard him voice his disappointment like that before and it saddened her greatly. Dyce asked so little of her and she felt useless that she could not give the man a son, something he wanted very badly. Before the mood became too heady, she collected her shawl and pulled it around her shoulders.

"Then let us speak no more of such things, not tonight," she said. "There is a feast for today's victors and I shall be in attendance. Must I go alone?"

The smile was back on Dyce's lips. "My beautiful wife in a sea of men?" he snorted. "I think not. I must go if to only beat them away."

Isabeth laughed softly. "I do not think you have to worry,"

she said, rubbing her belly. "There aren't many men who find a pregnant woman attractive if she is not carrying his child."

"True enough."

Reaching out, he adjusted her shawl in a very fatherly gesture and then took her hand, leading her from the tent and out into the deepening night.

The feast for the evening was being held in the open, which was unusual. The Earl of Teesside had a small hall that had filled to capacity quickly, so the majority of the guests were in the bailey of his small castle, lit up with dozens of torches against the night sky. There were heavy tables laid out, all of them full to bursting with food and drink. Near the center of the bailey, a massive fire belched sparks and smoke into the night sky as musicians played a lively tune.

Isabeth thought it was all quite exciting and fascinating. On their small outpost in Yorkshire, they didn't see much frivolity like this. Such delights were rare, so she took it all in, watching women dance with knights and soldiers, a mixing of classes because the tournament brought together so many social castes. The earl had his castle open to everyone in attendance, regardless of social standing, and everyone seemed to be gathered.

It made for great fun.

Dyce pushed through groups of people, hunting for a place to seat his wife, while Isabeth let him take the lead as she took it all in. She watched men gambling in a group, rolling bones or dice, while still others were singing in direct conflict with the musicians playing their instruments. She grinned when the men started slapping each other because they were singing out of tune.

Dyce brought her to the end of one of the big feasting tables were several knights were gathered, plowing into a meal of boiled beef and peas. Off to her right, Isabeth was watching a group of women whisper to each other and point at her. They were obviously scrutinizing her and Isabeth stared back at them, perhaps in a challenge. She was very good with gossipy women. Still holding her hand, Dyce began to speak.

"Good men," he said. "I think you may have met my wife years ago, but she has come with me to this festive tournament and I am honored to reintroduce you to her. This is my lady wife, the most beautiful woman in the entire world, Isabeth de Brito. She is very excited to join us this evening even though her health is delicate. Choose your conversation subjects accordingly."

There were grins all around the table at that comment which was more like a threat. Dyce wouldn't tolerate subjects that might singe his lady's ears. The first man that stood up and faced Isabeth was a man she'd met before, though it had been a long time ago. He smiled and dipped his head politely.

"Lady de Brito," he said. "Do you remember me? I am Ronan de Wolfe."

Isabeth knew the name and she knew the man, though only through her husband. She honestly hadn't remembered what he looked like. "Of course I remember you," she said, her green eyes twinkling. "They call you The Shield."

Ronan grinned. "An old name," he said. "It was given to me by my grandfathers, once, because I am the unstoppable force, though your husband will not acknowledge my greatness."

Isabeth giggled. "I believe he does," she said. "Your name is spoken regularly in my household as the man my husband loves most in this world."

Dyce made a face. "Do not listen to her, Roe," he muttered.

"She is lying."

Isabeth laughed softly. "Never would I do such a thing," she said. "You speak of Ronan de Wolfe as if the man can walk on water so, of course, I know him very well."

"You do not."

"He is like a brother to me now, Dyce. You have made it so."

Everyone started chuckling at Isabeth's wit. Ronan pulled out a chair for her. "Sit down, my sister," he said. "Sit and tell me all of the things Dyce says about me and then I shall decide whether or not to punch him in the mouth."

Someone put a full cup of wine in front of Isabeth as she sat down, laughing when Dyce tried to push Ronan aside and sit next to her. But Ronan was having none of it – he shoved Dyce back and sat down on her right.

"I assure you, he only says good things," she said. "He speaks very fondly of you. He says you are from the great de Wolfe family in Northumberland."

Ronan nodded. "I am, my lady," he said. "My grandfather was the Earl of Warenton, William de Wolfe."

"And your father?"

Ronan cocked his head thoughtfully. "He is a bit more complicated," he said. "Suffice it to say that he is garrison commander of Roxburgh Castle, as Baron Sydenham, but he splits his time between Roxburgh and Castle Questing, the seat of the de Wolfe empire. My father is a very busy man these days."

Isabeth was listening politely. "I'm from Yorkshire so I am not completely familiar with the families of Northumberland, but my husband says your family is quite large."

Ronan nodded. "We hold most of the important castles and

properties in Northumberland," he said. "We also hold Carlisle Castle. If you know anything about my grandfather, then you know he was a great knight, the Scourge of the Scots before King Edward ever held that distinction. My family, as a whole, is still the last line of defense between England and the Scots. You may thank me now."

Isabeth giggled. "My gratitude is endless," she said, but she sobered somewhat. "I can hear the pride in your voice, my lord."

Ronan grinned. "Pride, indeed," he said. "But also truth. I only speak the truth."

Someone distracted him with a comment and he turned away as good-natured insults were lobbed, but Isabeth found herself watching the man. What she hadn't remembered was how handsome he was, making her feel the least bit giddy now that she had a good look at him. She was married, of course, so nothing clandestine ever came to mind, but she appreciated a handsome man when she saw one.

Ronan was definitely that man.

He was big and blond, very blond, with a faint beard of dark blond whiskers. He had blond lashes and brows, and dark, piercing eyes. He had enormously wide shoulders, enormous arms, and equally enormous hands that dwarfed her own. There was nothing about him that wasn't exquisite in a male beauty sort of way. Perhaps he wasn't the tallest man she'd ever seen, but he more than made up for it in just his gigantic size and strength.

It was no wonder that Dyce admired him so.

With thoughts of Ronan lingering in her mind, innocently, she turned for her cup of wine. Dyce had managed to push the man seated to her left out of his chair, so he was in the process of filling a trencher for her from the food that was laid out on the table. As he put the meal in front of her, one of the women who had been gossiping and pointing approached the table. Clad in the finest wine-colored silk, she was open in her curiosity.

"I do not know you," she said to Isabeth. "Who are you?"

Isabeth turned to see a pretty woman with dark hair, dark eyes, and slightly crooked teeth standing behind Dyce's chair. Dyce stood up as the lady spoke.

"Lady de Wolfe," he greeted. "This is my wife, Lady de Brito. I do not believe you have ever met. Beth, this is Ronan's wife."

Lady de Wolfe's gaze was intense upon Isabeth, the smile on her lips forced. "My lady," she said. "It is a pleasure to meet the wife of my husband's dear friend. I cannot imagine how we have never met before."

Isabeth smiled timidly. "Nor I," she said. "It is an honor to meet you, Lady de Wolfe. I do hope it will be the first of many times to come."

Lady de Wolfe's smile turned genuine. "What a charming thing to say," she said. Then, she tapped Dyce on the shoulder. "Get up and let me sit with your wife. I should like to speak with her."

Unhappily, but obediently, Dyce stood up and pulled the chair out for Lady de Wolfe, who took it and commandeered Dyce's cup of wine. She cozied up to Isabeth in a way that made Isabeth somewhat wary.

Suddenly, the woman seemed to want to be her best friend.

"You must tell me all about yourself," Lady de Wolfe said. "Where is your family from?"

"Yorkshire," Isabeth said, resisting the urge to lean away

from a woman who was sitting quite close to her. "I am a de Royans."

Lady de Wolfe cocked her head. "Bowes Castle or Netherghyll?"

"Netherghyll."

"Ah," Lady de Wolfe said. "Your father is a Yorkshire warden?"

Isabeth shook her head. "A brother to the warden," she said. "He did not hold the title."

"Where did you grow up?"

"Briarfield Castle, my lady."

Lady de Wolfe reached out and patted her hand. "Let us not be so formal with each other, shall we?" she said. "Please call me Marian. My family is the House of de Grey. Surely you have heard of them."

Isabeth sensed something haughty in that statement. *My family is richer than God – of course you have heard of them.* "Of course I have," she said steadily, though truthfully, only vaguely. "And please call me Isabeth. I should like us to be friends and friends are not so formal, as you have pointed out."

"Isabeth," Marian said, running the name over her tongue. "What a lovely name."

"Thank you, Marian."

Marian lifted her cup. "See?" she said. "We are good friends already."

Isabeth lifted her cup and drank because Marian did. The woman seemed to be staring at her an awful lot, as if she were studying her. Her gaze moved over her, lingering.

It was like being digested, bit by bit.

"How long have you been married?" she asked.

"Almost ten years."

Marian's eyebrows lifted. "Children? Many, I would think."

Isabeth didn't like the way she said it, an assumption that was both rude and painful. She found herself not wanting to tell the woman that she was pregnant, as if that were any of her business. It wasn't. That beautiful secret was for her to share at her discretion, and she didn't want to share it with this bold woman.

"In ten years, one would presume so," she said, avoiding giving her an answer. Then, she veered the subject away from her. "How long have you been married?"

It was clear that Marian liked her wine because she took another large gulp. "The same as you," she said. "Almost ten years. My father was determined that I should marry a de Wolfe son, so I did. Handsome, isn't he?"

Isabeth turned to glance at Ronan, who was still in conversation with the knights at the end of the table. "Indeed," she said neutrally. "You are quite fortunate. And you have children?"

Marian nodded. "Three," she said. "Three daughters. Mayhap if I had given birth to a son, my husband would no longer ignore me."

It was a statement of both self-pity and accusation. She said it loud enough so Ronan could have heard it, but he didn't acknowledge it. He continued speaking with his friends. Unsure what to make of the comment and feeling uncomfortable, Isabeth forced a smile.

"You are still young and very beautiful," she said, trying to be positive. "I am sure there will be many sons to come over the years, so I would not fret."

By now, Marian's smile was gone completely and so was her wine. She was looking off into the courtyard, seemingly disinterested in the conversation now.

She set her cup down.

"Mayhap," she said, rising to her feet. "Please excuse me."

Without another word, she was gone, leaving Isabeth feeling confused at her abrupt departure. As she watched the woman walk away, Dyce reclaimed his seat next to her.

"Thank God she's gone," he muttered, tossing the cup she drank from off the table and hunting around for another one. "I am sorry she forced herself upon you."

"Why? She was good conversation."

"What did she say?"

Isabeth shrugged. "Nothing of note," she said. "She asked where I was from and how long we had been married. She asked if we had any children and I avoided giving her an answer. I did not want to tell her of the child in my belly, for it is none of her affair. It is our secret, Dyce, and no one else's. At least until we can no longer keep it a secret."

He couldn't disagree. "Did she say anything else?"

"She told me that she had three daughters."

Dyce found another cup and poured himself a full measure. "And not one of them belongs to her husband," he muttered. When he saw the shocked look on Isabeth's face, he was immediately regretful. "I am sorry, my sweet. Please… do not repeat that."

Isabeth frowned. "I will not," she said. "But what do you mean? You've never spoken of Ronan's wife. I only knew he had one because, as you have said, I met her once, long ago. What is this disdain you show for her, Dyce?"

Dyce pulled her chair closer to him and away from Ronan so the man hopefully wouldn't overhear. "I do not speak of her because she is not worth the breath out of my mouth," he said.

"There has never been a more disloyal, repugnant wife in the history of history."

"Why? Tell me."

"Because those two never should have married," he said, his voice low as he lifted his chin in Ronan's direction. "They only married because Marian seduced him and her father forced Ronan to marry her. That is the worst reason of all."

Isabeth thought that sounded rather sad. "I am sorry to hear that," she said. "I know you hold Ronan in great esteem. I am sorry his marriage is not a happy one."

Dyce snorted. "Happy?" he repeated as if outraged at the mere suggestion. "Marian de Wolfe does not let something like a marriage slow her down. She has had more men in her bed than a London prostitute and her daughters are not Ronan's children."

Isabeth gasped at the thought. "Truly?"

"Truly," Dyce said, eyeing Ronan to ensure the man didn't hear him. "Ronan let her seduce him in a moment of weakness and it has cost him everything. Now, he turns his back as his wife beds lotharios from France, men who take Ronan's money from his very own wife. Truly, 'tis a mess, Beth. Poor Ronan."

Shocked, Isabeth found herself looking at Ronan through new eyes. That handsome, charming knight had a dark secret, or perhaps not so much a secret if Dyce was gossiping about it. Marian had all but disappeared and Isabeth wondered if it was because she was off finding lotharios in full view of her husband.

It was a rather shocking thought.

"But why doesn't he stop her?" she hissed. "He is her husband and he can stop her – can't he?"

Dyce shrugged. "It is complicated," he said. "She's a de

Grey, one of the most powerful political houses in the north. On the other hand, he's a de Wolfe, one of the most powerful military families in the north, so there is a great risk of creating political upheaval should he offend her family."

Isabeth frowned. "Should *he* offend *her* family?" she repeated, aghast. "From what you have told me, she is the one creating the issue. She should be concerned with offending the House of de Wolfe, I would think. Do they not have bigger armies?"

"Indeed, they do," Dyce said. "De Wolfe could easily crush de Grey, but de Grey is very powerful, politically. It is a very difficult situation and I suspect Ronan has been counseled to look the other way to avoid a massive upheaval."

"Is he a negligent husband, then? Is that why she wanders?"

Dyce shook his head. "Not from what I have seen," he said. "Ronan is a good man, Beth. His heart is good and his soul is pure. He's simply in a terrible situation, so do not judge him by it. He was young when he married Marian and it was simply a mistake, one she punishes him with daily. Women like Marian should never marry. They are a plague upon men of good faith."

Isabeth wanted to ask more about the situation, but Ronan turned in their direction and Dyce shut his mouth, at least for the moment. It would do no good for Ronan to hear him gossip about the state of his marriage, something he was sensitive about.

But something he pretended not to care about.

"Are you still here?" Ronan said to Dyce. "How can I coerce your wife into telling me deep and dark secrets about you if you are still here?"

Dyce flashed a grin. "She would never betray me so."

"Then you *do* have deep and dark secrets."

Dyce laughed, moving to pour himself more wine from the pitcher on the table. "If I do, then she would know them all," he said. "Did I ever tell you that I met Isabeth when she was a young girl? About nine years of age, in fact. I was newly knighted and, even back then, she was the prettiest thing I'd ever seen."

Ronan was smiling, looking between the pair. "So you have known each other a long time."

"A very long time," Dyce agreed. "She has been everything to me for a good deal of my life. I do not have a big family like you do, Roe. Beth *is* my family. All of it."

"And you are a fortunate man," Ronan said. "When you have children, you will be even more fortunate."

Dyce eyed Isabeth, who gave him a little grin. They both liked and trusted Ronan, and Dyce was ready to burst with the news. "It is funny you should say that, my friend," he said. "We are not telling anyone yet, so please do not repeat this, but Isabeth is with child."

Ronan laughed with delight. "My best wishes to you both," he said. "What wonderful news."

"Thank you, it is."

Ronan couldn't help but chuckle at the prideful father and the blushing mother. "There is a great deal to think about now," he said. "Children will change everything."

Dyce flashed his teeth. "I hope they do," he said. "We have been disappointed before, which is why we've not told anyone yet. When we are certain the child will be born safely, we will spread the news."

Ronan lifted his shoulders. "That is understandable," he said. "You must ensure your wife is well taken care of, of course. Do you have help for your wife when she delivers the child? You said you had no family and that is usually a job for female relatives."

Dyce nodded. "We have a midwife," he said. "Why? Are you offering up your female relatives?"

"If you need them."

Dyce patted him on the side of the head. "That is very generous of you," he said, looking at Isabeth. "We shall discuss it and if my wife would like women around her for comfort, then I shall send word."

Ronan smiled at the lovely woman. "Please do," he said. "I can send my mother and my sister at the very least, and probably more female cousins. I think my mother has delivered more babies than a midwife. Our family seems to keep having them."

Dyce snorted. "That is because the House of de Wolfe gives birth in litters, not just one child," he said. "How many cousins do you have again?"

Ronan lifted his eyebrows. "Too many to count," he said. "My grandparents had nine children and many of those children have had multiple children. I think at last count, I had over seventy cousins. When I tell you that de Wolfe's are all over the border, I was not jesting. We really are."

Dyce looked at Isabeth, smiling as he did so. "We hope to have dozens, as well," he said. Then, he caught sight of a great subtlety being brought out of the kitchens, a massive almond pudding shaped like a castle. He immediately stood up. "I shall procure some of that for you, Beth. Roe, entertain my wife for a moment."

With that, he dashed off, leaving Isabeth and Ronan watching him plow through the crowd to get to the dessert.

Isabeth laughed softly.

"He is quite determined to ensure I have some of that pudding," she said. "Honestly, I do not even like almond milk. You would think he would remember that."

Ronan grinned. "He is a good husband to you, my lady," he said. "He is trying to do something nice."

"He is," Isabeth agreed. "And speaking of husbands, I met your wife earlier. She was very friendly."

Ronan seemed to lose some of his humor. "I am glad, my lady."

"Please," Isabeth said, putting a soft hand on his arm. "Call me Isabeth. I told your wife to call me by my name also. It seems odd to be so formal with one another, especially when you are Dyce's very favorite person."

The warmth was back in his eyes. "I think *you* are his very favorite person."

She smiled. "True," she said. "But as far as men go, you are greatly admired by my husband. He does not make friends easily, so thank you for being kind and congenial with him. I have always wanted to thank you for that."

Ronan shrugged. "Dyce and I have always gotten along," he said. "We understand each other and that is important. But I will agree that he seems like a lonely man at times, which is strange because he is well-liked. No one can say a bad word about him."

Isabeth could see Dyce in the distance, demanding a larger slice of the almond pudding. "He is a good man," she said simply. "And I do hope you and your wife will visit us soon. Mayhap when the child is born. I am sure Dyce would like to celebrate the birth with his friends."

Ronan dipped his head gratefully. "I would be honored," he said. "You're living at Ravenscar, are you not?"

Isabeth nodded. "We have been there for a few years, since Dyce's father passed on," she said. "It's a rather big manse on the edge of the sea with an enormous herd of sheep. Dyce makes a very good Lord Farmer, by the way."

Ronan chuckled. "I seem to remember hearing him say that, though he does not speak too much on the subject," he said. "I think he is concerned we might all think him a sheepherder rather than a knight, so all he speaks of are his days with your father at Briarfield and his days of fostering at Oakhampton Castle."

"He holds the title of Lord Ravenscar, so he's not completely a peasant."

"I know. But we still make sheep noises at him once in a while."

Isabeth giggled as Dyce appeared, bearing an enormous plate of almond pudding. He set it down in front of his wife triumphantly, eager for her to take a bite. Isabeth picked up her spoon, smiled wanly, and scooped up a small amount which she reluctantly put in her mouth. That pleased Dyce immensely and he picked up his own spoon, taking a huge bite for himself. He encouraged his wife to eat more than she wanted to and, not surprisingly, had to retire early from the feast with a bellyache. Dyce returned her to their tent and waited until she went to sleep before returning to his friends and drinking the night away.

Tomorrow was going to be a victorious day.

CHAPTER THREE

D E WHINFELL HAD some friends.

As dawn broke over the tournament field and the first knights lined up against each other to the roar of the enthusiastic crowd, the very first pass was a violent one as a de Whinfell ally ended up nearly breaking the neck of his opponent. He was disqualified as his opponent was carried off the field and the knight protested, loudly, for a half-hour before the field marshals made him leave. But that brutal first pass set the tone for the rest of the day.

There were men out for blood and, unfortunately, they found it.

Ronan had seen it all unfold before him like some horrific nightmare. Dyce had been the third round that morning, after two brutal bouts, and tensions were on the rise. Ronan and Titus had tried to convince Dyce to withdraw but when he wouldn't do it, they counseled him on the best way to face his opponent, who was a de la Londe knight. Everyone knew de la Londe knights were some of the most brutal in England, a house descended from mercenaries and favored by King John those many years ago. They had wealth and property, but they were a house that men stayed away from.

Yesterday, the de la Londe knight had used an illegal move to brutally unseat his opponent. He'd been disqualified but lodged a protest that went on well into the night. The head field marshal finally acquiesced and now Dyce had to face that nightmare. But no amount of pleading could convince him to withdraw.

Not even the mention of his wife, who was sitting in the stands.

Ronan had used Isabeth as a last resort, but Dyce was convinced he would make her proud. She had come to see her husband compete and he was going to give her that honor, convinced that Ronan's concerns were for naught. After that, there wasn't much more to say until his very first pass found him impaled on an illegal spear-tipped joust pole that had gone into his chest and out through his back.

The crowd, cheering wildly in excitement, gasped in collective horror at the sight.

Ronan remembered running onto the arena floor along with Titus and several other men as Edward, Axel, and Christian attacked the de La Londe knight. As they pulled the offending knight off his horse and began to beat him severely, Ronan and Titus dropped to their knees beside Dyce, who was still alive. Titus pulled off his helm as Ronan steadied him because he was laying awkwardly. The tip of the joust pole had broken off when he'd fallen, so he had a four-foot piece of wood and steel protruding from his body in both the front and back of his torso.

Ronan would never forget the look of surprise on Dyce's face when the man's helm came off.

"Steady, Dyce," Ronan said evenly. "We'll get you moved to

your tent and the physic can remove this thing, but steady on, lad."

Dyce looked at him with unnaturally bright eyes within his pale face. "Is it bad?"

"Nay," Ronan lied, forcing a smile. "It only looks bad. You'll be as good as new soon."

Dyce coughed, spraying blood all over himself and onto Ronan, indicative of the fact that the wound was, indeed, bad. The lance had done enormous and irreparable damage and they all knew it.

Even Dyce.

"You never were a good liar," he said thickly because of all of the blood in his mouth. "You tried to warn me, Ronan. I know you did and I would not listen. You must not blame yourself for this."

He reached out, grabbing Ronan's hand and holding it tightly, as if afraid to let go. Over to their right, Edward and Axel and Christian had beaten the de la Londe knight unconscious but the knight's men had taken exception to that and a big brawl was going on. The field marshals were trying to contain the chaos as de Wolfe soldiers emerged onto the field, preparing to side with their knights. Half went to the brawl, half to Ronan and Titus as they knelt beside Dyce. They were there to help but also to shield the dying knight from the crowd, who were on their feet. Women were weeping, men were pale, and through all of it, Ronan held Dyce's hands tightly.

But his heart was breaking.

"The only person to blame for this is lying in a heap thanks to Eddie and Axel," Ronan said after a moment, a lump in his throat. "He played one of his dirty tricks on you."

Dyce nodded, closing his eyes and groaning because his

body had shifted and the pain was overwhelming. "Dirty," he muttered. "Dirty, indeed. It happened so fast."

"I know."

"I did not even get my lance into position."

"He did not give you time."

"Will he be punished?"

"Aye," Ronan said simply, watching Dyce's eyes roll around in his head. He knew time was very limited and the loss, the grief, was eating at him already. "Dyce, is there anything you need? Anything you want? Tell me what you want me to do for you and I shall do it."

Dyce's eyes opened again and he flashed his teeth, now bloodied from all of the blood he was coughing up. "There is only one thing you can do for me," he rasped. "My wife, Ronan. You must promise to take care of Isabeth."

Ronan's brow rippled in confusion. "Take *care* of her?"

"Please, Ronan."

"But surely she will want to return to her family. I shall afford her a full de Wolfe escort and…"

"Nay," Dyce said, tugging on his hand and interrupting him. "She has no family. *I* am her family. When I am gone, she will be all alone and my son… please, Ronan… tell my son about me. Tell him how much I loved him though I'd not yet met him."

That lump in Ronan's throat was growing larger. He managed to nod, unable to speak, when he noticed pale blue fabric next to him. He turned to see the very subject of their conversation kneeling in the dirt next to her husband.

Isabeth.

The woman had come out of the stands and Ronan never even heard her. Quiet, composed, but eyes that were strained with grief, she was the model of grace as she bent over and placed a gentle hand against her husband's forehead.

"Be at ease, Dyce," she said softly. "I am here. I will not leave you."

Dyce gazed up at Isabeth, the same loving expression on his face that he'd always had when he looked at her. "My love," he murmured, blood dripping from his lips. "I do not want to leave you."

Isabeth forced a smile, her hand stroking his forehead. "Do not speak so," she said. "Let Ronan's men take you back to our tent. I will tend you."

"Nay," he said shortly, spraying more blood. "You must not exert yourself."

"Nonsense," Isabeth said, looking to Ronan. "Take him back to our tent so the pole may be removed."

Ronan looked at the woman. No hysterics, no tears. Simply quiet determination. Her world was crumbling and she was displaying grace and dignity in the face of such turmoil. It was incredibly impressive at such a difficult time and he admired her greatly for her control.

But her request was unrealistic.

"It is better not to move him, my lady," he said quietly. "It will cause him great pain."

Her mouth worked as if she wanted to argue with him, but she thought better of it. Ronan could see that she knew her husband was as good as dead, just as they all did. She was simply being positive for Dyce's sake. Or perhaps for her own. In any case, Dyce weakly grasped her arm and brought her hand to his lips, leaving bloodied lip prints as he kissed her.

"I love you," he muttered, visibly weaker. "Ronan has promised to look out for you. Obey him as you would me, Beth. He will take care of you now. He is your master."

Isabeth looked at Ronan in shock, who gazed back at her with a great deal of reluctance. It was all over his face as she stared at him, seeing his reluctance but unwilling to verbalize it. The man had just been given a burden that no man should have to accept, something a lesser man would have denied or passed off to another. But not Ronan.

Like it or not, he was accepting that burden.

A pregnant widow.

"As you wish," she said, her eyes still riveted to Ronan until she managed to tear them away. "Until you are better, I shall do as he wishes."

Dyce squeezed her hand, as much as he was able now that the life was nearly out of him. "Forever," he muttered. "Obey him forever. Listen to him. Our son… Ronan will be good to him. I trust him.. with… your life… I…"

He sagged after that, dropping his hand. His eyes closed and as the others watched in horror and grief, he took two or three unsteady breaths before finally falling still.

Sir Dyce de Brito was no more.

Fighting off tears, Ronan stood up, jaw flexing with emotion as he watched Isabeth fold herself over her husband's head and weep softly. His blood stained her pale blue dress as she wrapped her arms around his lifeless body, cradling it gently.

It was the saddest thing Ronan had ever witnessed.

And that infuriated him.

A man's life had just ended and the world was still going on around them. Nothing had come to a halt when Dyce's life had stopped. Everything was going on, moving on…

It was an insult.

An insult to Dyce.

The brawl was still happening and Ronan saw a release for that rage. He plunged into the fray, delivering devastating blows with just one punch. With his maternal grandfather's powerful size, and Kieran Hage had once been the strongest man in the north, no one wanted what Ronan was dishing out. It was less than a minute after plowing into the brawl that men began to disengage. De la Londe men were scattering, leaving the de Wolfe soldiers winded and Edward, Axel, Christian, and Ronan ready to take on half of England. They'd lost a friend and those responsible were going to pay.

That meant the de la Londe knight, who was in a bloodied, unconscious heap. His men tried to take him away but Axel and Christian refused to release him, instead handing him over to the de Wolfe soldiers as a prisoner. When the field marshals tried to force the de Wolfe men to release him under penalty of all of the competing knights being disqualified, Ronan threatened to bring the de Wolfe army down to Middlesbrough and raze the town.

The de Wolfe men were allowed to remain and the de la Londe knight remained in their custody.

Through the chaos and confusion and rage, Ronan and Edward managed to clear out the de Wolfe soldiers but the knights remained. A physic, in the employ of the Earl of Teesside, came to see to Dyce and they allowed the man to examine him even though he was dead. Titus had remained with Isabeth throughout the fight, but Ronan realized as he looked at her that it should have been him.

Dyce had asked it of him.

I trust you with her life.

The physic had a couple of helpers, men who had brought a blanket to cover up Dyce. They removed the broken lance from his body and quickly covered him up, lifting him off the ground gently as Ronan went to Isabeth and helped her to her feet. She was trembling, shocked and grieved, and he and Titus managed to walk her off the arena floor between them, each man with an arm. They walked her all the way back to the de Brito tent where Dyce was placed, wrapped up tightly in the blankets the Teesside physic had brought.

And that was where he remained the rest of the day and into the night.

Ronan never left him. Now that the chaos of Dyce's fall had faded away, the shock of the man's death only grew more jarring as the day went on, so much so that when it came time for Ronan to compete, he defaulted and gave the victory to his opponent.

But he hardly cared.

Evening fell.

There was a feast that night yet again for the winners of the day and the sounds of revelry and smells of food wafted upon the cool night air into the encampment where Ronan had been standing vigil at the entry to Dyce and Isabeth's tent. He'd been watching Isabeth the entire day as she sat next to her husband's body, softly weeping, offering her food and drink that she refused. He'd promised Dyce he'd take care of the woman and had no idea where to start or even what to do. He had no idea where his own wife was, otherwise he would have sent for her.

But he knew he was very much alone.

He always had been.

"How is she?"

Jolted from his train of thought, Ronan turned to see Titus standing behind him. The man was clad in his jousting armor and Ronan looked him over.

"Grieving," he said. "Did you win?"

"I did."

"Good."

He returned his attention to the scene inside the tent and Titus came to stand next to him, observing the pregnant woman as she prayed beside her husband's body. Ronan heard him sigh faintly.

"What now?" he asked quietly.

Ronan shrugged. "I do not know," he said. "But I think I have gotten myself into a mess. You heard him, Titus – he asked me to take care of his wife and child. I could not deny a dying man so now his burden has become mine. I've been standing here trying to decide what should be done."

"And?"

"And I think I need to speak with my father."

Titus nodded. "Of course," he said. "But meanwhile, *what* are you going to do?"

Ronan shook his head slowly, his gaze riveted to the beautiful woman in the bloodied pale blue silk. "Whatever Lady de Brito wants to do, I suppose," he said. "But first, I must have Dyce taken away so he can be prepared. The priests from St. John the Evangelist are waiting to take him away. The Earl of Teesside sent them."

"And then what?"

"He returns home, wherever that may be."

"What do you mean?"

"I mean that Dyce had his small outpost, but that was a gift from his wife's father," he said. "Dyce said she had no other family, and I know he had no family, so I have no idea where she wishes to bury the man."

"Then you'd better ask."

That was what Ronan had been thinking for the better part of the afternoon. Asking Lady de Brito what she wanted to do but giving the woman time to grieve before he did. It wasn't as if they needed to move Dyce home tonight. Or even tomorrow.

But soon.

"This is an unhappy duty," Ronan muttered after a moment. "I cannot even grieve my friend's death because, now, it seems I am responsible for his wife. I must present a strong front for truly it is not my right to show sadness. It is hers. I will not take that away from her."

Titus knew that. His gaze drifted to the lady in the darkened tent. "He should not have asked it of you."

"He had no one else."

Titus sighed faintly, thinking that he was glad it hadn't been him. It very well could have been since he'd been there at the end, too. Gently, he slapped Ronan on the back.

"I am going to remove my protection and then go to the feast," he said. "I'll have food sent to you and the lady."

"That would be appreciated."

"The de la Londe knight still hasn't awoken from the beating he was dealt."

There was a sense of satisfaction to hear that and Ronan was glad. "Good," he growled.

As Titus headed off, Ronan broke from his position at the tent flap and moved into the tent itself. Darkened and smelling of smoke with a faint hint of a woman's perfume, he approached Lady de Brito.

"My lady?" he said softly. "I am very sorry to disturb you, but we must take Dyce away to be prepared for his return… home. I realize this is an uncouth question to ask, but I must. Have you decided where you wish to have him buried?"

Isabeth had been sitting so still that one would have thought she was asleep sitting up. Not a muscle moved and her eyes were closed, but when Ronan spoke, she slowly opened her eyes, turning to look at him.

"Ravenscar, I would think," she said, sounding hoarse and weary. "It is our home, after all. My father gave it to us. Did he ever tell you that?"

Ronan nodded his head. "He told me," he said. "We had many conversations about you over the years, when we would meet up on the tournament circuit or he would come north to visit me, and he would speak of Ravenscar. He did tell me that it was a gift. But he also never brought you along on any of his visits north, I noticed. Why is that?"

Isabeth smiled weakly. "Because he did not like to expose me to the dangers of travel," she said. "I think you know how protective he was of me. He treated me as if I were the most precious glass, so fragile that a mere breath of air could shatter me."

"Is your health poor, my lady? If so, I did not know."

Isabeth shook her head. "My health is fine," she said, though it wasn't exactly true. "Dyce simply worried."

"Even so, I did not mean to make light of it."

"You did not," she said. "But it is of no matter because, truthfully, I am not much interested in going places. I like my corner of the world because it is safe and it is mine. Now I see what happens when I travel with my husband, out of that safety."

Her smile faded and her attention turned back to Dyce, who was starting to turn a bluish tinge because he'd been dead a few hours. Ronan took a moment to study the woman, who was a truly exquisite specimen. He could see why Dyce had been so enamored with her. He'd seen it last night, too. Isabeth had an aura of beauty around her that was not easily found with her luminescent green eyes and porcelain skin. Her hair was brown, but it had glimmers of gold and red all through it, fashioned into a bun at the nape of her neck. But her lips… they were plump and shapely and quite kissable, as Dyce had said many times.

Ronan couldn't disagree.

But this exquisite beauty was in distress and Ronan had to help. Not only for Dyce's sake, but for the lady's sake as well. She was pregnant and widowed, a nasty combination as far as society was concerned. Ronan began to feel the twinges of protectiveness. Dyce had been quite overprotective of her and, now, Ronan was starting to see why. There was something about the lady that a decent man would want to protect.

There was grace and fragility there.

"What happened was a tragedy, my lady," he said after a moment. "But what happened was an evil act and the man who did this has been punished. Dyce has been avenged, so take comfort that his friends would not let this travesty go unanswered. Now, we must take care of you. We are all friends of Dyce and it is our privilege to do this for him. We shall return him to Ravenscar if that is your wish."

Isabeth nodded faintly. "I think so," she said. "You have visited Ravenscar a couple of times. I remember. But it has been a long time."

"Too long," Ronan said. "I am sorry my visits were not more frequent but having a big family like I do means one is kept quite busy. And speaking of families, Dyce said he was your only family. Is that because he did not wish for you to return to your father? Was there some disharmony there? As you said, he was quite protective over you and I would not wish to go against him."

Isabeth shook her head. "My father died a few years ago and his castle, Briarfield, was inherited by a cousin who has made it clear that I am not welcome. 'Tis sad, really. When we were children, we were friendly but when he grew up, his wife did not like me for some reason. I believe she is the one who banished me from Briarfield, not my cousin."

Ronan understood the situation now. "And Dyce has no other family?"

"Not close family," Isabeth said. "But he has great friends, like you, so we never felt completely alone."

The circumstances were coming clear. Dyce had been right – Isabeth really *was* alone. That didn't make things easier for Ronan, to be sure, but the more he spoke to her, the more he realized that he wasn't entirely reluctant to take on the duty of her care. She was polite, witty, and well-spoken and he liked that.

He smiled weakly.

"Nay, my sister, you are never alone," he said. "You told Dyce that I am like a brother to you, thanks to him, so I am pleased to assume that role since you do not have a brother. But in doing so, I will make you a pledge – I will never lie to you and I will never do anything that I do not completely believe is in your best interest. Do you trust me?"

Isabeth nodded solemnly. "Dyce did," she said. "I do, too."

Ronan smiled faintly. "Good," he said. "Now, as your brother, I would ask that you please let us take Dyce away so that he may be prepared to return to Ravenscar. And you must eat and rest. We must take care of Dyce's son."

Isabeth hesitated a moment, instinctively putting her hand

on her barely-rounded belly as she turned to Dyce one last time. She knew that Ronan was right so she nodded briefly, once, and Ronan immediately went to the tent flap, motioning to the soldiers and the three priests who had come from St. John the Evangelist's parish. Ronan went back into the tent to Isabeth, helping her to stand and moving her out of the way as the soldiers and priests went about their business. Ronan couldn't help but notice that Isabeth stood stiffly as her husband's body was removed from the tent. When he was finally gone, the tent seemed so oddly empty.

Deathly still.

"Is he really gone?" Isabeth murmured. "As quick as the blink of an eye… is he truly gone?"

Ronan nodded slowly. "Aye, my lady."

"I shall never see him again."

"Nay, my lady."

Isabeth lowered herself back onto the chair she'd been sitting on all day, plunking down as if the strength in her body had suddenly left her. For a moment, she simply looked dazed.

"While he was here, I could look at him and see him and not feel as if I were alone," she said. "But now… now, I am alone."

Ronan could feel her despair – the confusion, the loss. Being a compassionate man, something he'd inherited from both sides of his family, he simply couldn't leave her like this.

He had to offer what comfort he could.

"I do not know if this will help, my lady, but I will relay something to you," he said quietly. "My grandparents were married for over six decades and when my grandfather passed away about fifteen years ago, we were all devastated. William de Wolfe had lived a very long and very healthy life and his passing had been unexpected. He passed away in his sleep and my grandmother remained with him, in bed, for most of the day before we were able to remove him, but strangely enough, my grandmother wasn't in hysterics. She was very composed. She even washed my grandfather's body and helped dress him before he was put in his crypt, all the while tending him carefully. When my father tried to convince her to leave him so that she could rest, my grandmother refused. She told my father that this was what she had always been meant to do, that the marriage of two people does not end when one of them dies. When my grandfather died, it was still her duty to take care of him. When we tried to comfort her, she was the one who comforted *us*."

By this time, Isabeth was listening intently. "She sounds like a remarkable woman."

Ronan nodded swiftly. "She was," he said. "The point I was trying to make was that she said death does not end true love. She said that, to her, it was only as if my grandfather had stepped into the next room. Or mayhap he'd gone on a battle march, which he'd done many a time. That was how she viewed his death – that their separation was only temporary. He wasn't truly gone. Dyce isn't truly gone, my lady. Mayhap he's only stepped into the next room if it helps you to think that."

As Ronan watched, Isabeth's luminous eyes filled with tears that eventually spilled over. She closed her eyes tightly, looking away as more tears coursed down her cheeks.

"Thank you," she said softly. "That is a good way of putting the situation. You are very kind to take the time to do so."

She continued to weep softly and Ronan watched her lowered head, thinking that she was such a gentle and pathetic creature. He knew Dyce would be frantic with worry, wanting to take care of her, to shield her, things he'd been doing since the day they married and before. Now, Isabeth was going to have to face her life without the man who had always been there for her.

Ironic, he thought. *My wife probably wouldn't shed a tear were I to die.*

That thought sent him out of the tent.

Ronan was out in the encampment before he realized he'd even moved. He came to an unsteady halt, forcing himself to focus, to think about why he'd just run away from a pregnant woman he'd sworn to protect. He'd just bolted like a fool. And then, it occurred to him.

Jealousy.

He was jealous.

Dyce, his dear friend, a man he was mourning, had a woman that Ronan could only dream of. While Dyce had married a sweet and compassionate woman, and Ronan knew that because, over the years of their friendship, Dyce had only spoken of his wife and their wedded bliss, Ronan was married to a woman who treated him with apathy and discourtesy. Marian ran amok and took whomever she pleased as a lover while Isabeth was true and faithful, mourning her husband as he should be mourned.

As Ronan himself would never be mourned.

God, what a mess his life was.

Slowly, he turned back towards the de Brito encampment. It really wasn't that far away. Men were milling about, leaning over a cooking fire, and the tent where Isabeth was remained still and dimly lit. Ronan just stood there and stared at it, feeling stupid and confused.

But dutiful.

Always dutiful.

He retraced his steps back to the tent.

By the time he got there, a soldier sent by Titus appeared bearing boiled beef and vegetables. Ronan indicated for the soldier to give the food to Lady de Brito, which he did, while Ronan remained outside of the tent, unwilling to go inside and see that lovely, grieving woman.

The one who made him feel so envious.

He just couldn't shake that feeling.

CHAPTER FOUR

"RAVENSCAR? WHERE IS that?"

It was morning in the de Wolfe tent where Marian was just rising from a night of very little sleep. While Ronan had spent most of the night at the de Brito encampment, sitting by the fire as Lady de Brito slept inside her tent, he'd returned to the de Wolfe encampment just before dawn only to be told by his sergeant in charge that Lady de Wolfe had returned not four hours earlier, drunk and smelling of wine. She'd been accompanied by a young knight who had left her off to go about his own way.

Ronan's men were used to seeing such things when it came to Lady de Wolfe.

Ronan had returned to his encampment shortly before dawn and, with his wife snoring in her bed, had fallen asleep on a separate cot. Unfortunately, they didn't have all the time in the world to sleep because he intended to depart Middlesbrough for Ravenscar that day, a journey that would take at least two full days of travel if they moved swiftly.

But Marian had been resistant from the very moment he told her of their plans and, now, voices were being raised.

A standoff was coming.

"Ravenscar is Dyce de Brito's manse about two days to the south," Ronan said with strained patience. "I must escort Dyce home for burial."

Marian's face screwed up with disbelief and confusion. "Why?" she demanded. "Ronan, Dyce has his own men to take him home. Why must you go?"

"Because I promised I would," he said simply. "I promised Dyce that I would see to his wife and I need your help to do so. You know it would not be proper for me to go with her, alone. I need your presence, if nothing else."

Marian's jaw dropped in outrage. "I did not make the promise – *you* did," she said. "His wife is not my responsibility. Though I do not mean to be unkind, I do not even know the woman."

Ronan looked at her with contempt. "She has no one," he said. "Dyce asked me to see to her and I told him I would, so it would be polite if you were to give the woman some comfort as we take her husband home for burial. You may not love your husband, but she loved hers. Try to show some understanding."

The knives were already sharpening at this early hour. That wasn't unusual with them, but Ronan was worried about a scene. Marian had no restraint when it came to their arguments and he didn't want to feed the gossip mills with whispers of Ronan de Wolfe's screaming wife.

Still… sometimes, he just couldn't help himself when she was being difficult.

And Marian knew it.

"Why should I care who the woman loves or does not love?" she hissed. "She has no bearing on my life, nor does her husband. And I would watch the accusations about love between spouses if I were you. I do not recall you showing me any, so do not accuse me of being loveless when you commit the same sin."

"I have not accused you of anything. I have simply stated a fact."

"Your facts, Ronan, which are never mine."

"Mine are the truth. Yours are fantasy."

"Cease your belligerence," she spat. "I will not listen to it. Go do whatever you promised to do and I will wait for you here. The tournament is not over yet and I have come for the spectacle, so I have no intention of leaving."

Ronan was gearing up for another nasty comment but he knew it would only spiral the situation and, at the moment, he was trying to gain her cooperation. It wasn't often he needed it but, in this case, he did.

Wearily, he scratched his head.

"Don't you ever become tired with the arguing?" he asked, trying to defuse the situation a little. "All we do is argue, Marian. There was a time when we didn't argue at all."

She was still frowning, still angry from the conversation, but she didn't want to reminisce with him. She waved an irritable hand at him and turned for the tray of food that had been brought in for her to break her fast.

"I do not wish to discuss it," she said. "I am staying here. Go do what you must do."

Ronan watched her inspect the warmed beef and gravy along with thick slices of white bread and butter. "I must escort my friend home and his widowed wife," he said. "You are a de Grey. Your family is entrenched in protocol and manners. I would like you to show some to Lady de Brito, who has just lost her husband. It would be a gesture of goodwill and would be an excellent demonstration of de Grey compassion. Will you not do this for your family's name?"

He didn't even bring up the de Wolfe name anymore because she didn't care. She loathed having to carry the name de Wolfe, so he invoked the name of her family and prayed it would do the trick. He waited with anticipation while she slowed her movements and sighed heavily.

"Must you always manipulate me like that?" she finally asked.

Ronan could hear, by the tone of her voice, that her guard was lowering. He'd hit a vein. "It is not manipulation if it is the truth," he said. "It would be a gesture of goodwill to know that you and I escorted Lady de Brito home to bury her husband. Word may even get back to your father and it would make him proud, so please, Marian. Please go with me. It would be the proper thing to do."

She looked at him, sighing with exasperation again. "How long will we stay?"

"Long enough to bury the man and no longer."

Marian rolled her eyes and looked back to her food. "If you promise."

"I do."

Marian picked up her spoon. "Very well," she muttered. "I will eat and dress and go with you to see Lady de Brito. Mayhap I can help her in some way. Pack her things for the journey, mayhap."

"I am sure she would appreciate it."

Marian didn't care. She waved him off and dug into her food, signaling the end of the conversation. Ronan fled the tent at that point, relieved to be out of her presence like he always was. Being around Marian was like a weight on his shoulders he couldn't shake. He hated that their relationship had deteriorated so badly, for he would at least like to have a pleasant one. Even if he didn't love her. Once outside in the light of the new morning, his attention inevitably turned to the de Brito camp.

It was off to the northeast, not far from where he was, so he headed off in that direction, catching sight of Titus being dressed by Edward and Axel and a couple of squires. Titus had an early round that morning and, more than likely, would end up in the final round somehow. Edward and Axel were competing later on that day, as Ronan understood it, but Christian had been defeated against a professional opponent the day before. There were knights that only rode the tournament circuit and Christian had gone up against one of them.

It had been a sobering experience for the young knight.

Ronan grinned when he thought of his cousin, so full of passion and ego. His mother was Ronan's father's twin and his father was Ronan's mother's brother, so they were related on both sides. De Wolfe family ties could often be quite confusing. While most of the cousins had fortunately inherited some, or all, of Grandfather Kieran's cool demeanor, Christian was one of the rare individuals that had inherited their grandmother, Jemma's, fiery personality.

The lad was all Scots.

"Roe!"

Ronan came to a halt, turning to see the very object of his musings heading in his direction. Tall, with a crown of dark blond hair and green eyes, handsome Christian Hage waved to his cousin as he trotted in his direction.

"Well?" Ronan said. "What has you up at this hour?"

"Titus," Christian said, frowning. "He says that you are escorting Lady de Brito and her husband home today."

Ronan nodded. "I am."

"He told me to go with you. He's going to take the escort home with Eddie and Axel."

"Home" in the vernacular of the de Wolfe empire simply meant they were taking the escort back to whatever de Wolfe castle or property it had originated from. All of them – Titus, Edward, Axel, Christian, and even Ronan – served at different castles, but they mingled from time to time as manpower was shifted from one to the other, usually dictated by either Scott de Wolfe or his twin brother, Troy, the eldest de Wolfe brothers and the heirs to the empire. Technically, Scott was the Earl of Warenton, but Troy co-managed alongside him, making for a powerful and unbeatable team.

"Excellent," Ronan said. "I welcome your sword and I know Dyce would, too."

Christian's gaze drifted over to his older cousin. "I did not have the chance to express my condolences, Roe," he said. "I know that Dyce was your friend. It is difficult to lose a friend like that."

Ronan nodded. "It is," he said with resignation. "Although I've seen such a thing happen before at tournaments, I've never seen something like that so egregious. What about the de la Londe knight, anyway? Has he regained consciousness?"

Christian shook his head. "Teesside's physic does not think he ever will," he said. "He thinks the man is going to die."

Ronan hardened. "Good," he said. "Let him linger in a stupor until death claims him. It is more merciful than what he did to Dyce."

"His men are demanding his return."

"He is our prisoner. They can have his corpse when we're finished with it."

"Teesside came to Titus this morning, wanting to negotiate for the man."

Ronan shook his head. "Unless Teesside wants the ire of de Wolfe, he'll stay out of it," he said. "In any case, I am going to see Lady de Brito now and I want you with me. You can see to the preparation of the de Brito escort as we return Dyce home, but I also want you to ensure we have a way to transport his coffin. See to it, will you?"

"Of course."

With that, Ronan headed off for the de Brito encampment once more with Christian now on his heels. As he drew close, he could see that two of the four tents had already been dismantled and they were loading up the provisions wagon they'd brought along. He also saw Dyce's black and white warhorse tethered, tearing through a bucket of grain. The animal had run off when Dyce had been mortally wounded, but someone had evidently returned the expensive animal. He gave the beast a pat, looking it over for injuries, before turning for the big tent where Lady de Brito was. As Christian headed off to take care of his tasks, Ronan cleared his throat.

"Lady de Brito?" he said, standing next to the tent flap. "It is Ronan, my lady. May I enter?"

There was a pause before the tent flap was abruptly pulled back, revealing Isabeth in the early morning light. Dressed in a heavy woolen traveling garment in a color of yellow that was most becoming, she nonetheless appeared pale as she forced a smile at Ronan.

"Good morn to you, my brother," she said, her eyes twinkling dully with mirth. "I am glad you have come. I wish to speak with you."

She stepped back into the tent and he followed, remaining

by the tent flap and closing it when she indicated that he should. In spite of her pale appearance, she seemed more energetic this morning. Determined, even. He could sense that simply by the way she was holding herself.

"How may I be of service, my lady?" he asked.

Isabeth faced him in the dim light, the sounds of the encampment around them permeating the canvas walls. Men were shouting, dogs were barking, and birds were chirping but, at the moment, they were only focused on each other.

Something curious was in the air.

"As you can imagine, I did not sleep much last night," Isabeth finally said. "Mostly, I was thinking. Thinking about Dyce, about my future. Everything has changed now."

Ronan nodded sympathetically. "That is understandable, my lady."

"Indeed," she said. "But I also thought about you, Sir Ronan. All jesting aside, you and I are literally strangers and what Dyce asked of you was not fair. He should never have asked you to take care of me. I am not your responsibility."

Ronan was beginning to understand why she seemed so determined. Clearly, she'd been thinking long and hard about her situation and his involvement in it and had come to some conclusions.

But he had conclusions of his own.

"Nay, lady, you are not, but I cannot go back on my word," he said. "I promised Dyce that I would ensure your safety and that is exactly what I intend to do."

Isabeth's gaze lingered on him for a moment, studying him. "But what does that mean, exactly?"

He shrugged. "It means that I shall escort you and Dyce home," he said. "It means that I will ensure your well-being and safety once we reach Ravenscar."

"Do you intend to remain at Ravenscar, then?"

"To be truthful, I do not know. I've not thought the matter through to its logical conclusion."

Isabeth sighed faintly, moving for a chair. "I have," she said. "Please sit, Sir Ronan."

He lowered his big body into the nearest chair. "Just Ronan, my lady. We needn't be so formal."

"Then you must call me Isabeth. This *is* peculiar, isn't it?"

He gave her a half-grin. "A little," he said. "But above all, I want to do what is right by Dyce. You were clearly the most important thing in the world to him and that is something I do not take lightly. He was my dear friend and I would fail him miserably if I did not take care of the most important thing in his life – you. Do you understand my perspective?"

Isabeth nodded. "I do, indeed," she said. "But do you understand mine, I wonder? Dyce asked you, a married man, to become my guardian. Have you told your lady wife any of this?"

Ronan nodded. "I have, my lady," he said. "She will be accompanying us to Ravenscar."

Isabeth lost some of her determination, some of her stiffness then. "I see," she said. "And… and she is agreeable to this?"

"She is, my lady."

"She does not mind that you have a widow as your ward?"

"She understands that I am a man of my word, my lady. She will help."

Isabeth wasn't sure what to say after that. "If your wife is agreeable, then I suppose my concerns are for naught," she said. "She is a very compassionate woman to allow her husband to have a grown woman as a ward. But I still feel as if I will be a terrible burden to you."

He smiled faintly. "You will let me worry about that," he said. Then, he stood up. "Now, if that will be all, my wife will come in a short while to help you pack. As I said, she would like to help if you are agreeable."

Isabeth nodded reluctantly. "If you are certain it will be no trouble."

"No trouble at all."

He turned for the tent flap, but she stopped him.

"My lord," she said. "Ronan. If, at any time, I seem ungrateful, please know that I am extremely grateful for everything. It is not a lack of gratitude that fuels my hesitation, but my great concern that my husband's request has complicated your life. You are very gracious to keep your word but please know that if you decide it is too much, I will completely understand. I would never want to be a burden to you."

He looked at her, that exquisite woman in the yellow garment. Her hair was braided on this day and the braid was wrapped around her head, giving her the appearance of having a halo. It was fitting considering she was quite angelic. She simply didn't seem like the burden he'd thought she was the day before.

Somehow, the burden was getting lighter.

She was simply a nice woman he felt sorry for.

"And you shall not be, I assure you," he said. "My wife will be here shortly to help you finish packing and then we shall depart when you are ready. I am mustering the escort as we speak. It will probably take us a couple of days to reach Ravenscar but I will try to keep the pace easy, for your sake."

Isabeth smiled bravely. "You need not worry over me," she said. "I am stronger than I look."

His eyes narrowed at her, but it was good-natured. "Then

you shall come in handy should we need an additional sword," he said, watching her laugh. She had a sweet little laugh. "Take heart, my lady, that our journey to Ravenscar will be uneventful. I intend to make it so."

With that, he dipped his head politely at her and quit the tent, heading straight for Christian, who was gathering the de Brito men and explaining that they would be departing that day. Ronan announced to the men that he would be taking command of the de Brito escort, by Dyce's request and Lady de Brito's approval, and the men seemed eager to please the de Wolfe knights. Ronan and Christian gave the orders and the de Brito men hurried to do their bidding. Even after the knights headed back to their own encampment, the de Brito soldiers were ensuring everything was prepared for the coming departure.

The day, already, was moving briskly.

CHAPTER FIVE

S HE DIDN'T WAIT for Ronan.

In fact, Isabeth didn't wait for anyone. She most especially didn't want to wait for Lady de Wolfe. The woman hadn't given her a good impression the day before. Isabeth was feeling weary and anxious and Dyce's passing left an ache in her chest that she couldn't seem to overcome. It pressed against her heart, making it difficult to breathe, and Lady de Wolfe's presence wasn't going to help.

It was only going to make it worse.

Therefore, she quickly packed her things, and Dyce's things, and emerged from the tent to announce that they were departing immediately. The soldiers were confused by the command but carried out Lady de Brito's orders. They superseded any de Wolfe orders. As they were breaking down the large tent and gathering the baggage, Isabeth caught sight of their provisions wagon, the one they'd brought with them from Ravenscar.

She could see a simple pine box secured to it.

That pressure on her chest grew worse at the sight. Her stomach rolled. Perhaps she hadn't loved Dyce the way a wife should love a husband, but she had been very fond of the man. He was someone she'd known more than half her life, more like a brother and a best friend even though he was her husband. There was an attachment there, though hers was much different than his was.

It was an attachment that would probably never be broken.

In the light of the new day, the reality of his death crashed down on her again. She still couldn't accept that he was gone. It didn't seem real. As the soldiers raced around her, loading up the wagon, she made her way towards the casket as it lay, still and lonely, upon the wagon bed. Isabeth went to it, putting her hand on it, fighting back the lump in her throat.

She wanted to get him home.

The escort was ready in less than a half-hour. Everything had been quickly loaded onto the wagons and everything was secured. Not wanting to ride the palfrey she had ridden all the way from Ravenscar, Isabeth had the soldiers fashion a place for her in the rear of the wagon where she could sit next to Dyce's casket. Making herself comfortable alongside old Gerta, the de Brito escort departed Middlesbrough a couple of hours after sunrise.

They headed east, to the road that led down the coast.

The area was heavily agricultural this close to the sea, with rich soil that had been farmed for centuries. The Danes, the Angles, and the ancient tribes had all found this land to be quite fertile, growing their grains and vegetables. Sitting in the rear of the wagon, Isabeth was quite warm with the blankets and hides that the soldiers had used to make her comfortable, and she could smell the salt of the sea. Overhead, gulls cried and the clouds began to roll in from the east. It wasn't fog, but perhaps more of a storm or two coming ashore.

The scent of rain was in the air.

Isabeth had been on this road before. Ravenscar was a coastal village, highly dependent upon the fishing trade and rather isolated, so this was the main road that went north into Middlesbrough but also south into Scarborough. She'd been along it a hundred times in her life, either with her father or with Dyce, and she found it incredibly lonely to be traveling along the rocky, sandy road with Dyce's casket. Even though she was surrounded by soldiers and accompanied by her maid, it simply wasn't the same. She was still alone. It was indicative of how her life was going to be from this point forward and it was difficult not to feel self-pity along with the confusion.

With Dyce gone to plan every moment of her future, she was going to have to plan it herself.

As the day headed towards noon and they were nearing the village of Easington, the soldiers at the rear of the escort began to take up a cry. Isabeth's head popped up, trying to see what had their attention, and she could see a lone rider racing down the road towards them. The escort began to move aside to allow the rider to pass, but as he drew closer, they could see that it was a knight.

A de Wolfe knight.

And he was riding hard.

Isabeth caught sight of him, too, knowing without even seeing the man's face that it was Ronan. It couldn't be anyone else. The sergeant in charge of the escort asked her if she wanted to stop and, with reluctance, she gave the order. The escort ground to a halt as the knight thundered up behind them, heading straight for the wagon where Isabeth was just rising to her knees.

From the size of the man, her suspicions of Ronan were

confirmed even before he showed his face. As she watched anxiously, he dismounted his warhorse and tethered the animal to the wagon bench before approaching Isabeth.

He held out his hands to her.

"A word, Madam," he rumbled.

Isabeth didn't reply. The tone of his voice frightened her so she wasn't sure what she could say other than she was completely guilty of leaving him behind. She stood up in the wagon bed, preparing to climb out, but he grasped her around the waist and easily lifted her out. Then, he tucked her hand into the crook of his elbow and forced her to walk several feet away from the big ears of the soldiers. Only when there was a sufficient distance between them did he come to a halt, lift his visor, and face her.

The dark eyes were rolling with fury.

"I do not know whose bright idea it was to try to escape me, but this will stop here and now," he said, his voice low. "Whoever gave the order should know that I do not take attempts to force me to break my word lightly. Not much infuriates me in this world, but dishonor does. I have been made to look dishonorable and I will not tolerate that. Now, who should I speak to about this? Who gave the order to leave Middlesbrough without me?"

Isabeth was looking at him with great fear. "I did," she confessed. "I did because… because I do not think you should be forced to keep your word to a man who should have never asked such things of you in the first place. I am absolving you of that duty, Sir Ronan."

"It is not your choice, Lady de Brito."

There was anger in every syllable, mostly because he was right. It wasn't her choice. However, Isabeth had made it her choice and now she had a furious knight on her hands, one who took his promise to Dyce seriously. Perhaps she hadn't realized that before as much as she did at this moment. More than anything, she'd offended him.

"Mayhap it is not," she said, her composure starting to slip. "But you will forgive me, my lord, when I say that this is my situation. This is my life now and I must do as I feel best. You do not have any bearing on my life from this point forward and I do not need your help. Dyce spent his life trying to protect me and treating me like a fragile little thing, and that is something you and I have discussed. But in his last moments, he did not have the right to ask you to assume his responsibility when he was gone. He was my husband and you are not. If I do not want your assistance, it is within my right to refuse you."

She was trembling by the time she was finished, her eyes filling with tears. Ronan could see that he'd upset her, but the truth was that he was upset, too. He'd just spent the past three hours riding like the devil to catch up to the escort that he was supposed to be in charge of, so Isabeth's attitude wasn't unexpected. He knew she was resistant to his presence. Perhaps he thought he could assert himself and she would acquiesce.

But she didn't seem to want to.

At that point, he did the only thing he could do – he backed down.

"It is," he said quietly. "But I wish you would not. I very much want to help you, my lady. Dyce was my dear friend and I feel as if I would be wronging him greatly if I simply let you go about your life without my help. I would worry over you."

Isabeth sniffled. "I am not trying to be difficult, my lord, truly," she said. "But I simply want to go home and I do not want to be inconsiderate to people I hardly know simply because my husband asked you to watch over me. I do not need watching over. I simply wish to go home and stay there."

The storm clouds that were gathering overhead began to let loose with fat droplets of water. One hit Ronan in the cheek and he looked up, seeing that the rain was indeed coming. Frustrated with the situation and knowing it wouldn't be resolved in the next minute or so, he looked around, noting there was a village up ahead, one he'd stayed in before when he'd come south. He knew there was an inn there, a small one, and it would fill up in this weather if it hadn't already.

"You'll not be home tonight," he said, taking Isabeth by the elbow and turning her back towards the wagon. "There is an inn in town. We'll stay there tonight. It will give my escort a chance to catch up to us."

Isabeth let him lead her to the wagon. "Your escort?" she said. "You have more men coming?"

Ronan nodded. "More men and my wife," he said. "I believe Marian would like to be of some help to you during this time. If you have other friends or family you would like me to send for, I will do that, but until then, Lady de Wolfe and I are glad to be of some comfort."

Isabeth thought about Marian de Wolfe and the mere thought of the woman made her stomach churn. "Although I appreciate your intentions, I do not need your comfort," she said. "I have my maid with me. She is comfort enough."

Ronan lifted an eyebrow. "Having a maid is not the same as having the company of a woman of your station."

The battle lines were forming and Isabeth went on the offensive. "My lord, I know you are doing what you believe you should do," she said. "But I genuinely do not want company right now, not even your lady wife. If I have not made that clear, then I shall do so now. I do not know Lady de Wolfe well and I would feel as if I needed to be hospitable and I simply do not feel like that right now. I do not have the strength. I wish to be left alone."

She was speaking more firmly than Ronan had ever heard her, indicative of the seriousness of her statement. But all of this was still new, and she was disoriented. She didn't truly know what she wanted, or so he thought. That was the entire reason he wasn't leaving right away – women had a tendency to change their minds and he wanted to be there when she changed hers.

"Come," he said, grasping her by her slender waist and lifting her up into the wagon again. "We must find shelter."

He didn't give her a chance to argue with him. He whistled loudly between his teeth, getting the escort moving, and the wagon moved out quickly. Isabeth had been on her knees, knocked onto her bottom when the wagon lurched forward.

The entire escort moved into the village.

The rain was starting to fall a little heavier as they pulled into the little seaside village of Hinderwell. There was a small district with some merchants and a town well, and the only inn in town sat on the south side. It was called The Fox and Rabbit, with a hand-painted sign on driftwood over the door. As the wagon pulled up to the entry, Ronan was waiting for Isabeth, lifting her out of the wagon again and shouting for someone to bring her bags.

Isabeth found herself ushered into the warm, stale inn whether or not she wanted to be.

Fortunately, the common room was only about half-full and the innkeeper nervously ran to the entry door as a knight, lady, and soldiers started pouring in. The first thing Ronan did was demand a room for the lady and the innkeeper was quick to comply. He provided a room overlooking the livery yard behind the inn, so it was relatively quiet.

Isabeth was being pulled around by Ronan, who had taken charge in a way Dyce had never had the presence or strength to do so. It was quite impressive and quite intimidating, but she let him pull her into the rented chamber as a servant wench brought in peat and kindling. The innkeeper was ordering the servant about in frantic tones as someone brought in Isabeth's bags. She only had two of them, satchels made from canvas, and they were tossed onto the relatively big bed. In fact, the entire chamber was large for a rented room and she unfastened her cloak, looking at her surroundings as she did so.

"I'll have food and a bath brought to you," Ronan said, standing by the door. "Is there anything else you require?"

Isabeth turned to look at him. "Possibly Gerta," she said. But then, she shook her head and tossed the cloak onto a chair. "I suppose not. I'd rather be alone."

Ronan glanced around the chamber. "It may get cold tonight with the storm," he said. "I will have the innkeeper send more blankets."

She stopped him. "Nay," she said. "I do not require anything further and I think you have done more than enough. In the morning, you may return back to Middlesbrough and I will continue on to Ravenscar."

She wasn't deviating from her demands to be left alone. He'd hoped that she would become accustomed to his presence since he was resolute to keep his word to Dyce, but she wasn't having any of it. She was still as stubborn as ever.

Ronan stared at her a moment before sighing heavily.

"Madam, you will not give me orders," he said. "I will not have this conversation with you again, so let *me* be clear. I understand your wish. I understand that you wish to be left alone. But I made a promise that you cannot force me to break, so stop trying. I will go with you to Ravenscar and I will attend the burial of my friend. If you do not like it, keep it to yourself, for your ungrateful ramblings are becoming tiresome."

Isabeth's cheeks flushed a dull red. "I am *not* ungrateful," she said. "I simply want to be left alone. Why can you not honor my wishes?"

Ronan's dark eyes flashed. "Because they are not Dyce's wishes," he said. Then, he jabbed an enormous finger in the direction of the stables where the wagon had been brought to rest. "There is a dead man outside in a pine box, one of the finest men I have ever known, and I will obey his wishes to the letter. Your protests reek of disobedience and ungracious behavior and Dyce would be ashamed of you. Stop acting like a selfish fool and start behaving like the wife of a good and decent man."

His words were harsh, harsher than they should have been, and her eyes filled with tears. She turned her back on Ronan and the sounds of her quiet weeping filled the air. Ronan watched her gently heaving shoulders but he didn't move to apologize. He meant what he'd said and she had to know that, once and for all. He wasn't going anywhere.

Without another word, he quit the chamber and shut the door quietly.

☙

"SHE'S NOT SELFISH, you know."

Ronan had been sitting in the common room of the inn, in a chair that had been placed before the fire. He'd been staring into the flames for the better part of three hours, drinking ale as the world went on around him. The ale was particularly strong, locally brewed, and flavored with apples. He could taste them. But he also tasted straw and whatever else managed to make it into the brew. But the soft voice behind him had his attention and he turned to see a very old de Brito soldier standing there. When their eyes met, there was no fear in the old man's eyes.

Only truth.

"Who?" Ronan said.

"Lady de Brito," the old soldier said. "I brought her satchels into the chamber. I heard what you said to her. If I was a younger man, I'd call you out for it."

Ronan was torn between amusement and annoyance. But he could see from the man's expression how serious he was, which tempered his reaction. He'd said something very brave. Or very foolish. Ronan's response would determine which.

Therefore, it was measured.

"I do not believe that is any of your affair," he finally said. "I can handle the lady without any advice."

The old soldier sighed heavily, scratching his nose. "She's *not* selfish, my lord," he said. "She is one of the most giving and compassionate ladies you'll ever meet. What you said to her… it was hurtful. She did not deserve it. I thought you should know."

The old man said it with some emotion, leading Ronan to believe he was somehow emotionally attached or emotionally involved when it came to his young mistress. Not in a romantic sense, but in the sense of humanity. Perhaps he'd known her most of her life. Perhaps she reminded him of his daughter. Or perhaps he was simply fond of her. Whatever the case, he was astute enough to know that the old soldier wasn't speaking out of turn.

He meant what he'd said.

"What's your name?" Ronan finally asked.

"Bibby, my lord."

"You know that Sir Dyce asked me to look out for his wife, do you not?"

The old soldier nodded. "I do, my lord."

"Sir Dyce was my dear friend and I gave the man my word."

"I understand, my lord."

"Then you must also understand that I am in a difficult position," Ronan said. "Lady de Brito seems not to want any assistance, but I gave Dyce my word. I must honor my word no matter what she wants."

The old soldier nodded in resignation. "I know, my lord," he said. Then, he hesitated a moment before continuing. "May I speak freely, my lord?"

"You've been doing a pretty good job of it already."

The old soldier grunted, a flicker of a grin on his lips. "She's afraid," he muttered. "My lord has taken care of her since she was a young girl. He married her when she was barely of age and he's been a father to her more than her own father. I don't know if the lass knows how to even think for herself because Lord Dyce did her thinking for her, and her father before him. For the first time in her life, she has to make a decision and she's afraid."

Ronan lifted his shoulders. "Of what?" he said. "The decision for me to accompany her to Ravenscar has already been made."

Bibby shook his head. "That's not what I meant, my lord," he said. "Lady de Brito is afraid of being a bother. She's afraid of causing you trouble so she is trying to make the decision *not* to cause you trouble, if that makes sense. The lass doesn't have a selfish bone in her body, I assure you. She's very kind and thoughtful of others to the point where it would even be detrimental to herself. When she tells you that she wants to go home and be alone, it's because she's frightened to be a bother."

Ronan sighed faintly. "She is *not* a bother," he said. "She should not worry about me. If I did not want to do this, I would have told her so. But I do. I want to show respect to my dear friend and his wife by carrying out his final wishes."

Bibby scratched his head. "Then may I give you some advice?"

"I wish you would."

"She's not afraid to speak her mind," he said. "You've seen that. The lass will tell you what she thinks because I've seen her do it. But when she tells you to leave… just ignore her. Don't fight with her. It just hurts her feelings when she's only thinking of you. At least, she's trying to. Truthfully, Lord Dyce and her father kept the lass so isolated, she has difficulty communicating sometimes because Lord Dyce always did it for her. This is the first time she's had a voice all her own, with no interference from him."

He made sense and Ronan appreciated his candor. "How long have you known Lady de Brito?"

Bibby's grin broke through, revealing missing teeth. "I used to serve her father," he said. "I was part of her dowry."

"Then you've known her all her life."

"All her life, indeed."

Ronan eyed the old soldier, thinking that perhaps he *had* been too harsh with Isabeth when she was evidently only thinking of him – but not communicating it very well. He'd never in his life met a socially awkward woman, but that was apparently what he had on his hands. He never would have guessed it by her wit the first day of the tournament, before things turned so terribly bad, but perhaps that was because Dyce was by her side. Perhaps his presence gave her confidence. But Dyce wasn't by her side any longer and perhaps Isabeth didn't know what to think or how to manage what she was now in charge of. Ronan realized he needed to make her feel comfortable in this strange new world she found herself in.

A world with no husband speaking for her.

"Thank you, Bibby," he said. "I shall amend my ways accordingly."

The old soldier simply nodded his head and headed out of the inn. Ronan watched the man go before standing up, thinking on his next course of action. Initially, he was going to leave Isabeth alone this night but he was coming to think that might not be wise. Her first night without her husband, in a strange place, with a strange future ahead of her. She was understandably disoriented.

He'd be less than a friend if he allowed her to feel such loneliness on this night.

Ronan knew that a bath had been brought to her as well as a meal because her chamber door was in his line of sight and he'd seen the servants going in and out. He'd seen the bathtub go in and he'd seen it come out. A food tray, too, but he hadn't noticed if it was empty when it was removed. He'd been too busy paying attention to his own thoughts and wants.

Therefore, he went back to the kitchen and spoke with the old couple there who did the cooking. They showed him the tray that had come out of the front room, the room they called the King's Room, and it was a full tray. Nothing had been touched. They were going to feed it to someone else and Ronan gave them his blessing to redistribute the food, but he also ordered a fresh meal.

He watched the wife, an elderly woman with wild gray hair tied up with twine, dish out stew from a large pot over the hearth. Bread and butter joined the stew on a new tray. They had some kind of almond dish but remembering what Isabeth had said about almonds, he passed that over for an egg dish that had been baked that morning. They were hard boiled eggs that had been rolled in a fish paste and breadcrumbs and fried in fat. The old woman warmed them up before putting the dish on the tray.

Armed with a tray loaded with food as perhaps a peace offering, he headed towards Isabeth's rented chamber.

03

SHE SHOULD HAVE been exhausted, but she simply wasn't.

Isabeth stood at the window, overlooking the kitchen yard, seeing the Ravenscar wagon parked partially in the barn. She could clearly see Dyce's casket, which had been covered with an oil cloth that was weighed down with rocks. A storm was raging at this hour, having blown in off the sea, and the de Brito soldiers had done their best to protect their lord's remains. But all Isabeth could do was stare at the casket.

Was she truly being selfish?

Was this entire incident caused by her selfishness?

As the shock of Dyce's passing began to settle, several things began to occur to her, not the least of which was the fact that she had been pestering Dyce to compete in the Middlesbrough tournament ever since he'd told her about it nearly a year ago. Dyce usually only competed in the smaller tournaments because, truthfully, he wasn't terribly practiced at it, but the Middlesbrough tournament was a much bigger tournament than he'd been used to, attended by the professionals who followed the circuit. And she'd encouraged him to compete so she could attend.

Perhaps it really was her selfishness that brought her to this point in her life.

With a heavy sigh, Isabeth turned away from the window and sealed the oil cloth so the wind wouldn't blow it around. Her chamber was quite warm, as the fire in the hearth was burning brightly. She'd taken a bath that evening, washing with lavender-scented soap that Dyce had bought her, and she'd soaked until her skin wrinkled up.

She'd lain in the water, her full breasts right at the waterline, running her hands over her barely rounded belly and thinking of the child growing inside of her. But the hands on her belly moved to the fluff of curls between her legs, a part of her body that Dyce had claimed for his own. He had probed, touched, stroked, tasted, and kissed the junction between her legs and there had been a few times when he'd brought her pleasure, but not much. Sometimes, when Dyce touched her, she would close her eyes and imagine it to be someone strong and handsome and exciting. She knew it was wrong, but Dyce's touch had never meant that much to her.

That was something she'd resigned herself to.

Truth be told, she was young and virile. Dyce had shown her a taste of the pleasure a man could give a woman. As she lay back in the water and stroked herself, she easily brought herself to a climax, something old Gerta had told her was bad for the child she carried. It wasn't as if old Gerta knew she touched herself so sinfully, but the superstitious old woman had told her not to climax when her husband made love to her.

That really wasn't difficult.

When the bath grew cool, she finally climbed out and dried

off before the fire. Donning a heavy lamb's wool shift with long sleeves and a high neck, something to keep her warm on this stormy night, she'd dried her hair by the fire, running her comb through it until the titian locks dried into soft waves. The storm raged on outside and she knew she should try and get some sleep, but she simply wasn't tired. She was spiritually and mentally exhausted, but sleep… it wouldn't come easily this night. As she sat and pondered the bed a few feet away, there was a soft knock at her chamber door.

Curious, she pulled her shawl from one of her satchels and wrapped it around her shoulders as she approached the door.

"Who comes?" she asked quietly.

"Ronan, my lady," came the reply.

Wondering what the man wanted at this late hour and suspecting he might have returned to yell at her again, she was hesitant to answer the door. But then she was fearful that he might kick it open, so she threw the bolt and slowly lifted the latch, opening it just enough so that he could see one eye.

"What is it?" she asked warily.

Ronan lifted the tray. "I come in peace," he said. "May I enter?"

The one eye looked at the food on the tray for a moment. "I am not hungry, my lord."

Ronan maintained the faint smile on his lips. "But mayhap your son is," he said quietly. "I would wager that you have not eaten all day and you must think of Dyce's son. You would not starve a child, would you?"

That shot holes in her resistance. After a moment, she shook her head in surrender. "Nay," she said, opening the door to admit him. "Come in."

Ronan entered the very warm chamber and set the tray

down on the table. The fire was blazing in the hearth as the storm raged outside. He turned to see that Isabeth was still back by the door, still eyeing him warily, and he stood away from the table and indicated for her to sit.

"Please," he said encouragingly. "Eat it while it is still hot."

She took his invitation but it was reluctantly. She sat down, shawl clutched around her shoulders, eyeing all of the food on the tray. When she reached for the cup of wine, she realized that it was warm and she took a healthy swallow.

All the while, Ronan watched her closely.

"My lady, I am sorry the past two days have been so difficult between us," he said quietly. "May we calmly discuss the situation? I fear our emotions may have gotten the better of us."

Isabeth was cutting into the boiled egg, but she paused and looked up at him. "I am not certain what there is to discuss."

"I think there is a lot to discuss," Ronan said, trying not to sound too forceful. "I was harsh with you earlier and I apologize, but I know you understand that a knight's word is his bond. I promised your husband something and I cannot go back on my word. You were married to an honorable man, so I know you understand how important honor is to a knight."

She turned back to her egg, cutting more slowly. "I understand."

"Then you realize I am not leaving you."

She sighed heavily. "I suppose I do."

She seemed quite sad. Ronan wasn't heartless – he understood that she was feeling defeated. Her husband had died and now she had a knight she could not shake, grimly determined to be of service whether or not she wanted him to be.

"My lady, I promise to be as unobtrusive as possible," he said. "I will follow your orders. Other than leaving, I shall do as you please. How can I make this situation easier for you? How can I help you?"

Isabeth picked up a piece of the egg and put it in her mouth, chewing slowly. "I am not entirely sure," she finally said. "I do not think you can help me at all. What… what I mean to say is how does one go on after death? This is not how I imagined the rest of my life. I always thought Dyce would be with me, so how does one go on with an unexpected future?"

It was an extremely candid question in an unguarded moment and Ronan took it seriously.

"May I share something with you?" he asked.

"Aye."

Ronan thought carefully on what he would say next. "When I was around seven years of age, my father was killed in battle in Wales," he said. "My mother and father had known each other all their lives and when news of his death came, I remember that my mother sat in her chamber for days on end, simply staring from the window. She wouldn't eat and she hardly slept. Although I was young, I felt as if my entire life had ended. I loved my father very much, you see, and although losing a father is not like losing a husband, the sense of loss is still great. Even back then, my grandmother insisted that my father wasn't really dead… he'd simply stepped into the next room. That is what I told you before, the way she chose to view death. Think of it that way – that Dyce has simply stepped into the next room and you must carry on as if he is going to return at any moment. That means you live your life in a way that would bring him honor and when your son is born, you raise the boy to know his father as if Dyce has been there all along."

By that time, Isabeth was looking at him. "And your mother?" she said. "Did she pretend that your father had just stepped into the next room, too?"

Ronan nodded. "She did," he said. "For a while, anyway. Then, she met her next husband and that helped ease her grief. She had something to look forward to at that point and her life continued in a happy way. But I should tell you that in my father's case, he really *had* just stepped into the next room, for he returned five years later a changed man."

Isabeth was curious at that statement. "What happened?"

Ronan pulled up the nearest chair and sat down wearily. "He received a terrible head wound in an ambush," he said. "My grandfathers and my uncles thought that he was dead and because they were outnumbered by the Welsh, they were forced to leave him behind. As it turned out, he wasn't dead. He was saved by a Welsh warlord who healed him. Unfortunately, because of the head injury, my father did not remember who he was or where he came from until years later. But he returned and I have always been grateful."

Isabeth's eyebrows lifted. "That is a miraculous story."

"Indeed, it is," he said. "But I think the point is, for you, to take every day as it comes, focus on your son, focus on Dyce's properties and administer them in a way that would make him proud. Keeping busy will help ease the grief."

Isabeth lifted her shoulders. "But I do not know the first thing about administering his properties," she said. "He did everything himself. He told me that my head was too pretty to be filled with useless knowledge."

Ronan smiled faintly. "That is also why I am here," he said. "Although your head is quite pretty, I do not agree with Dyce when it comes to useless knowledge. No knowledge is useless. I will teach you everything you need to know and you will be an excellent student."

Her brow furrowed. "How do you know?"

His smile broadened. "Because you are bright and witty," he said. "I saw it the first night at Middlesbrough when you told Dyce that I was your brother because you knew so much about me. I still hope that you will always consider me your brother, my lady. I would be honored."

Isabeth's gaze lingered on him before she returned to her egg. "That night at Middlesbrough seems so long ago," she said. "So much has happened since then."

He watched her pick at her egg. "Aye, it has," he said. "But you are made of strong stuff. This will not sink you."

She sighed faintly. "It feels like it already has."

"Nay," he said quietly. "I am your boat in rough seas. I will not let anything sink you."

Isabeth looked at him, grinning in spite of herself. "You do not look like a boat."

He snorted. "Have you ever been on a boat?"

She nodded. "Once," she said. "Dyce took me to Calais when we were first married. The boat made me so sick I could hardly eat anything. I vowed to never go on a boat again."

Ronan broke down into laughter. "And here I am, comparing myself to a boat," he said. "I am coming to think that was not the right comparison."

Because he was laughing, she grinned. "Mayhap not," she said. "But it was appropriate. When one sinks, one needs a boat."

"I hope this boat will not make you sick."

She giggled. "Surely not," she said, looking more relaxed than he'd seen her since Dyce's passing. Finally, he was getting a glimpse of that witty woman again as she warmed to the conversation. "And you don't smell like the rotten sea, which is refreshing."

He, too, was relaxing with the conversation at hand. "That you know of," he teased. "I'm far enough away that you cannot smell my barnacles."

Isabeth burst into gales of laughter. She also took another bite of her egg because the humor was helping her appetite. "What an enticing thought," she said, though she didn't mean a word of it. "How does Lady de Wolfe feel about the smell of barnacles?"

Ronan's smile faded somewhat. He couldn't tell her that his wife didn't care how he smelled. Or looked. Or thought. They hadn't been intimate in years, not since his last daughter was born and he knew the child wasn't his. He couldn't tell Isabeth that he didn't have a relationship with his wife like the one she had with Dyce, where there was genuine caring.

Nay, he couldn't tell her that.

To admit it would be to admit failure.

"I suppose it's all part of the de Wolfe allure," he said, avoiding the question. "Tell me about Briarfield. I've never been there but know the area. To the west in the moors, isn't it?"

It was a change in subject. If Isabeth noticed, she didn't let on. She went on like normal, finishing up her egg and cutting into the second one. "Aye," she said. "It is about a day's ride from here. And it was a rather idyllic upbringing, I suppose. My mother, my father, me, and no trouble that I can recall."

"Where did you foster?"

"Nottingham," she said. "My father did business with the castle and knew the lord, so I fostered there for a few years. I met Dyce right before I left to foster."

"How old were you?"

"About nine," she said. "I went to foster when I was nine

years of age and returned when I was twelve because my mother couldn't stand to be parted from me. She said that three years was enough."

He nodded in understanding. "It is difficult on the parents, to be sure, unless you can't stand your children and are eager to be rid of them."

He said it with a twinkle in his eyes and she grinned. "You have children, do you not?"

Ronan struggled not to lose his humor completely. "Anne, Esther, and Priscilla."

"Where do they foster?"

Ronan averted his gaze, shifting on his chair now that they were on the unhappy subject of the offspring that bore the de Wolfe name.

"Anne and Esther are at Northwood Castle," he said. "Priscilla is at Castle Questing, though she is still a little young to foster. Mostly, she is staying with my mother, who lives at Castle Questing."

Isabeth was devouring her second egg, interested in the conversation. "You must miss them terribly," she said. "I know that I must send my son to foster, but even as I think on it, it makes me so very sad. I have never understood why young children must be sent away from those who love them."

Ronan shrugged. "It is the custom," he said. "They go to learn great and noble things. They go to learn how life is different at homes other than their own. It is all part of their education. It was part of yours and part of mine."

"Where did you foster?"

"Kenilworth," he said. "I was trained by the master knights of Kenilworth before returning to Northumberland and serving in any number of my family's properties. The past few years, however, I have been at Roxburgh Castle because it is so active."

"What does that mean – active?"

"It means the Scots are bent on throwing out the English and claiming the castle for their own," he said. "It is a very volatile location."

Isabeth nodded in understanding. "I have never seen a battle in my life," she said. "Briarfield is not a contested castle, nor does anyone want it badly enough to fight for it, so it has not seen a battle in one hundred years."

Ronan grunted. "I have seen battles since I was a small lad," he said. "In fact, I even fought a few as a young boy."

She frowned. "The House of de Wolfe forces children to fight?"

His grin was back. "Nay, not like that," he said. "After my father died, I felt it my duty to take up arms in his stead. Remember that I was only seven when he died, so there were times when I would follow the army to a skirmish and do my best to smite the enemy."

Her eyes widened. "And you were never injured?"

"Never. But I did get a grandfatherly beating or two."

Isabeth chuckled. "But it did not stop you."

"Never," he said. "In case you have not realized it, I can be rather stubborn when it comes to doing something I feel strongly that I must do."

"Like honoring your word to a dying man."

"Exactly. Or fighting in my father's stead, even as a child."

Isabeth's gaze lingered on him for a moment, a twinkle to her eyes. "Very well," she finally said, as if surrendering. "I understand now."

"What do you understand?"

"That I cannot be rid of you no matter how much I want

to."

His eyes glimmered at her. "Now you understand every-thing, Madam."

She nodded in resignation. "You are a stubborn man, Ronan de Wolfe."

He chuckled. "Stubborn is where I begin," he said. "Where I end, no one knows. I've yet to find any ending to anything about me. Everything that I am is continuously expanding, ever-reaching. I will go on forever."

Her smile was warmer and more relaxed than it had ever been before. "I would believe that," she said. "Therefore, I will give you permission to return to Ravenscar with me. But given the circumstances… you will forgive me if I am not the most gracious chatelaine. I will try, but there may be times when I simply do not feel like…"

She trailed off and the mood of the conversation took a downturn. However, in this case, Ronan understood completely and it didn't feel as if things had turned sour between them. Not in the least. In fact, he felt as if they had more common ground now.

As if they understood each other better.

"Not to worry," he said quietly. "If you feel as if you are sinking, remember that I am your boat. Barnacles and all. All you need to do is ask and I shall move heaven and earth to grant your wish."

All Isabeth could do was smile in response, unsure what more to say. This conversation between them had been the most productive conversation yet, without arguing or unhappy feelings. It wasn't as if she'd changed her mind about him or his wife – she still didn't want either one of them at Ravenscar – but she knew it would be a losing battle to try and keep them away.

She wasn't very good at fighting battles.

Therefore, the conversation died. They sat in relative but not uncomfortable silence until Isabeth finished her food, every last crumb, and Ronan took the tray away. Their time together, for the moment, was over. Leaving the woman to sleep, he had a feeling of peace he'd not had when he'd entered the chamber. Peace that things were going to be well, after all.

At least that was the hope.

Until Lady de Wolfe and her entourage entered the inn.

That was when things started to become difficult again.

CHAPTER SIX

ISABETH NOTICED SOMETHING about Marian right away.

She kept looking over her shoulder at one of the men riding at the rear of the column. Given what Dyce had told her about Marian de Wolfe, perhaps she was simply being overly suspicious. Truthfully, she shouldn't have even cared what Marian de Wolfe did but, somehow, she found it fascinating that a woman should be so unfaithful to her husband with his full knowledge.

Isabeth hadn't been oblivious when Ronan had changed the subject away from his daughters the night before. As soon as he mentioned them, he had changed the focus of the conversation and Isabeth had simply gone with it, unwilling to discuss something that was clearly unpleasant to him.

Not that she blamed him.

But Marian was coming to fascinate her as a woman who did what she wanted regardless of whether or not it was proper. Or, perhaps, that was only the gossip. Not knowing Marian, she wanted to give the woman the benefit of the doubt but that was increasingly difficult as Marian continued to look to the rear of the column, spying someone back there and smiling coyly before she turned back around and faced forward. Once, Isabeth thought she caught a glimpse of a smile on one of the knights who had come with Marian.

Isabeth seemed to recognize the knight as one she'd seen at Middlesbrough. She'd seen him sitting at a table at the feast the first night of the tournament and she had seen him the next day simply in the crowd. Though she'd lived a somewhat sheltered life, she wasn't a fool. She was astute when it came to men and women and emotion, and what she was seeing between Lady de Wolfe and the knight was something more than simply friendliness.

There was flirting going on.

She wondered if Ronan was aware.

Isabeth kept going back to what Dyce had said about the situation. *Poor Ronan*, he'd said. *Marian de Wolfe does not let something like a marriage slow her down. She has had more men in her bed than a London prostitute.* The politics of the situation were sticky given that the marriage was between two of the largest families in the north, but the fact remained that Ronan had a trollop for a wife. The more the escort plodded along south towards Ravenscar, the more Isabeth could see how Marian was so wrapped up in herself and in the knight she was trying to flirt with that she didn't care who noticed her behavior.

And Isabeth had been watching ever since they had left the inn.

The situation had been very odd. Marian had arrived very late the previous night and she'd barely been ready to depart that morning when Ronan mustered the escort. In fact, she had them all waiting in the kitchen yard as she dragged herself out of the inn, followed by two women and three soldiers carrying her baggage. She looked as if she'd brought everything she owned with her, which made Isabeth's two satchels seem rather meager. She was so tired that she'd barely said two words to Isabeth before the escort headed south.

And that was where Isabeth found herself now – sitting in the wagon bed next to Dyce's casket, watching Marian aboard her gray palfrey, flirting with the knight at the rear of the column. Ronan was at the head of the column and Isabeth found herself watching him, feeling sorry for the man who had so much honor in him that he kept his word with a dead man. It was a most confusing situation.

He was a most confusing man.

As the morning deepened, old Gerta provided Isabeth with something to eat because she hadn't broken her fast at dawn. Truth be told, she didn't feel much like eating because the child in her belly made her feel nauseous sometimes, but the bread and cheese and boiled apple juice managed to settle her stomach a little. She was just finishing it when one of Marian's ladies trotted up to the wagon bed and held out a sack.

"Lady de Wolfe insists you eat this." The woman with the high forehead and severe wimple spoke with a lisp. "She says that you must keep your strength up."

Isabeth eyed the sack. "What is it?"

"Pork and egg pie, seasoned with honey," the woman said, dropping the sack in the wagon bed because Isabeth wasn't fast enough to take it in-hand. "You must eat it."

Isabeth thought the woman quite demanding for a mere servant. "Thank your lady for her kindness," she said, though she would have been quite content saying nothing at all. "I appreciate it."

The woman's gaze lingered on her. "Prove it," she said. "Eat what Lady de Wolfe has been gracious enough to give you."

"I will when I am hungry."

That wasn't what the woman wanted to hear. "Lady de Wolfe has given you a command," she said. "You must keep up your strength. We are being forced to escort you home because of your husband's unfortunate accident and the least you could do is obey your hostess."

So much for Isabeth's attempts to be polite. Her eyes narrowed.

"I do not like your tone," she said. "Lady de Wolfe is *not* my hostess. She is not my anything. Her husband was a dear friend of my husband and Sir Ronan is escorting me and my husband back to our home. Now, go back to your lady and remain there before I throw this pie in your face."

The woman geared up for a retort but Marian was suddenly there, resplendent upon her white mare. She put up a hand, mostly to her lady. "Enough," she snapped quietly. "Go to the rear and stay there, Lenora."

The woman bowed her head obediently and reined her little horse around, heading back to the group of de Wolfe soldiers who were bringing up the rear. Marian watched her go before smiling wanly at Isabeth.

"She is used to dealing with very difficult people," Marian said, a half-baked attempt at an apology. "Sometimes, she is difficult herself. It seems that you and I have not had any time to speak to one another this morning, so I wanted to send you the pie in greeting. I do hope you slept well last night."

It was a ridiculous and forced question, simply to be polite, and Isabeth resisted the urge to roll her eyes. This was what she didn't want to do – be polite and carry on a conversation with a woman she was increasingly feeling a dislike for. If Marian's lady was haughty, it was because Marian set the example. That had been evident since nearly the moment they'd met.

"I did," she said shortly. "My lady, I am grateful that you have taken your valuable time to accompany me to Ravenscar, but I told your husband that it is unnecessary. Surely I am keeping you from something far more important you wish to be doing. I have no desire to impede you like that."

Marian's wan smile turned stiff. "You are not impeding me," she said. "It is my husband who is impeding me. He is to blame."

"And I told him I did not want him to come with me to Ravenscar but he insisted. Please know I have not asked him to come with me. Quite the opposite."

Marian's smile faded as her gaze raked over Isabeth. "Why shouldn't he want to come?" she asked. "A lovely young widow? Of course he should want to come. The more you tell him to go away, the more he will remain by your side. He wants to be the first to comfort you."

It was a terrible thing to say. Isabeth thought she might be trying to compliment her at first, but she quickly decided that wasn't the case. It was a blatant insult, quite surprising considering she and Marian had only had civil words before. Still, it was clear that the woman was bitter and her first hint was that savage lady-in-waiting who had hinted at her mistress' unwanted journey to Ravenscar.

Clearly, Marian blamed her.

"My lady," she said slowly. "When you and I met at the feast the other night, I was quite certain that we would be friends."

"We said so, didn't we?"

"A friend would not say to me what you just did."

Marian's brow rippled with confusion until she realized that

Isabeth was on to her not-so-subtle insult. "I simply meant that he was a good friend of your husband," she said, backtracking. "It is right that he should want to comfort you."

"I do not want his comfort," Isabeth said steadily. "And that is not what you meant. If we are friends, Marian, then friends do not lie to one another. They do not insult one another. I have asked your husband to leave and he has refused, so if you believe he wants to comfort me, then it is not my fault. I have given him no encouragement. But if the man is looking to comfort a woman other than his wife, mayhap the fault lies with the wife."

All hint of warmth or friendliness was gone from Marian's face as she realized Isabeth hadn't minced words. "You dare say such a thing to me?" she hissed. "I shall forgive you this time because you are grieving and out of your mind, but watch your tongue, Woman. I will not be so forgiving the second time."

Isabeth sized her up, thinking that she really was a nasty piece of work. Usually, she wasn't so confrontational, but grief and travel and Marian's passive-aggressive behavior had weakened her composure. Marian had made her position on the situation clear.

Isabeth would do the same.

"You can sling insults but you are offended when one is lobbed back at you?" she asked. "That must be the spoiled, highborn wench in you. Women who are used to hurting others and expecting no retaliation in return. If that is the case, then you have insulted the wrong woman. Treat me the way you wish to be treated, Lady de Wolfe. If you insult me, I will assume you wish to be insulted in return, for I will not cower to your bad behavior."

Marian's mouth popped open in shock and outrage. "You

little piece of filth," she growled. "I shall tell my husband what you have said to me. He'll have something to say about it."

Isabeth cocked an eyebrow. "Say anything you wish," she said. "I will happily tell him about the knight you've been flirting with for the duration of this journey. You did not think I saw the winks and smiles you've been passing him, did you? My husband warned me about you. It seems that he was correct."

Marian's mouth shut and her face turned red. Her lips worked as if she wanted to say something but couldn't quite bring forth the words because she knew if she did, Isabeth would toss them right back at her. She wasn't used to that, not in the least, and the fact that Isabeth had noticed the flirting she'd been doing with the young knight she'd met in Middlesbrough had her rethinking her next move. It wasn't as if she had been particularly discreet about it, but for someone to call her out on it…

"Bitch," she muttered.

"At least I am not a harlot."

The retort came fast and succinctly. It was like a slap to Marian. Her head snapped back, her eyes widened, and she jerked her palfrey around, heading back to where her women were riding. Isabeth watched her go, rather pleased with herself because she had met Marian de Wolfe on her own terms and she had held her own. The lines of battle had been drawn and she wasn't sorry in the least. She just wanted to go home and she wanted that witch of a woman to leave her alone. But she wasn't unrealistic. Time would tell if Marian kept her mouth shut and stayed away.

Or if her sense of highborn vengeance meant Isabeth was in for trouble.

CЗ

RAVENSCAR CASTLE WAS more of a fortified manse than a castle, nestled on a cliff overlooking the North Sea. In the days of old, Northmen would land on the sandy beaches and the castle had seen more than its share of raids and sieges, but that hadn't happened in a hundred years. The Northmen bypassed Ravenscar for the larger settlements to the north. Isabeth had never been afraid living here. In fact, she loved it deeply. The smell of the sea, the sounds of the waves, and the damp breeze that would caress her face. All of it was treasured.

She was very happy to return home.

But she was also very sad.

Dyce had adored Ravenscar. It had been part of his blood even though he hadn't been born there. It didn't matter to him – he'd loved it the moment he first saw it and Isabeth still saw him standing on the battlements, looking out to sea as the damp north wind lifted his dark hair.

The ghost of Dyce was already there.

As soon as they'd arrived in the rather vast bailey, they were met by the majordomo of Ravenscar, Odo Norbreck. The old man had served Isabeth's father, a rather stout one-eyed man who had served the Earl of Alnwick at one point in his life. He was savvy and efficient, and one look at the casket on the wagon and he knew what had happened. His old face had been filled with sadness. He had greeted Isabeth with sorrow and she had explained the situation to him, including the de Wolfe guests. After asking the majordomo to see to the needs of their visitors, she retreated to her chamber and locked the door.

It was too much.

That's what Isabeth kept repeating to herself. All of it was just too much – Dyce's death, the de Wolfe escort, Ronan's insistence that he accompany Dyce's body home and, finally, her encounter with Marian. Yet again, her life seemed to be out of her hands, now with Ronan so determined to carry out Dyce's final wish. It was true that she had somewhat reconciled herself to Ronan's presence, but now that they were back at Ravenscar, she simply wanted everyone gone.

It was too much.

Not long after retreating into the bedchamber she used to share with Dyce, Isabeth fell asleep and slept for the rest of the day. She missed Marian demanding the best chamber in the manse and demanding separate chambers for her ladies only to be told that the best chamber belonged to Lady de Brito and the only things suitable were a series of small rooms in the small southern wing. She missed Marian arguing with Odo, who eventually told her that she could either take the rooms or go sleep in the stables. When Marian complained to Ronan, he told her the same thing and walked away.

Begrudgingly, she took the smaller chambers.

As Isabeth slept in an exhausted stupor, she also missed Ronan taking charge of Dyce's casket. There was a small church nearby called St. Mary's and Odo had informed him that Sir Dyce had expressed interest in being buried there, so Ronan and Christian went into the small village of Ravenscar and made the arrangements. With no vault, they selected a spot for him near the altar. The mass was scheduled for the next day.

Isabeth finally awoke near sunset with a headache, the scent of a fish stew heavy on the air. Since they were feeding additional men, she knew that Odo had ordered a stew, something plentiful and filling, but Isabeth couldn't stand the smell. It was one of several things that made her gag these days, so she sealed up her windows with her oil cloth curtains, hoping to keep the smell at bay.

She let old Gerta know that she was awake, finding the woman in her usual alcove right outside the chamber door. Gerta was never far from Isabeth, like a faithful dog, and the old woman rushed to prepare her lady's bath. She grabbed a serving wench who was busying herself in another chamber, sending the girl down to the kitchens to order the bath, before following Isabeth back into her chamber.

"How are you feeling, lass?" she asked.

Isabeth went to her satchels and opened them up. "Better," she said. "I suppose I should go into the village and speak with the priests about burying my husband. I shall go in the morning to make the arrangements."

Gerta began unloading the satchels with enthusiasm. "That is not necessary, my lady," she said. "Sir Ronan has already done that."

Isabeth paused and looked at her in surprise. "He has?"

"Aye."

Isabeth pondered that bit of information. "I see," she said after a moment. "It seems to me that he was assuming much by doing that. I should have done it."

Gerta shrugged. "I'm sure he was trying to be helpful," she said. "He seems very… helpful."

"You mean very bold."

Gerta lifted her eyebrows as she went to the large wardrobe in the chamber, garments slung over one arm. "He's not the bold one," she said. "His wife has been demanding since she arrived. All she does is complain. She hates the chambers she and her ladies are sleeping in, she hates the cold wind from the sea… I've heard the other servants tell stories about her already.

She's very angry that she doesn't have the biggest chamber at Ravenscar."

Isabeth eyed her. "Is she creating problems?"

Gerta opened the wardrobe and hung one of Isabeth's finer garments on a peg. "She's causing a stir, for certain," she said, trying to be diplomatic. She wasn't usually so tactful, but she didn't want to upset her lady's delicate condition. "Her women are quite demanding, also."

That didn't sit well with Isabeth. Considering how Marian's lady had treated her, she could only imagine how she was treating the de Brito servants.

"What have they done?" she asked. "And do not spare me, Gerta. What have they done?"

Gerta hung up the last garment. "It's difficult to say…"

"*Gerta*?"

The old woman sighed heavily and looked at her. "The women spent time in the kitchens, overseeing what is being cooked, making sure everything is to their lady's liking," she said reluctantly. "The cook was saving two big sides of beef, but they demanded that the cook boil it immediately and then they took the best for her. When the servants do not move fast enough, they slap them."

Isabeth's mouth popped open in outrage. "*Slap*?"

Gerta nodded sadly. "Aye," she said. "Today has been a difficult day, my lady, but no one wanted to bother you with such things. You are grieving and we understand that."

Isabeth's eyes were still wide with shock and rage. "Has no one told Sir Ronan?"

Gerta shook her head. "No one will speak ill about Lady de Wolfe to her husband."

But that didn't include Isabeth. She did not have to remain

silent and she wouldn't. She stared at Gerta for a moment before moving to the ice-cold water in the basin near the bed and quickly splashing water on her face before lathering a small, lumpy bar of soap that smelled like lavender and washing her face with the froth. She splashed water on it again and dried her face with a small towel, embroidered with flowers, before rushing over to the wardrobe.

"Help me dress," she snapped softly.

Gerta did. Between the two of them, they managed to get her out of her traveling gown, the one she'd fallen asleep in, and dressed her in a shift and a simple garment of a soft blue. The dress itself was nothing more than long sleeves, a bodice that clung to her torso, and a flowing skirt, but she wore it like a goddess.

Gerta ran a comb through her locks several times before braiding her hair, a long braid that trailed down her back, and secured it with a blue ribbon. She did all of it as she followed Isabeth around the chamber as the woman hunted down slippers and a shawl. Once she was fully dressed, she put the shoes on her feet and the shawl around her shoulders and quickly quit the chamber.

But Gerta remained behind.

She had a feeling there was about to be an explosion.

Ↄ

"I AM NOT asking you to leave," Isabeth said. "I have come to the unalterable conclusion that you will not leave until you feel your oath to my husband is fulfilled. But that same oath does not hold true to your wife. She made no pledge to Dyce and if we are being perfectly honest, I do not want her here. She is creating chaos during a time when I do not need it, my lord. I want her to go."

Surprisingly, the tone wasn't harsh or critical. It was more a plea. Ronan had been standing with Christian, looking over a spectacular view of the sea beneath a full moon on a stunningly clear night, when Isabeth approached him on the battlements. Christian quickly excused himself, leaving Isabeth alone with Ronan. Before he could even greet her, she was laying out her case.

Pleading with him.

"I am sorry to hear this," he said. "I had hoped that she would bring you some comfort. What, exactly, is she doing?"

Isabeth cocked her head. "You do not even know what your own wife is doing?"

"If I knew, I would not ask."

Isabeth was trying very hard not to launch into an angsty tirade. Her search for Ronan had taken some time, during which she had seen one of Marian's women in the great hall as she snatched something from a servant. But that was all she saw and it was enough.

She wanted Ronan to do something about it.

"Her women are rude and demanding," she said. "I have a feeling you know exactly what I mean. They demand the best rooms, the best meals, and when my servants do not move fast enough to their liking, they slap them. I know you had hoped she would be of some comfort and I appreciate your effort, but she is creating chaos in my world and I want her out of it."

Ronan sighed faintly. Truth be told, he had been following his own tasks that day and, as usual, he simply ignored his wife and whatever she was doing. He never paid any attention to her, so he had no idea what the woman and her two haughty ladies were up to even though he should have suspected.

Marian had complained to him about the rooms she had been assigned and he'd ignored her complaints. Therefore, he wasn't surprised to hear that she was creating problems.

And he was embarrassed.

"I see," he finally said, his voice quiet with resignation. "I am truly sorry, Lady de Brito. I thought she might settle down and be a good companion. Unfortunately, I had no choice but to bring her. I hope you understand that."

Isabeth could hear the distress in his voice, but it was more than that. There was a coldness when he spoke of his wife, something she had noticed before. Though she hadn't really seen the pair together except on the journey to Ravenscar and the first night of the Middlesbrough tournament, her experience was enough to know that there was a complete disconnect between them. He didn't speak to her and she didn't speak to him. They preferred to go on as if the other one didn't exist.

That kind of marriage baffled her.

She could see that Ronan was genuinely regretful. But she couldn't help sense that he was trying to pretend everything was well between him and his wife. He'd brought her along, like a dutiful husband, so he wouldn't be completely alone with a new widow. It suddenly occurred to Isabeth that it was the exact reason he'd brought his wife along – to protect Isabeth's reputation. Nothing would be worse than gossips whispering about a new widow and a married knight.

That being the case, then the woman's presence was... necessary.

Now, she was starting to see it.

"I do understand," she said after a moment, her stiff stance relaxing. "Believe me, I do. But she is creating turmoil and if she will not behave herself, then I must ask that you both leave. And no amount of honor-bound pleading is going to change my mind. I understand that you cannot remain alone with me, as it would be improper, so if she cannot behave, then you must both leave. This is creating strife and disorder that makes a terrible situation worse. I need peace and your wife is not allowing me to find it."

Ronan knew that. From the expression on his face, he'd known it all along. "Then I will find her and tell her so," he said. "Please accept my apologies."

Isabeth shook her head. "There is no need for you to apologize," she said. "If there is one thing I have learned about you, it is that your intentions are true. You are determined to do the honorable thing. This is simply one of those difficult situations."

His gaze lingered on her in the moonlight. "You are very understanding," he said. "That is an excellent quality."

She shrugged. "Whatever I am, I learned it from Dyce," she said. "He was very patient and understanding. And… and I believe I owe you my gratitude for something else. I was told that you have already seen the priests at St. Mary's?"

The subject shifted and Ronan nodded his head. "I did," he said. "While you were sleeping, my cousin and I went into the village to speak to the priests. We selected a burial spot next to the altar. I hope that is agreeable."

"Very agreeable," Isabeth said. "Thank you for taking the initiative."

"It was no trouble."

A brief silence followed, but it wasn't awkward. The conversation had become soft, almost gentle between them. None of the irritation Isabeth had been feeling when she had first come to the battlements. That stubborn, determined knight she'd been butting heads with was a man with problems, just like everyone else. But in his case, it happened to be his wife. A highborn woman who shamed him and treated him like the dirt beneath her feet. Isabeth had heard about it before she ever really became acquainted with Ronan and now that she'd spent time around him and his wife, she could clearly see that the rumors were true.

In truth, she felt a little sorry for him.

That had her stance towards him softening just the slightest.

"Have you heard it yet?" she asked, turning her attention out to sea.

Ronan had been looking at her, now distracted by her question. "Heard what?" he asked.

Isabeth pulled her shawl more tightly about her shoulders. "The Koloss," she said as the breeze lifted the tendrils around her face. "The devil of the sea. He's out there, you know, waiting to snatch unsuspecting men and drag them to their doom."

Ronan stared at her for a moment before grinning. It was an unexpected turn in the conversation but a welcome one. "Ah," he said. "*That* Koloss. Nay, I've not heard him. Does he speak often?"

Isabeth fought off a grin. "Often enough," she said. "The men in these parts tend to be a very superstitious group. They believe in sea monsters and trolls and demons who feast on the flesh of men. There is a particular group of younger soldiers in Dyce's army who are very superstitious. They wear talismans, among other things, so sometimes Dyce would go down to the lower part of the manse, the area that faces the sea, and call up to the men when they were on sentry duty. He would growl and hiss and tell them that he was the Koloss. Then he would laugh so hard that he would nearly choke."

Ronan started laughing at the mental picture of Dyce playing tricks on his own men. "That is a wicked man who would do such a thing," he said. "But I love him all the more for it."

Isabeth was giggling, too. "It was quite dastardly," she said. "He would do it every time they had the night watch and they never caught on."

"Never?"

"Never!" she insisted. "He would tell them to do things like hit each other in the nose or go down into the bailey and spin circles, and everyone thought they were mad. It was the source of great humor for Dyce and his sergeants."

"And me," Ronan said, his eyes twinkling. "I fear that I must carry on that tradition. You will tell me when those men are on duty again and I shall do the same thing."

Isabeth snorted. "Who is wicked now?"

Ronan put up both hands in surrender. "I never said I was a perfect angel," he said. "There are some traditions worth keeping. This is one of them."

Isabeth eyed him, still smiling. "You will not teach my son this tradition."

Ronan hung his head, laughing softly. "If he is anything like his father, I will not need to," he said. Then, he eyed her more closely. "Speaking of your son, you are not properly dressed to be out in the cold like this. Let me escort you back inside."

Isabeth waved him off. "No need," she said. "I will go now. But about Lady de Wolfe…"

The humor between them quickly faded as they reverted to that unhappy subject. Ronan put up a placating hand. "I will speak with her immediately," he said. "You needn't worry."

Isabeth didn't want to contradict him, but given the behavior she'd seen from Marian, she wasn't entirely sure that was true. "Thank you," she said. But she paused and looked him in the eyes. "However, I am serious, Ronan. If she continues to behave poorly, you must both leave. I do not need the additional distress."

She used his Christian name, indicative of how truthful she was being, and he nodded solemnly. "I know," he said quietly.

"This is a situation wrought with strife already. I do not need the addition of a lady who cannot behave herself."

"I understand."

"I hope you do."

With that, she left the battlements but Ronan followed anyway, going down the narrow spiral stairs before her and steadying her as she took the steps. They reached the bottom together and he forced a smile, dipping his head at her politely before heading off, presumably to find Marian. But he was heading in the direction of the great hall and knowing that Marian was in the manse the last she had heard, Isabeth headed back to the manse.

She had an idea.

Truth be told, she was feeling the slightest bit guilty about their harsh words earlier that day. The more time passed, the more she was relenting, but only a little. Isabeth wasn't usually so cutting or brutal, but Marian had pushed her beyond her limit. She had been tired and her belly had been upset, making for a brittle combination. Though she still didn't excuse Marian's behavior, or that of her ladies, this was her home and she was chatelaine. She would be a poor hostess indeed if she didn't at least try to make peace with her guest before she had the woman thrown out. Perhaps if she did, and Marian was at least somewhat reasonable, perhaps she wouldn't need to leave at all. Considering the woman didn't seem to have any respect for her husband, she probably wouldn't listen to Ronan, anyway, so perhaps this was all up to her.

She was going to try.

The interior of the manse was warm as she entered. There was a hearth in the entry as well as in every room in the place because of the damp climate next to the sea. Dyce was constantly cold, so every hearth was lit as soon as the sun began to set and sometimes even before. As Isabeth paused by the fire, holding out her hands to warm her icy fingers, she was met by Odo, who had just come from the kitchens. A hearty fish stew was steaming away, he told her, but Isabeth already knew about the boiled beef that Lady de Wolfe had demanded so she asked him about it.

That's when the man's demeanor changed.

It was difficult for the proud man to be humiliated in his own domain, by guests no less, so he reluctantly told her that Lady de Wolfe had demanded the boiled beef only for herself and her ladies. They were not to give it to anyone else, she had instructed, putting Odo in a tight spot. That beef was meant for pies the cook was going to make, so once Isabeth heard about her guest taking food that wasn't hers, her determination that she should try to make some peace with Marian vanished.

She wasn't sure why she'd been foolish enough to entertain those thoughts in the first place.

Assuring Odo that he could use the beef no matter what Marian said, she left the majordomo in the entry and headed towards the south wing where Marian and her ladies had been housed. Smaller rooms, but they were comfortable, although she was certain Marian didn't think so. The more she walked, the angrier she became. Up a flight of steps to a landing and then up another small flight of steps that took her to the smaller southern wing where there were four small chambers.

The first thing she heard was singing.

It wasn't very good singing, either. Someone was trilling a tune and unable to stay on key. There were sconces lit along the stone walls, lighting the way as she followed the sounds of the singing, which she soon realized wasn't singing as much as it was gasps of delight that turned into high-pitched groans. The groans became a tune.

It was all quite strange.

The sounds were coming from the last door on the left. This was a chamber that had a view of the moonlit sea but it could also be a very damp chamber. Perhaps someone was ill with all of that strange noise that was emanating from the chamber. Hearing those gasps and groans had her puzzled, so much so that she didn't bother to knock. She simply lifted the latch, which wasn't locked. More singing, more gasping.

Isabeth stuck her head in.

What she saw shocked her.

God knows, given what she knew about Lady de Wolfe, it shouldn't have. But it did. Marian was laying on a small bed, her skirts around her thighs as a man's head disappeared between her legs. As she watched in disbelief, the man lifted his head and she could see that it was the knight that Marian had been flirting with on the journey to Ravenscar. His face and mouth were in between Marian's legs, clearly feasting on her private parts, and Isabeth only knew that because Dyce had done it to her, many times. She knew exactly what was happening.

Outrage filled her.

The door slammed back on its hinges.

"Shame on you," she hissed. "Shame on you for doing

this… *this* with a man who is not your husband! How dare you use my home to conduct your unsavory activities!"

The knight, startled, leapt to his feet but ended up stumbling and went down to one knee as Marian sat bolt upright, pushing her skirts down. Her features were wide with shock.

"*You!*" she gasped. "You were spying! You had no right to spy!"

It was a weak protest at best, but Isabeth was livid. "Everything my husband told me about you is true," she hissed. "He said you had more men in your bed than a London prostitute and now I can see that he was correct. Know that I will not provide a chamber for you to engage in your affairs, Lady de Wolfe. Whatever illicit activities you participate in, do it somewhere else. It will not be here."

The knight was on his feet again, backing away from Isabeth and trying to make his way around her so he could make a break for the door, but she whirled on him.

"And you," she seethed. "What is your name?"

The man was young, good-looking, with dark hair and dark eyes. She hadn't gotten a good look at him until now and she could see that he was handsome. "Gaspard," he said in a heavy accent. "Gaspard de Maurienne, my lady."

Isabeth cocked an eyebrow at him. "I want you to go to the stables," she said through clenched teeth. "Go there and stay there. Do not leave until I come for you. Do you understand me?"

The knight nodded, once, and fled as Isabeth turned to Marian, who was just climbing off the bed. Never in her life had she felt such contempt for another human being and after a moment of staring at her, she simply shook her head.

"Do you know why I came here tonight?" she said, disdain

in her voice. "I came to speak to you about your women and the way they have been treating my servants. I had hoped to have a civil conversation with you and tell you that your ladies are not welcome to abuse my servants, but it seems that the filth they are has trickled down from you. You are pure, disgusting filth, Marian. I want you out of my home immediately."

Surprisingly, she had nothing more to say. She was so disgusted and shocked from what she had seen that more words of condemnation wouldn't come. She turned for the door, but Marian stopped her.

"Where are you going?" she demanded. "To tell my husband?"

Isabeth paused, turning to look at her. "Would I be telling him something he already knew?" she asked. Then, she shook her head. "Nay, lady, I will not dirty my tongue by speaking of what I saw unless I am forced to. But you… you will leave now. You will tell your husband that you are leaving this night. If you do not, then I will tell him that I have banished you and I will tell him why. Therefore, you will tell him that you are leaving voluntarily."

Marian was trembling with rage, with turmoil. Her dark eyes narrowed. "What do you know about anything?" she muttered. "What do you know about me and my life? Of life in general? You live in a pathetic little outpost in a dirty little town and I will not be judged by you. You are nothing more than a peasant."

"Better a peasant than a whore," Isabeth said quietly. "No matter where you come from or how fine your family, you are nothing more than a common whore. You should be ashamed of yourself but, clearly, you are not. You're no better than the women who service the soldiers. More than likely, that is where you will end up someday."

Marian's lips were working as if she wanted to say something but she couldn't quite bring it forth. But that was only momentary. One minute, she was standing a few feet away and in the next, she was grabbing Isabeth's arm and digging her fingernails into her tender flesh.

"You know nothing," she hissed at her. "Keep your mouth shut or you will pay the price."

"Let me go."

"Do you understand me?"

"I will tell you once more to let me go."

"You do not give orders!"

Isabeth didn't stay another word. She lashed out her free hand and struck Marian in the face with an open palm, sending the woman staggering sideways. There was blood on her nose as she brought her head up, her eyes wide with accusation and outrage.

"I give orders in my own home," Isabeth said steadily. "Touch me again and I will defend myself. Now, I have told you to leave. If you are not gone in an hour, I will be forced to tell your husband what I saw. Is this in any way unclear?"

Marian was cornered. Frightened, angry, and cornered. She wasn't used to anyone contradicting her wishes and rather than respond, or attempt any kind of a rational reaction, she grabbed the first thing within arm's reach and threw it at Isabeth, clipping her on the shoulder. She'd thrown a pewter cup that still had a little wine in it from earlier in the day. The cup clattered to the floor and what was left of the wine sprayed onto Isabeth.

After that, the fight was on.

CHAPTER SEVEN

"WHAT ARE YOU going to do?" Christian asked softly.

Ronan eyed his cousin. They were in a small outbuilding where visiting knights were usually housed, according to Odo, but it was cramped and uncomfortable and dark but for a couple of fat tapers burning on the table in the tiny common room. That's where Ronan had found Christian when he'd entered the outbuilding, sitting in that teeny common room, trying to repair a nasty scratch on the leather of his expensive boots. He'd told Isabeth he'd find Marian, but he hadn't.

He'd gone looking for Christian instead.

"I do not know what I am going to do," he replied. "Chris, I came here because of Dyce and for no other reason than that. I had to bring Marian – you know that. I could not have come alone with Dyce's widow."

"I know."

Ronan threw up his hands. "All I need is for something to get back to my father, or worse, Marian's father," he said. "You know how that man smothers everything in his world. Edmund de Grey controls everything and what he cannot control, he still tries to control. It has been that way for ten long years and if he thought, for one moment, that I was somehow being unfaithful to Marian with the widow of a good friend, he would go to war against my father. He would not even ask questions – he would simply show up at Roxburgh with an army."

"I *know*," Christian said patiently. "Roe, you have done nothing wrong in this case but you risk looking like a weakling if you do not do something about Marian. Lady de Brito is right – you cannot have your wife turn Ravenscar into chaos. That is not fair to Lady de Brito."

Ronan shook his head slowly. "Nay," he said. "It is not."

"Which brings me back to my question," Christian said quietly. "*What* are you going to do?"

Ronan stood there a moment, refusing to look at him. He seemed more interested in the floor than in providing an answer. When he did speak, it was soft with regret.

"I have tried, Chris," he said. "You know I have tried. I have been trying for ten years, but she will not… she does not…"

"She's a bitch in heat," Christian said frankly, but he held up his hands quickly in apology. "I know I should not say it, but that's all she is, Roe. She was like that before you met her, when you met her, and after you married her. Edmund de Grey thought that marrying her off would keep her from jumping into men's beds, but that has not worked. You tried to keep her happy, but she is the kind of woman who will never be happy with just one man. She should have never married at all."

Ronan sighed faintly. "But she did marry and I am the one who is saddled with her," he said. After a moment, he shook his head. "When Dyce was killed and his wife mourned him deeply, do you know that I was jealous? If I die tomorrow, no one will mourn me so deeply. Not like a wife should mourn a husband. Certainly, my family would mourn me. My friends would mourn me. But my wife… she will dance on my grave and throw a feast, a joyful feast, celebrating my death. That is what Marian will do. She will not weep one tear for me."

Christian snorted, an unhappy sound. "Uncle Blayth should let you get an annulment," he said. "Or a divorce. You can, you know. You can provide proof of adultery. Your daughters, as pretty as they are, do not look like you in the least. Everyone knows they are not your children."

Ronan shook his head before the man was even finished speaking. "You know I cannot," he said. "I would be risking the entire House of de Wolfe against the House of de Grey and we need them like they need us. It is out of the question."

Christian was disgusted on his behalf. "So you are the sacrifice," he said. "The human sacrifice to have a strong alliance with a major northern family."

"It seems that way."

"That's because it is that way," Christian said. Then he paused as an idea came to him. "Roe… I just thought of something."

"It is probably nothing I haven't already considered."

"Have you considered making the woman so miserable that she'll seek the divorce?"

Ronan nodded wearily. "Of course I have, but it is impossible."

"Why?"

"Because it will anger Edmund de Grey and he'll march on Roxburgh."

"But our army is *bigger* than de Grey's," Christian reminded him. When Ronan continued to shake his head, Christian grew annoyed. "So you are a martyr for the rest of your life because you let your wife do as she pleases? It makes you look like a weak fool, Roe. You let that woman walk all over you."

"As my father has told me, it is better than ruining an important alliance."

"What would it take for you to stand up to your father and tell him that you are divorcing Marian no matter what he says?"

Ronan lifted his shoulders. "I do not know," he said honestly. "Nothing. Something. Anything. I simply do not know."

Christian could see how defeated Ronan was and he blamed the man's father. He was the one who had brokered the marriage and who forced Ronan to remain trapped in a miserable affair. It wasn't that Christian didn't understand the importance of politics for he most certainly did. He was a de Wolfe and they were schooled in such things from an early age. It was more that he hated to see Ronan – big, handsome, gentle, but also quite deadly Ronan – be made a fool of by a woman who wasn't worthy of him. Marian de Wolfe was no better than a common whore and everyone knew it.

But Ronan couldn't, and wouldn't, do anything about it.

It was a terrible situation in so many ways.

"As you say, Roe," he said, resigned. "But know that I do not like the way that woman treats you. I never have. No one does. She's simply not worthy of you."

"So you've said."

"It's true."

"Then who is?"

Christian rolled his eyes at the question. "I seem to remember several young women who would have been very grateful to have been Lady de Wolfe," he said. "Who was that lass from Sedburgh? Iris or Heather or something?"

Ronan smiled weakly. "Wintersweet," he said. "Wintersweet de Leia. A lovely woman."

Christian grinned. "One of many who would have fallen at your feet at the first mention of marriage," he said. "But instead, you had to marry the harpy. It is one of life's unexplained horrors as far as I'm concerned."

"Mayhap so, but you needn't keep reminding me at every turn," Ronan said. "There is nothing I can do about it, so just… stop."

"But…"

"*Please*, Chris. I need your advice, not your condemnation."

Christian finally put up a hand in surrender. "Very well," he said. "I am sorry. I do not mean to make you feel bad. I simply do not like what she does to you."

"Nor do I. But scolding me does not help the situation."

"Then what advice do you need that I've not already given you?"

That was a good question. Ronan already had the man's advice and he knew what he should do – send Marian out of Ravenscar. But his father had him so paranoid about creating an incident that would alienate the House of de Grey that it was easier to ignore the problem than to act on it. That's what Christian didn't seem to understand.

Ronan wiped his hands over his face, wearily.

"I suppose I know your thoughts on the situation," he said. "I suppose I should…"

He was cut off when a soldier suddenly entered the outbuilding, slamming the door back on its hinges. Light from the moonlit night streamed in through the doorway.

"My lord," the soldier said. "You must come. There has been a fight."

Ronan frowned. "You do not need me to intervene," he said. "Where are the sergeants?"

But the soldier shook his head. "Not a soldier's fight, my lord," he said. "Your wife. You must come."

Ronan was out of the outbuilding in a flash.

℈

MARIAN'S LADIES, WHO she had evidently sent away so she could carry on her tryst with the young French knight, returned in time to see Isabeth with a fire poker in her hands, whacking Marian on the arms and back with it as the woman tried to run from her. That had been all they needed to go after Isabeth and try to fight her, but Isabeth was in the flight or fight mode at that point. Seeing Marian's ladies rush towards her, she began swinging the fire poker with a vengeance.

It was clear from the beginning that neither Marian nor her women were used to anyone fighting back. They reigned with terror wherever they went, slapping and shoving and making demands, so the fact that the chatelaine of Ravenscar fought back was something of an anomaly. They weren't sure how to respond other than to try and slap her, but Isabeth was in panic mode. All of those heightened emotions during early pregnancy were in full bloom as she found a target for her anger, her fear, and even her grief.

Marian was that target.

Her ladies couldn't get near her as she cowered in a corner and screamed. Isabeth had brained one of the ladies on the side of the head and she was on the floor, dazed, as the second lady stood out of range and bellowed at her. All Isabeth could do was order them to leave, to go far away from Ravenscar. But they had no intention of leaving so it was a screaming match as Isabeth stood with her back to the wall, poker raised as the women screeched at each other.

Servants and soldiers began arriving.

Odo was the first one to appear to settle the situation, but he ran directly into the woman who was bellowing at Isabeth. She shoved at him, thinking he had come to harm her, and he stumbled back through the door. That brought Isabeth with her poker and she struck the woman with it, defending Odo, and ended up cracking her across the neck and jaw. She fell to the ground, next to her dazed comrade, as Marian screamed from the corner at the top of her lungs.

No one seemed quite sure what to do. Isabeth was panicked, with a poker as a weapon, two women were down, and Marian was simply screaming incoherently. That was how Ronan found the group as he stood in the entry, trying to figure out what in the world was going on. But his gaze immediately moved to Isabeth, who was the only one armed. It looked to him as if she had attacked Marian's women, but he sincerely couldn't believe that. Not without provocation.

He called to her, forcing her to focus on him.

"My lady," he said steadily. "Lady de Brito? What has happened here?"

Marian, seeing her husband, rushed towards him but that brought panic from Isabeth, who thought she was being attacked again. She began swinging the poker wildly, forcing Marian to retreat. Even Ronan retreated out of range of the waving poker.

"My lady?" he said again, louder this time. "What is amiss? What has happened?"

Isabeth looked at him and he could see that she was absolutely terrified. "They… they attacked me," she said, tears pooling in her eyes. "I came to speak to Lady de Wolfe to tell her that slapping my servants was unacceptable but, instead, she challenged me. She grabbed me and would not let go. She threatened me and tried to hurt me, so I fought back. Then her women came in and they attacked me, so I was forced to defend myself."

Ronan grunted unhappily at the tumultuous turn of events. "My lady, I told you that I would see to Lady de Wolfe," he said. "I told you that I would deal with her. You did not have to come to her yourself."

"I did," Isabeth snapped. "When I left you, you headed in the opposite direction of where she was. I had no way of knowing when you would speak with her, so I came to do it myself."

She was right. After speaking with her, he hadn't gone off to find Marian immediately. He fully admitted to himself that he'd gone to find Christian because he was so embarrassed to deal with his wife's behavior that he simply had to take time to summon his energy to address the situation, but that delay had cost him.

His apathy when it came to Marian had cost him.

And Isabeth.

At the moment, he realized just how terrible this entire situation was and his focus shifted to Marian, who was back to cowering in the corner. He felt like a fool for ignoring her when, clearly, she was creating such a horrific problem for Isabeth. He'd been told that – and he acknowledged that – but still, he'd delayed dealing with it.

But no more.

The time had come to take a stand.

"It is my understanding that you are creating an intolerable situation, Marian," he said, addressing her informally in front of everyone. "I am told that you are making demands and that your women are slapping Lady de Brito's servants. Is this true?"

Marian's hands came away from her head and her eyes widened as she looked between Isabeth and her husband, realizing that Isabeth had already complained about her before she ever saw her with the French knight. That brought indignance.

It brought rage.

"As your wife, my position is the greatest wherever I go," she said, thrusting her chin up as if daring everyone to defy her. "You are a de Wolfe. I am a de Grey. My wishes shall be met in my own household and in any other household, it is the host's duty to ensure my needs and wants are fulfilled. I need not explain this to you."

Ronan had heard that imperious tone too many times to count. "It is also your duty to be a gracious guest," he said steadily. "You have not been that while at Ravenscar. You have shamed the de Wolfe and de Grey names with your behavior and the behavior of your women, and now you attack your hostess?"

Marian's gaze flew to Isabeth. "She… she attacked me first!"

Ronan knew something about his wife – Marian was selfish and outrageous, but she was also cunning. It would be her word against Isabeth's because no one had been present when the trouble started. Reluctantly, Ronan looked at Isabeth for clarification of the situation, but she simply shook her head.

"It is not true," she said softly.

It was clear by Ronan's expression that he believed her, but he was trying to get to the bottom of things. "What happened when you first arrived?" he said. "Did you exchange words?"

Isabeth looked at Marian. She knew that if she didn't strike hard and strike fast that Marian might end up remaining at

Ravenscar as long as Ronan did. He'd made it clear he wasn't leaving and Marian seemed to want to manipulate the situation. And above all, Isabeth was tired of these people. Not Ronan so much, but certainly Marian. She'd told Marian that she wouldn't tell Ronan what she saw, but her word of honor wasn't going to hold up against a woman of Marian's disrepute. She could just tell that Marian was going to do anything and everything to discredit her in front of Ronan.

Isabeth wasn't going to let her.

"We did not at first," she said, her focus returning to Ronan. "I was coming to speak with Lady de Wolfe when I heard strange sounds coming from her chamber. Her women were nowhere to be found, so I approached the door. I heard what I thought was a gasp, as if she might be ill, so I opened the door to find Lady de Wolfe on the bed and a man between her legs. You want to know the truth? Now you have it. She attacked me because I saw her fornicating with another man and if you do not remove her from my home, Sir Ronan, then I shall order my husband's men to throw you both bodily from Ravenscar. I am sick with grief over the death of my husband and you have brought this horrible woman into my midst, making the situation far worse. I will never forgive you for that."

With that, she tossed the poker aside and stormed out of the chamber, tears in her eyes that quickly streamed down her cheeks. Odo was behind her, rushing after her, having heard what she'd said. He was heartbroken for his young mistress, following her until she reached the stairs before coming to a halt. Isabeth raced up the stairs alone to the living chambers above, slamming the door and bolting it once she reached her rooms.

She lay on the bed and wept.

CHAPTER EIGHT

"**I** HEARD WHAT happened," Christian said. "It's all over the garrison."

The night, having been so clear at sunset, was starting to fog over as the mist from the sea began to roll in. The dank, dark, mysterious mist was folding in over the uncertainty of all of Ravenscar. Things were happening, people were in turmoil, and it had nothing to do with Dyce's passing. There was something beyond that grief, something that Marian had selfishly created, a maelstrom that had enveloped the quiet and peaceful manse and taken attention away from the man whose burial was to take place on the morrow. Ronan had just come from the manse to the yard, his features lined with stress as he encountered his cousin.

"Where is he?" he demanded.

"Who?"

"That French knight," Ronan said. "De Maurienne. He accompanied Lady de Wolfe from Middlesbrough."

"Did you notice him when he was part of her escort?"

Ronan's jaw flexed. "I did," he said. "I do not interfere in Lady de Wolfe's business of who she hires to ride escort unless he is a man of ill repute, but I knew nothing of de Maurienne."

"Now, you know."

"Now, I do. Where is he?"

Christian had the unhappy duty of telling him the truth. "Gone," he said. "I saw the man with Lady de Wolfe's maids not long ago, but he has since departed. He is long gone, Roe."

Ronan didn't seem too surprised to hear that. "I take it you heard that he was involved."

Christian didn't want a rehash of their earlier conversation about Marian and her infidelity, mostly because he didn't want to gloat about his correctness in the face of Ronan's shame. "I heard," he said simply.

Ronan didn't waste any time on a conversation that he didn't want to have in the first place. He simply wanted to get on with it, with what he needed to do.

"I want you to have an escort prepared for my wife," he said. "She is departing at dawn for London."

Christian's eyebrows lifted. "London?" he repeated. "Why?"

"Because she asked to go," Ronan said, his jaw ticking faintly. "She wants to visit her cousin, Millicent, in London and I have agreed. Truthfully, I have given her little choice in the matter. It is best that she leaves and stays far away from me."

Marian had been to London many times in her life, visiting her cousin on her father's side, so it was not an unusual request. Millicent de Haydon was a spinster, rich and alone, and Marian loved to go to London and take advantage of her. But Christian could tell simply by looking at Ronan that this request was different.

There was something in his expression that was different.

As if something, for him, had changed.

"Then I'll make sure the escort is ready," he said quietly.

"How many men will you send with her?"

"Twenty."

That was a shockingly low number for such a long trip, but Christian didn't argue with him. He was in full support of Ronan sending the woman away, alone if necessary. But he felt very sorry for Ronan, a man with a stellar pedigree, a great family, and close friends, but a man who literally had no control over his marriage.

Life was a cruel jokester sometimes.

"The escort will be ready," he said. "I'll prepare a wagon as well. Provisions and all that."

"And for her baggage."

"Of course."

Without anything more to say, Ronan simply turned away and headed back towards the manse. He couldn't even look Christian in the eyes any longer, knowing how the man felt about Marian and the situation in general because he was afraid he would see a lack of respect in the man's expression. A lack of respect for a husband with a wife who had no regard for him, who had never had any regard for him, and for a husband unable to do anything about it. Ronan had always been the rather quiet type, congenial and much loved by his family, but the House of de Wolfe was full of assertive men. Men who took life as it came and met it bravely. Though Ronan wasn't lacking in bravery in any case, sometimes his type of calm manner could be taken as a weakness.

Ronan had been dealing with that his entire life.

His greatest fear was that his family would see him as weak.

But he couldn't dwell on that at the moment. He had other things to contend with, not the least of which was a wife he'd locked up in her chamber. Marian was bolted in for the night and he'd left orders that only he would release her in the morning so that she could depart for London. Since he'd never seriously punished her for anything she'd ever done, because he simply looked the other way out of sheer indifference, she had been shocked that the man had actually taken a stand. He could still hear her cries of outrage as he bolted her into her chamber.

Quite honestly… it had felt good.

Somehow, in that small action, he felt as if he'd reclaimed some of his dignity. Marian had been running all over him since the day they were married and his position had been to ignore it. To pretend it didn't bother him. At first, it had bothered him greatly but as the years passed and children were born who clearly weren't his, he'd grown numb to it. He told himself it didn't matter and, eventually, it didn't. At least, he thought it didn't until he'd locked Marian in her chamber and had felt the smallest twinge of satisfaction.

That told him that he wasn't as numb to it as he'd pretended to be.

Entering the manse, his destination was Isabeth's chamber. He wanted to assure her that Marian was leaving on the morrow, as he'd promised. He made his way up to the living level of the manse where there were generous rooms with fine views. It was late, and he suspected she might be asleep, but he was willing to take the chance that she wasn't. Perhaps she was waiting for confirmation that her horrible guest was indeed leaving. Reaching the big double doors of the master's chambers, he lifted a hand and knocked softly.

The reply was immediate.

"Who comes?" came the muffled response.

"Ronan, my lady," he said quietly.

A few seconds passed before he heard the bolt thrown. The

door creaked open and he found himself gazing into Isabeth's beautiful face, illuminated by the single taper she held in her right hand. She was in a heavy sleeping shift with a thick shawl pulled around her shoulders. It was strange… he'd always thought the woman to be beautiful but, at that moment, there was something more he was thinking. How Dyce had been a very fortunate man to look upon that face on a daily basis, to love a woman so completely that she consumed his entire being. He could clearly see why Dyce had loved her so much. There was everything to love about her, at least in Ronan's opinion. He found himself wondering what it would be like to love a woman so completely that she would be part of him and he part of her. He must have been daydreaming a little too long because Isabeth's eyebrows rose as she looked at him.

"Well?" she said. "Did you want something?"

Shaking himself from his thoughts, and slightly embarrassed for it, Ronan nodded.

"I came to inform you that Lady de Wolfe will be departing on the morrow," he said. "I have made the arrangements. She is locked in her chamber for the night, so you needn't worry. She and her women will not be roaming the halls during the night."

Isabeth was visibly relieved. "Thank you," she said sincerely. When he nodded briefly and turned to leave, she stopped him. "I am sorry it came to this, my lord. I truly am. I know you tried to do something fine for me and I appreciate it."

He looked at her. "Trying and failing," he said. "For that, I am sorry. I hope you will not hold it against me."

She shook her head and opened the door wider. "Nay," she said. "In fact, please come in. I would like to speak with you."

He did. The chamber was almost unbearably warm as he entered, but he didn't comment on it. She was comfortable and that was all that mattered, even if he was already starting to sweat. She left the door open, however, so that old Gerta in her alcove could keep watch as she went to sit near the ridiculously blazing hearth and indicated for him to sit opposite her. He came to sit down, discreetly moving the chair away from the fire so he wouldn't melt. He saw Isabeth grin.

"Too hot?" she asked.

He smiled weakly. "A little."

"Dyce used to move the chair all the way across the room."

Ronan chuckled softly. "May I?"

"Of course."

He moved it far enough away so that he wasn't in danger of heat stroke but he was still close enough to have a normal conversation with her. No shouting across the room, as it were. Isabeth watched him get comfortable.

"As you can imagine, I have had a lot to think about," she said. "This evening in particular."

"I can imagine," he said with a tinge of irony. "The return to Ravenscar has not gone as planned."

She shook her head. "You misunderstand," she said. "I have not been thinking about your wife. You will forgive me, but she is not worth the effort. I mean no disrespect to you, my lord, but your wife is not like you."

"What do you mean?"

"I mean that you are kind and dedicated," she said. "Your wife… she is a selfish woman. I am certain that I am not telling you something you do not already know and I am sorry if my honesty offends you."

He shook his head. "It does not," he said. "She *is* very selfish. But in fairness to her, she was raised that way. It is her father's fault. He raised her to believe she could do no wrong and to do as she pleased, in any situation. I am sorry that she has shown no restraint while a guest in your home."

Isabeth waved him off. "I am coming to see that it is not your fault," she said. "You are correct when you said she has shown no restraint. Even in my own home, she tried to give me orders. That is what you saw earlier – she really did attack me. I have the wounds on my arm to prove it when she grabbed me and sank her nails into me. I hope you do not think I would have actually attacked a guest in my own home unless pro-voked."

"I never thought that."

"Good."

"Is that what you wished to speak to me about?"

"Nay," she said. "I… I hope it will not be too much of an imposition if I ask you a few questions."

"What about?"

She sighed faintly, pulling her shawl more tightly around her shoulders as if to ward off what was to come. "I have no father to speak to, you understand," she said. "The only male relative I have is my cousin, the same cousin who does not wish to have me at Briarfield, so I was hoping you could help me."

"I would be delighted to."

She looked at him, fear in her eyes though she was desper-ately trying not to show it. "My future has changed drastically in just a few short days," she said. "In the grand scheme of things, your wife and her behavior does not matter. She is leaving tomorrow and I shall never see her again. But I suspect I will continue to see you, at least for a short time."

Ronan nodded. "Until Dyce is buried, which is set for the morrow," he said. Then he sighed sharply and sat forward in his chair, adopting a more casual stance. "But the truth is that I promised him I would take care of you. I hope you know that I simply cannot walk away forever. As you have come to see, my honor is important to me. I must ensure that you are safe and happy, so your future and that of Dyce's son are my responsibility."

Isabeth was watching him carefully. "That is what I have been thinking on," she said. "After we bury my husband tomorrow, what then? What should I do? What do I need to do? I do not know where to turn, so I must ask for your guidance."

Ronan's gaze drifted over her, looking so ethereal in the firelight. *If only I had a wife like this to retire with every evening,* he thought. It was odd how he felt such a sense of peace with Isabeth. Something about her was calming and soothing, as if she settled something inside of him. He wasn't sure how or why, but she seemed to have that impact on him.

He struggled to focus.

"And you have it," he said, pushing thoughts of her calming effect on him aside. "Are you sure you want to discuss this tonight? There is no great sense of urgency."

But Isabeth nodded. "There is," she said. "I must know what I should do next. What *should* I do next?"

Ronan could see that she'd been stewing about this, and for good reason. She was facing an unexpected and mysterious future, but all he could see was her vulnerability. She looked so lost and vulnerable and he very much wanted to help her.

Protect her.

Something was stirring in his chest, something he was trying very hard to ignore.

"Very well," he said. "If you wish to discuss it, then we shall. I do not want you to be afraid of the future. Now, you've asked what you should do after we bury Dyce. The first thing we must do is make a notification to his liege. Who is his liege?"

"My cousin," she said, a little fearfully.

"The one who does not wish to see you?"

"The same."

Ronan stood up and moved his chair a little closer to the fire and a little closer to her before sitting back down and giving her his focus.

"Let us speak frankly about him," he said. "Firstly, what is his name?"

"Oston," she said. "Oston de Royans."

"His wife?"

"Oston married Clemence de Fulke."

His brow knitted thoughtfully. "De Fulke," he repeated. "I've heard of the family near Kendal."

"I believe that is where she is from."

"And why does she not like you?" he said. "Did you have the same great friendship with her that you have with Lady de Wolfe?"

He was teasing her a little and she smiled weakly. "Nay," she said. "I do not even know her. I met her only once, at their wedding. Afterwards, my cousin made it clear that neither Dyce nor I were welcome at Briarfield again."

"Did you say anything to her that might have offended her?"

Isabeth shrugged. "I congratulated her on her marriage," she said. "That is all I ever said to her. But I remember Dyce commenting on how plain the woman was. Very plain and with marred skin, but her family was rich. Dyce said my cousin married her for her money. Mayhap someone overheard that."

Ronan fought off a grin. "That would be just like Dyce to

offend everyone around him and not give a lick," he said. "But it is of no matter, I suppose. Mayhap you can make amends when you write to your cousin to inform him of Dyce's passing. Mayhap he will be in a forgiving mood."

Isabeth's gaze was fraught with worry. "The only reason he kept Dyce at Ravenscar was because he was a good commander with a solid army," she said. "But with Dyce gone, there is a hole the must be filled with… someone. I am certain my cousin will want to have another garrison commander here, so what will happen to me? I have nowhere to go if I am told to leave."

She was beginning to tear up, frightened at the mere thought of leaving. Ronan's heart went out to her because he could only imagine the anxiety she must be feeling with a future so uncertain. Therefore, he scooted his chair closer to her and reached out, taking her hand gently. It was meant to be a touch of comfort, but the moment his flesh touched hers, that stirring in his chest began to burn.

"You need not worry about that," he said softly but firmly. "I will not let you be turned out in the cold. I will always look out for your welfare, whether it is here or somewhere else, but there is no world in which you would be left to fend for yourself. Do you understand?"

His touch had done something to her, too. It had calmed her, comforted her, flesh against flesh that assured her all was not doom in her world. Her champion was gone, but Ronan would take up the mantle in Dyce's stead. She could see that now. She'd spent so much time trying to chase him away that she never realized how much she really did need him, if only to give her some comfort that all wasn't lost.

Gazing into his eyes made her feel better.

"I do," she said. "But I do fear that Dyce's death will give my cousin an excuse to remove me from Ravenscar."

"Possibly," Ronan said. "But if that is the case, we will turn to my father for help and advice. There are a dozen or more de Wolfe properties. Mayhap one of them is looking for a lady just like you."

That sounded most comforting, but also a little confusing. "To do what?"

"Well," he said thoughtfully. "What *can* you do? What talents do you possess?"

She sighed. "Virtually none," she said. "Dyce did everything. But I can sew and I can sing. And I am very good with children."

"You see?" he said, squeezing her hand. "You can be a nurse. God knows the de Wolfes have herds of children. In fact, my Uncle Thomas, who is the Earl of Northumbria, has several children. Plus, his wife is the patroness of a foundling home. I am certain they would welcome your help and it would be a roof over your head, a place to raise your son. Would that be of interest to you?"

For the first time since he'd known her, Ronan watched Isabeth's eyes light up. "Very much," she said. "Will you ask the countess if she would accept my help?"

Ronan nodded. "I will do it immediately," he said. "Now, no more worrying about your future. I will help you find a good one, I promise."

She smiled faintly, looking into his exquisite face, feeling his enormous, warm mitt around her hand as something sparked in her chest. She wasn't sure what it was, but it was a tingle, making her feel the slightest bit giddy. At least, she thought it was giddiness but the truth was that she'd never felt that way in her life. All she knew was that it made her feel strangely alive and strangely happy during a time she'd not felt any happiness at all.

It was a curious sensation, indeed.

"I appreciate it," she said after a moment. "Dyce trusted you and so shall I. You were a very good friend to him, my lord. I know he loved you dearly."

His mouth twisted wryly. "And that's another thing," he said. "You keep addressing me as 'my lord'. I've let it go until now, but I shall tolerate it no longer. My name is Ronan and you said I was like a brother to you. Start acting like it."

She broke down into a grin. "You are right, of course," she said. "Considering what went on with Lady de Wolfe, however, I thought it best to…"

He cut her off, though not rudely. "I do not wish to speak on her any longer," he said. "Our dealings with her are through. You shall never see her again."

"But you will," she said quietly. "Won't she be angry with you for sending her away at my request? Truly, I am sorry if I cause any discord between you two."

He looked at her for a moment, the warmth in his eyes fading. "Madam," he said slowly. "Surely it has not escaped your notice that discord is all Lady de Wolfe and I have between us. There is no love lost there, not like you and Dyce. You and Dyce had a perfect marriage with mutual love and adoration. May I tell you a secret?"

Isabeth nodded seriously. "Of course."

He looked at her and she swore she saw a faint blush come to his cheeks before he looked away. "I should not be telling you this, but I will," he said. "The day Dyce was killed and you sat in the tent with him, all day, praying over him, I found that I was… jealous."

Isabeth frowned. "Jealous?" she repeated. "Why?"

He shrugged, as if it were all so very foolish. "Because my wife will never mourn me the way you mourned Dyce," he said. "You see, Marian and I were ushered into a somewhat forced marriage. I was young and foolish and I let her seduce me, and when she told her father, he demanded I marry her, so I did. But there was no love between us. Not even affection. It was a brief tryst, a bad decision, that became my life. Her father, and my father to an extent, saw it as a strategic marriage between two powerful families. But Marian has never honored her vows, as you have realized. What you saw… with the French knight… that was not the first time such a thing has happened."

He seemed quite ashamed of it. Resigned, but ashamed. This time, Isabeth squeezed his hand. "May I make a confession?" she asked softly.

He looked at her somewhat ironically. "Of course."

"Dyce told me about your marriage," she said, leaning forward and putting her free hand over his hand, the one that was clutching her fingers. "He told me everything and he was so very sorry for you. I already knew that she did not honor her marital vows long before I saw the French knight and mayhap… mayhap that was why I was so angry with her. You are a kind and thoughtful, handsome and honorable man, Ronan. She is a fool for not seeing how fortunate she is to be married to you."

He smiled in spite of himself. This deliciously sweet, compassionate and adorable woman was comforting *him* when he was supposed to be the one comforting her. It would have been so easy to…

"The only people who tell me that are relatives who must say such things," he said, trying to distract himself from less than proper thoughts when it came to the new widow. "I have never heard it from someone I was not related to."

"It is true," Isabeth insisted. "And since we are spilling our confessions, I have another to make."

"What's that?"

The smile faded from her lips as she sat back in her chair, gently pulling her hands from his grasp. Somehow, it didn't seem right to tell him what she was about to tell him while she was holding his hands. Nay, it didn't seem right at all.

"You say that you are envious of my marriage to Dyce," she said. "Truly, there is nothing to be envious of. Much like your marriage, we were more or less forced into ours. Wait… that is not entirely true. *I* was forced into it. Dyce wanted to marry me very much, but I… I did as I was told."

Ronan had to admit he was quite sorry she'd pulled away from him and resisted the urge to reclaim her hand. "But you two were very happy, it seemed to me," he said.

She shrugged. "*He* was very happy," she said. "Dyce was in love with me the moment he met me. He waited impatiently until I came of age, and that very day he asked my father for my hand. My father agreed and we were married immediately. I was never courted. I never had the chance to know other suitors or meet other men. I had known Dyce more than half my life and he was like a brother to me but nothing more. I was forced to marry my brother and there were times in the beginning when I would lay awake at night and weep because of it. To not ever know the touch of a man I loved as a wife should love a husband is quite tragic. I almost feel like my life was stolen away from me in a sense. But Dyce was a good man and I respected him greatly, so I had no right to be unhappy. But whatever you were jealous of, Ronan… it did not exist. I do not know if that gives you comfort, but it is the truth."

Ronan considered that carefully. Truthfully, he was surprised because he always thought there was great love between Dyce and his wife. The way Dyce told it, the woman lived for the mere sight of him, but as he thought on it, he realized that it was always Dyce who spoke fondly of his wife and whenever Ronan saw them together, it was Dyce who hovered and Dyce who showed affection. Isabeth simply went along with it.

"Odd," he muttered. "That we should both be in marriages we were forced into. But yours is far more successful than mine. At least you honored your vows, no matter how you felt about Dyce."

Isabeth smiled faintly. "As I said, he was a good man," she said. "He was honorable and true and he took great care of me. I always felt guilty that I could not return his feelings, though I did my best."

"Did he know?"

She hesitated before nodding. "He knew," she said with regret. "But it wasn't anything we ever spoke of. It was simply the way of things between us and we had a good life together. There was nothing to be unhappy over."

Ronan was coming to think he'd been very selfish thinking he'd been the only one in all of England with such a horrendous marriage. Not that Dyce and Isabeth's was terrible, because it wasn't, but the circumstances of their marriages were similar. Marriage of convenience, of strategy. But Dyce had fared much better than he had in that regard.

At least he'd married a woman worth loving.

"So now you have a new life ahead of you," Ronan said. "When the time is right, should I help you find a new husband? Mayhap that is what you would wish for instead of living in a foundling home. Mayhap you want a chance to find a man to love?"

Isabeth shrugged. "I've not thought on it, to be truthful," she said. "I know that Dyce would want me to be happy, but I also feel as if I would be doing him a disservice by marrying again. I've always thought a woman was only good for one marriage. To marry again… what man would want a woman used by another man?"

Ronan grunted as he stood up. "A woman like you could command a very fine husband who would be more than willing to overlook your first marriage," he said. "I would not worry overly if that is what you wish to do."

She watched him stretch his legs, moving to the hearth he'd tried so hard to stay away from, and hold out his hands to warm them. "I have nothing to offer," she said frankly. "I have no great dowry or lands or titles, so a second marriage for me is not expected. And… and it is not as if I can bear a new husband a dozen children. After ten years of marriage to Dyce, I've not been able to produce one living child and were I to marry again, I am sure my husband would expect children."

He eyed her. "But you carry a child now."

Isabeth nodded. "Aye," she said. "But it is still very early. Something can still go wrong as it has in the past."

"How many times?"

"Three. This is my fourth pregnancy in ten years."

Ronan had to admit that he felt some pity for her. A woman who couldn't bear a child was like a man who couldn't fight. Both were useless, at least in his world. But then again, Marian had yet to bear an offspring of de Wolfe blood in ten years, so the truth was that he didn't have any heirs after ten years, either.

Perhaps he and Isabeth were more alike than he realized.

"I think you are worrying about things that you should not worry about," he said. "I promised to take care of you and your son and I shall do that. Nothing will happen as long as I am around. I shall find the best physic for you to help you safely deliver the child. It is what Dyce would want, don't you agree?"

Isabeth drew in a deep breath as if to fortify herself and realized there was still hope. "Aye," she said. "He wanted this child so badly. He already has a name."

"What?"

"Maxwell."

Ronan grinned. "That's a Scots name," he said. "I shall have to have a talk with your husband about that. Once he is in his crypt, we shall have a long discussion about why you do not name an English child after the Scots. However, my grandmother was Scots and she named one of my uncles after her clan, so I suppose I am speaking out of both sides of my mouth."

Isabeth giggled. "I could not convince him to choose another name, either."

Ronan shrugged. "Then Maxwell it is," he said. His gaze lingered on her for a moment as he finished warming his hands by the fire. "Now, if that is all of the confessions we have between us, I shall bid you a good night. It is late and you must get some rest."

Isabeth stood up, taking a few steps in his direction. "It seems that you and I have become much better friends over the past several minutes now that we know each other's secrets."

His smile broadened. "We are family now, you and I," he said. "Dyce has made us that."

"He has," she said. "But had you not possessed the sense of

honor that you do, then his requests would have fallen on deaf ears. Thank you for not being deaf, Ronan. I shall never forget it. Or you."

There was great sincerity in her face and perhaps something more. Or perhaps Ronan only saw more. Whatever the case, he felt compelled to take her hand and bring it to his lips for a sweet kiss. She was so tender and delicious that he kissed her hand a second time before gently letting it drop. With a final smile, he left her chamber, heading out into the dark manse.

And leaving behind a lady with a thumping, slightly giddy heart.

CHAPTER NINE

The Village of Brompton

"DID YOU SECURE me the best room?"

The question came from Marian, though it was far more of a demand than a question. Her lady, the one who usually caused the trouble and slapped the servants, and who had forced the pork pie upon Isabeth when they'd traveled from Middlesbrough to Ravenscar, nodded firmly.

"Aye, my lady," she said. "You have the very best chamber. The innkeeper will show us to it now."

Marian was still on her palfrey. She refused to get off until everything was set – her chamber, her food, and her bath, so now that it had been confirmed, she was more than willing to part with her escort for the night. Men who would sleep in a barn or under a tree. She would spare no money for their comfort, mostly because they were de Wolfe men.

But there were several de Grey men mingled with the de Wolfe troops back at Ravenscar. That was usual since she'd brought five hundred of them as part of her dowry and they had been integrated into the de Wolfe army. In truth, there was no differentiating the de Grey from the de Wolfe men any longer because they were all Ronan's men, all sworn to him, but Marian treated them a little different.

She still separated the de Grey men from the rest.

There were a few back at Ravenscar even now, men her ladies fornicated with and who happily spied on Ronan for her. They always had, but in ten years of marriage, there had never been anything substantial for them to report on. Ronan was a good man, faithful to his vows, and that was all they ever reported. Even though that was the report she expected from Ravenscar, still, she wanted to know what was going on there. She wanted to know about that horrid Lady de Brito and any other details they could provide her because, deep down, Marian was a terrible gossip.

And she liked to spy.

So leaving Ravenscar wasn't the tragedy she made it out to be. In the end, she'd still have gossip fodder courtesy of the men she'd left behind. But the truth was that she had loyal de Wolfe soldiers with her and they, too, would report to Ronan on her activities on the road as well. Such was the game she and Ronan had played for ten years although, admittedly, it was far more her game than it was his.

With her lady's coaxing, she slid off her palfrey and stiffly walked into the inn. The sun hadn't even set yet but she was exhausted and wanted to stop for the night. She wasn't the best traveler which meant the trip to London was going to take several weeks. Her ladies led her inside, pushing aside anyone who came close to her, and took her into a short corridor. The last door on the left opened wide to reveal a large, comfortable chamber and a bath that was already being filled with hot water.

Marian entered the chamber and went to sit on the only

chair, planting herself wearily as servants rushed in and out, filling the old copper tub about half-full. One of her ladies quit the chamber while the other one, The Bull as Marian sometimes called her, hovered over the servants and slapped one on the back of the head when she wasn't moving fast enough.

The slap was like music to Marian's ears.

Once the servants were humiliated and finally pushed from the chamber, Marian settled down to enjoy her bath, which she lingered in until the water was cold. She'd been oiled and scraped and scrubbed until her skin was red and, finally, The Bull pulled her out of the bath and dried her off completely. As the sun began to set, Marian dressed in a warm shift and an incredibly expensive robe of brocade and ermine, something her father had given her and cost as much as a normal man made in a year. It traveled everywhere with her. Settling back to a supper of bread, stewed fruit, and a fish pie, she hadn't taken two bites when there was a loud knock at her door.

The Bull opened it.

The first thing Marian saw was her second lady, wearing a traveling cloak and looking exhausted. The second thing she saw was Gaspard.

The fish pie ended up on the floor.

"Gaspard!" she gasped as the young knight rushed into the chamber and went to his knees beside her. "How did this happen? How did you know I was here?"

Gaspard had her hands within his, kissing them gratefully. "Before I left Ravenscar, I told your maid that I would be nearby," he said. "I told her to send me word when you were alone so that I could return to you. But now I find you here!"

"But how –?"

"I told her where to find me," he said, cutting her off. "A

little village not far from here. She came to fetch me and told me that you have been exiled."

Marian squeezed his hands before throwing her arms around him, very glad to see him, indeed. "I have," she said. "My husband is a horrible and cruel man. I have told you this. He shows me no love or affection. You are the first man who has shown me such things, my darling, and I cannot be separated from you. I am so glad you waited for me."

Gaspard returned her feverish kisses, completely seduced by her lies. "He does not deserve you," he said. "I do not care if the man is a de Wolfe. He has no right to treat you so terribly."

Marian kissed him deeply. She needed a man to be chivalrous to her, to treat her as if she were the most important thing in the world. She always needed that. Since she'd met Gaspard at Middlesbrough, he'd done a good job of that and she'd done a good job of convincing him that she had a neglectful husband.

That would go on until she grew bored with him.

Such was the usual pattern.

"He has always been cruel to me," she said. "My father forced me to marry him and I did not want to. You have seen how he ignores me and discards me. I must have love, my darling, that only you can give me."

Gaspard pulled back, his dark eyes glittering at her as his big hands cupped her face. "I will only, and always, give my love to you," he said. "You have it forever if you want it."

Marian almost replied but it occurred to her that her women were still in the room, over by the door that was shut. They were pretending to listen for anything outside of the door, but Marian knew differently. She knew they were listening to every word said.

"You two," she snapped at them. "Out. Do not return until

morning."

The women fled, slamming the door in their wake. Only then did Marian return her focus to Gaspard, running her fingers through his dark hair, her features soft with passion.

"My life is full of tragedy," she said. "A cruel husband, a cruel family. I need you, Gaspard. I am going to London and you must come with me. Will you come?"

Gaspard nodded. "Of course I will," he said. "But where is your husband?"

Marian lifted an unhappy eyebrow. "At Ravenscar," she said. "He will be there for some time to come because of the Widow de Brito. I… I am certain that is why he sent me away, because he wishes to have her all to himself. He has always been so cruel to me, Gaspard."

"I know, *ma douce*."

"That is why you must not leave me."

Gaspard had no intention of leaving her. In fact, he'd found what he'd been looking for since he arrived in England three years ago – a wealthy married woman with an inattentive husband, a woman who was looking for a man to lavish money and attention on. As long as her husband remained aloof to her activities, Gaspard figured he was safe. He wasn't a fool – he knew who the House of de Wolfe was and he knew the House of de Grey. He knew they were both wildly wealthy and important, so to find a neglected de Wolfe wife was perfect for a man like him. All of the benefits without any of the responsibilities.

But there was a little more to it in his case.

He was greedy.

"I will never leave you, I swear," he said. "In fact, your husband is so terrible that I shall challenge him. I will punish him for what he has done to you. Would that make you happy?"

Marian's expression went from one of passion to one of surprise. "Punish?" she said haltingly. "But… but my husband is a de Wolfe. Have you seen how big he is?"

"I have."

"He will tear you limb from limb!"

Gaspard stroked her cheeks with his thumbs. "Then mayhap I should simply do away with him," he said. "His holdings, his estate, his money… everything would be yours and you can live where you please and do whatever you please. Your husband will never be cruel to you again."

Marian's eyes were wide when she realized what he meant. "You would *kill* him?"

"If you wish it."

Marian had never even thought about that. Ronan had his life, she had hers, and they never crossed paths. As long as that was the case, she was content to let him go about his business, but now, Gaspard had her thinking.

A world without Ronan would indeed be a world of unlimited wealth and lovers with no husband to complain to her father behind her back. Not that Ronan had, but her father would be less disapproving of her affairs if she weren't married. Oh, he knew about them but, much like Ronan, he simply looked the other way. But if Ronan were dead, she could do anything she pleased without the baggage of a husband. Perhaps she might even marry someone she actually *wanted* to marry. Not that she wished Ronan dead, because she didn't, but if he was gone…

Certainly, it was something to consider.

"I will think on it," she said after a moment, pulling him closer. "Meanwhile, you will travel to London with me and we shall have all the time in the world to consider what to do about my husband."

Gaspard could already feel himself growing hard as he swooped in on her, suckling her lips. "Anything you wish, *ma douce*," he said. "I am yours to command."

Marian liked the sound of that.

☙

IN A LITTLE church on the edge of the village about a mile from Ravenscar, Dyce de Brito was laid to rest on a misty morning.

But not without drama.

Just before sunrise, Ronan and Christian had released Marian and her ladies from their chamber and accompanied them to the small escort that would be seeing them into London. At first, Marian had been resistant and demanding. She even refused to go at one point, stubbornly refusing to budge, and that forced Ronan to bodily pick her up and carry her out of the manse.

Marian had been positively mortified and by the time they reached the courtyard, she'd settled down enough to where he was able to put her on her feet and she walked the rest of the way to her palfrey. After that, it was simply a matter of moving her, her women, and her escort through the front gates and out onto the road. Ronan and Christian had watched from the gates as if waiting for Marian to change her mind and try to dash back into Ravenscar.

But the escort finally faded from sight.

After that, there was a massive sense of relief as far as Ronan was concerned. Marian was out of the way, headed for London, and they could get on with what needed to be done on this day – bury his friend.

Dyce's burial was a solemn occasion and one with great dignity. Isabeth was clad in white, the traditional color of mourning, and Ronan escorted her to the church where villagers were already gathering to pay their respects. Word of Dyce's death had spread in the short time since their return to Ravenscar and, being well liked, many had come to give a proper send off to their liege.

Isabeth was quite touched to see everyone who had come to say their farewells to Dyce and as she headed towards the stone church on the edge of a windswept bluff overlooking the sea, people were rushing forward to give her sacks of food or flowers or other things, all of them offerings of respect for Dyce and his lady.

It was clear how much Dyce and Isabeth were loved by their vassals, but it came to the point where Gerta and a few of the soldiers were having to collect all of the offerings. Isabeth entered the church with only a bouquet of flowers, given to her by some children, while some of the soldiers were sent back to the castle with the remainder of the gifts.

With the smell of earth from the newly dug grave and incense burned by the priests that smelled of something equally dank and acrid, Dyce was laid to rest down in a dark, damp hole. Isabeth, Ronan, Christian, and a host of soldiers crowded into the small church and listened to the priest intone the mass in Latin and songs were sung as both a blessing and a sign of respect. Then, the prayers came and they lasted well into the morning, even as the fog lifted, before Dyce's casket was lowered into the ground near the altar.

When the mass was over, Christian ushered the soldiers out while Ronan remained behind with Isabeth. She stood near the grave as a few men began to fill it up again, tamping down the earth. In this parish, there were stones on the floor, paving stones, so once the earth was tamped down enough, they carefully placed the stones back over the top. The priest assured Isabeth that she could place a headstone over the grave with Dyce's name, but until then, there would simply be common stone over the grave.

And that was the end to the life of a good knight, great friend, and excellent husband.

It was difficult to describe the mood that had settled – sadness, confusion, resignation. All of those things filled the little church as Isabeth simply stood there and stared at the grave. The priest muttered words of comfort to her, assuring her that Dyce was with God, but that didn't help the myriad of feelings she was experiencing. No matter how Ronan reassured her that she would be taken care of, it was still disorienting and frightening to see the conclusion of the only adult world she'd ever known.

Today was the first day of the rest of her life… alone.

The realization was like a shot to the gut. A feeling of desolation spread out in her belly, filling her limbs until she could feel nothing else but utter despair. With a last look at the newly covered grave, she finally turned and headed out of the church where dozens of villagers were still gathered, still offering her words of condolence. She forced a smile at them as Ronan and Christian helped her push through the crowd to where her palfrey was waiting. But she walked right past the palfrey.

She kept walking.

The fog had lifted for the most part, with rays of sunlight peeking through the mist and creating golden beams of light on the sandy beach below the manse. A sandy beach where Isabeth and Dyce had walked many a time, speaking on their family, of their future, and of any number of things. Pulling the white woolen cloak more tightly around her slender body against the damp of the sea air, Isabeth took the path from the village down to the beach.

She continued to walk.

It was her moment to reconcile her alone status in the world. No longer would Dyce walk beside her. No one would until her son was born, but even a child was a poor substitute for a husband. Isabeth kept repeating the words over and over in her head – *I am alone, I am alone* – forcing herself to come to grips with the situation. Forcing herself to realize that no matter what came now, she was alone and her future was uncertain.

That was a difficult thing to swallow.

She kept falling back on Ronan's words, how he would ensure she had a place to go and a position in life, even if that position was watching over foundlings. He'd assured her that she didn't have to worry about her future and she believed him. Her focus turned from the sand at her feet to the sea, the dark waters that were churning at this hour, the waves as they crashed upon the shore. Perhaps the saddest thing of all was that she would miss Dyce's friendship, as they had been great friends. She wouldn't miss his scratchy kisses, she was sorry to say, nor would she miss his touch. That was a difficult admission, but it was an honest one. Only his friendship, his humor, his companionship would she miss.

Things would never be the same again.

Isabeth paused a moment, looking out to sea. As she did, she caught sight of something in her peripheral vision and realized it must have been Ronan. He was the only one who would follow her onto the beach to make sure she didn't throw herself into the waves in her grief.

"They say that the sea is constantly renewing itself," she said as the gulls cried overhead and the surf pounded. "It is life constantly renewing itself, always moving, never the same from one moment to the next."

Ronan, who was indeed a few feet behind her, turned to look at the water as well. "I did not grow up by the sea," he said. "You would know more of it than I would, but it is true that it is ever-changing."

Isabeth was still looking at the churning waters. "I feel as if I am the waves," she said. "I am crashing on a shore, smashing into a million droplets, and then retreating back into the water to become something different. Something new."

"That is not necessarily a terrible thing," he said. "Today marks the day that you begin your life anew. Dyce would want you to be strong in facing it. Do you feel strong, Isabeth?"

Her gaze lingered on the water. "I am not sure," she said. "I have little choice but to face it."

"You must be strong for Maxwell."

She nodded faintly. "I know," she said. Then, she sighed heavily with the great weight of an unborn child upon her mind. "What do I tell him of his father, Ronan? When he asks me about his father, what do I tell him? That he was kind and compassionate, but that he was only a mediocre knight who was killed by a better opponent in a stupid tournament that meant nothing in the end? What do I say?"

Ronan took a few steps in her direction. "You tell Maxwell that his father was a brave man with many friends," he said. "You tell him the truth. You tell him that he died surrounded by his friends and loved ones and that, in the end, his friends exacted revenge for the dastardly thing done to him. Dyce was avenged."

Isabeth turned to look at him, her gaze searching his face for a hint of what he might truly be feeling. "I shall tell him that his father's friend, Ronan, ensured that his son had a safe and healthy future," she said. "I think I shall tell Maxwell as much about Dyce as I will about you. He will know about the man who gave him life but also about the man who ensured his future."

Ronan was looking at her, too, into those mesmerizing eyes. "You make it sound as if I shall walk out of your life when my obligation to Dyce is over," he said. "My obligation will never be over, Isabeth. I will always look out for your welfare and Maxwell's welfare. I shall ensure he fosters in the finest homes and becomes a knight, like his father. I will see these things through, I swear it."

Isabeth smiled faintly. "I know you will," she said. "And we are grateful."

Ronan returned her smile, feeling that same trembling in his chest that he'd felt the night before when he looked at her. Something warm and quivery. He liked Isabeth – he liked her very much. He thought she was incredibly brave and dignified in the face of Dyce's shocking death and his respect for her was limitless.

But he also felt something more.

God help him, he did.

Quickly, he looked away.

"The breeze is rather cold," he said. "We should return to the manse. It is too cold for you out here."

He reached out to take her elbow as he spoke, gently turning her around in the direction they'd come from. But she took two steps and fell to her knees.

Ronan was beside her in an instant.

"What is wrong?" he demanded quietly.

She shook her head and struggled to stand up. "I… I am not sure," she said. "I feel very tired."

"Did you break your fast this morning?"

"Nay."

That was all Ronan needed to hear. Bending over, he lifted her off the ground and swept her effortlessly into his arms. Rather than resist him, Isabeth wrapped her arms around his neck, her head on his shoulder as he carried her back across the sand, back towards the path that led up to the manse.

In his arms, she was warm and soft and cozy, as light as a feather to his considerable strength. Ronan only realized later on that his pace grew slower the closer he got to the path. Slower and slower, not wanting to relinquish a moment of her in his arms. He'd never known anything like it in his life and by the time he reached the manse, Isabeth was in an exhausted sleep, clutched against his heart.

Ronan knew, at that moment, that he could never let her go.

And he was in for trouble.

PART TWO
RAVENSCAR

CHAPTER TEN

Early August

H E WAS LYING in wait.

Ronan was in the stairwell that led to the upper floors where the family quarters were, but these days, only Isabeth slept up there and her maid, Gerta, when the old woman could make the stairs. But over the past couple of months, that had been less and less and old Gerta tended to sleep on the floor below and send the younger maids upstairs to tend to her mistress' needs.

But he knew the habits of the maids. He knew they only came when they were called and when they were sent to Isabeth's chamber to clean it. They had already done that during the morning hours. Ronan had paid attention to the happenings in the manse even when he was going about his rounds, which on this day had been the monthly session of laws and measures. That meant anyone from Ravenscar's properties could come to the manse and plead their legal cases – sometimes it was farmers against farmers, sometimes a merchant against a thief, but it was one of the tasks that Dyce had carried out as the Lord of Ravenscar, something Ronan had stepped in to oversee because there was no one else to do it.

He'd taken to it easily.

The last two months, on the third Saturday of the month, Ronan had listened to cases and dispensed justice. He had a fair sense of justice thanks to his father and grandfathers and wasn't too heavy-handed when dispensing penalties. A man who stole milk from an old woman's goat to make cheese was sentenced to providing the old woman with cheese for an entire month. A farmer who took a fancy to another farmer's wandering dog was forced to give the owner two piglets in compensation as well as returning the dog.

In truth, Ronan was born to dispense justice because of his even temper and ability to see the situation from both sides. More than that, he enjoyed it. He was sliding into Dyce's role around Ravenscar quite easily, telling everyone that he was simply continuing the dead man's duties for a sense of security and continuity for not only the man's wife but for his vassals as well. He was simply being a good friend.

But that wasn't entirely the truth.

Hence the reason why he was lying in wait in the stairwell.

Just as he knew the maids' routine, he also knew Isabeth's. He knew every move she made. He knew she was down in the kitchens with Odo and the cook, supervising as they made enormous cauldrons of pea soup with carrots and onions. The previous winter had been mild so there were now apricots and cherries, and she had also been assisting in the making of stewed fruits and preserves. The fruits would be stripped of their skins and boiled with honey and spices, creating a delicious concoction that Ronan had most happily been spreading on his bread. Isabeth had been very clever with how they preserved the food for storage.

But, then again, Isabeth was clever in general.

That was something Ronan had come to see over the past couple of months. She was clever and bright, witty and charming, all things wonderful that had completely destroyed his restraint. That oddly socially awkward woman didn't seem to exist anymore. He remembered the days when he first arrived at Ravenscar and the mere sight of Isabeth made something tug in his chest. That tug had turned into a full-blown yank, something that exposed his heart and soul in a way he never thought possible.

And all of it exposed to Isabeth.

But it wasn't one-sided. Whatever he was feeling for her was catching because she felt it, too. When she realized it, she spent two weeks avoiding him and sending him missives through Gerta asking him to leave, but he didn't leave. He remained, which probably wasn't the smartest thing to do, but he felt more attraction to her than he'd ever felt for a woman in his life, something too strong to ignore. Truth be told, he felt like a giddy squire with his first love because it *was* his first love.

He felt as if he were walking on clouds, every minute of every day.

As he sat in the window seat of the stairwell, looking from the tiny lancet window and seeing the sea beyond, he had to smile to himself. Here he was, a man grown and mature, and experiencing love for the first time in his life. Unfortunately, it wasn't with his wife, but he'd quickly gotten over feeling guilty about that. He'd never before broken his marriage vows to Marian even though she had broken them more times than he could count, but this… this was different.

This was love.

He heard footsteps.

Knowing it was Isabeth, he sank back against the seat, knowing she wouldn't be able to see him from the direction she was coming. In fact, she walked right past him. As fast as lightning, he reached out and grabbed her from behind.

"I have been waiting here for an hour," he purred into her ear as he pulled her onto his lap. "Hours seem like years when you are not in my arms, Esa."

Esa.

He'd been calling her that for the past couple of weeks… *Eee-sa*… drawing it out in a dulcet tones, seducing her with her own name and watching her expression as he broke down her resistance. But he couldn't see her face as she sat on his lap, weakly trying to pull away. Still, he knew his whispered words were having an effect on her.

The woman turned to putty whether or not she wanted to.

"Roe," she whispered, her hands on his arms as he embraced her tightly, nuzzling her neck. "Please… not now…"

He ignored her, suckling on her earlobe as he ran his hands over her swollen belly, now much more visible as she approached her fifth month of pregnancy. But that belly was an aphrodisiac to him, a symbol of her womanly fertility that drove him mad with desire. Suckling on her earlobe, on her neck, had the desired effect as she stopped resisting, collapsing against him as his hands began to lift her skirts. When they were high enough, he snaked a hand underneath them, seeking the hidden jewel between her legs.

"Roe," she gasped and squirmed. "Do not… oh, God…"

His big fingers found the fluff of curls and he began to probe her, pulling one leg over his thigh so he had unencumbered access. One enormous arm moved up to clutch her around the chest, his hand finding a full breast, while the other did naughty things between her legs. It was enough to bring her to a climax almost immediately and when she began to gasp with pleasure, he turned her enough so that his mouth could claim hers. He kissed her deeply, feeling her honeyed walls contract around the fingers he had thrust into her.

She'd had her pleasure and now he wanted his.

Ronan had never wanted a woman so badly in his life. He'd bedded Isabeth for the first time a week ago and now, it was every day, sometimes two or three times a day. At night, he'd sneak into her chamber and take her once or twice before retreating back to the tiny knights' quarters in the bailey. So far, no one had gotten wise to it except for Christian, who was on to him. But Christian was so thrilled that Ronan had finally found happiness that he didn't say a word about it. As far as he was concerned, Ronan could do whatever he pleased with the de Brito widow.

It was about time the man found some joy.

Removing his fingers and pulling her skirt down, Ronan picked her up and carried her the rest of the way up the stairs and on into her chamber. Kicking the door shut with his boot, he bolted it before carrying her over to the bed. Usually, Isabeth protested his lust, trying to tell him why their actions were so terrible. Trying to reason with him when the truth was that neither one of them could control their passion towards one another. Even now, he turned her onto her side and slid the surcoat off her body, tossing it and her shift onto the ground. Quickly disrobing himself, as he was becoming quite adept at moving swiftly, he slid in behind her on the bed, wrapping his big arms around her.

Isabeth surrendered to the inevitable, eyes closed as his

mouth moved to the tender nape of her neck, kissing her softly as his big arms hugged her tightly. It wasn't long before his hands moved to her belly again, feeling the gentle rise of it against his flesh. He rubbed his hands over her stomach as his lips feasted on her neck.

Ronan was already so consumed by the woman that he could hardly think straight and he struggled not to let his excitement veer out of control. Even with his considerable power, he was extremely gentle with her.

He had been from the start.

"You are so beautiful," he breathed, his mouth on her shoulder.

"Roe," she whispered with her last shreds of common sense. "We shouldn't…"

His touch grew bolder, cutting off her last murmurs of protest, which she really didn't mean, anyway. It was the propriety in her speaking, the moral high ground because of Ronan's marriage, but that moral high ground had been sacrificed long ago to their true and growing feelings. He lifted her left leg, enough so that he had unfettered access to the region between her legs again. As he slanted his lips over hers, hungrily, he gently inserted a finger into her warm, wet folds.

Isabeth sighed with delight as his fingers stroked in and out of her a few times, mimicking the lovemaking they would soon be doing, and she gradually began to respond to him. He inserted two fingers into her, and then three, listening to her gasp softly. She was hot and slick and he knew that her body was ready to accept his.

The moment they'd both been waiting for.

Ronan wedged himself against her, his enormous arousal pushing at her buttocks. As strange as it sounded since he was bedding the man's widow, he'd been very careful of Dyce's son from the start, so he'd almost always taken her from behind so he wouldn't put any pressure on the babe. He knew how much the child meant to both of them. As Isabeth lay on her side, her arm upstretched around his neck, Ronan entered her from behind, his mouth to her neck as a hand moved to her breasts.

Isabeth groaned softly as he slid into her, his massive member filling her. With his mouth to her neck and his hand on her belly, he gently thrust again, sliding into her tight walls until he was completely seated. Isabeth closed her eyes and surrendered to him, as she had from the start, feeling things she had never felt before that were fed by the emotions she had developed for Ronan. Something that had come upon her so quietly, but so completely, that she still couldn't believe any of this was real.

She still couldn't believe she was in love with the man.

Ronan was fed by lust and desire as he thrust into her, a big arm holding her against him while the other roamed between her breasts and belly. As their passion grew and his thrusts increased, he moved to hold her left leg up by the knee, allowing him more freedom to wedge his big body between her legs from the rear.

Usually, he tried to make these moments last, but it was to no avail. All of the emotions he never felt for Marian, or any other woman, had come fast and hard for Isabeth and there was no restraining anything he felt for her. Something he'd tried to deny, but something that would not be denied. The love he felt for her superseded marriage, any alliance, de Wolfe and de Grey, becoming something that consumed his entire being and he didn't care one bit. In the prime of his life, he finally knew what it meant to love and be loved, nestled in this heavenly world of Ravenscar where he could pretend it was just the two of them and their happy life together.

God, he wanted it so badly that sometimes it brought tears to his eyes.

Isabeth's pants of pleasure brought him back to the world at hand and his fingers moved to the dark curls between her legs that were drenched with moisture from their bodies. He stroked her woman's center, feeling the hard little nub of pleasure buried deep within her slick folds. As he touched her, Isabeth suddenly stiffened and he could feel her throbbing walls around his arousal, pulling at him, demanding his seed. Another few thrusts and he answered her, spilling deep into her body, feeling wave after wave of pleasure wash over him.

There it was… that moment he lived for.

Even after he was spent, he continued to thrust into her, gently, feeling his arousal die but not wanting to relinquish this joy, not even for a moment. But he eventually slowed to a halt, his big arms pulling her close as he kissed her neck, her shoulders.

"I love you," he whispered. "Until the end of all things, I will love only you."

In his arms, he could feel her sigh faintly. "Please do not say such things."

"Why not?"

She grunted softly. "We have been through this, Roe."

"Through what?" he said, a hint of defiance in his tone. "Through the ridiculousness that is my life? Esa, you know how things are. Must I repeat it? Must I repeat that I have never loved Marian and that I was forced into a marriage with her and that she has given birth to three children who are not of my loins?"

She began shushing him quietly even before he finished

speaking. "Hush," she said, reaching back and putting her hand on the side of his head to quiet him. "Nay, we do not have to go through all of that again. I know the situation. I know how horrible Marian is. I know what a wonderful man you are and how much I love you, but it does not change things. You and I can never marry. We cannot be together forever so you must not… you must not say such things."

"Why not?" he demanded, sitting up as the mood was broken. He climbed off the bed, but not before pulling a coverlet over her to preserve her modesty. "You are all I have ever wanted in life, Isabeth. Do not tell me that I cannot have you forever. I will not survive if I cannot."

Clutching the coverlet to her chest, Isabeth sat up and watched him as he picked his breeches up off the floor and began to put them on.

"I am not entirely sure I would survive being separated from you, either," she said, trying desperately to be pragmatic in a world where Ronan refused to see reason. "But I have told you from the beginning that we must be reasonable. You are married and I… I am a widow."

He had his breeches up around his waist by this point, cinching up the ties. "You told me that you loved me."

"I do, but…"

"That is all that matters."

He was resolute in that. Resolute that he'd finally found love, as had she, and that was the only thing of consequence in their world. He was so blind to all else that it made conversations like this very difficult. Or, perhaps he wasn't blind as much as he was resistant. He didn't want to face the realities of what they were up against. Truth be told, neither did she. But she also couldn't live in a world of fantasy like he was.

"Then what happens when my cousin demands that I leave Ravenscar?" she said quietly. "Will I go north with you to the de Wolfe properties? Will I find a position in the foundling home and you will come to me when you can?"

He looked up from his breeches. "What do you mean?"

"I mean that you may love me, but you can never marry me," she said softly. "Marian has the title, the marriage, the prestige and respectability that a marriage brings. I will never be respectable because I am only worthy enough to be your mistress."

His gaze lingered on her for a moment before he returned his attention to the ties. "You are worth more than any woman in England," he said. "You are the most important woman in the world to me. You are the *only* woman to me. But you bring up a good point – will I leave you at the foundling home and come to you when I can, like a convenience? Nay, I will not. I have been thinking about this and I will send you to a property I own, one my father gave to me. You will live there and I will live with you."

Her brow furrowed in confusion. "How will you do that?" she said. "Where is this place?"

"It is called Halliden Castle," he said. "It is a very small outpost of Roxburgh and when my father took the garrison at Roxburgh, he gave me Halliden. It is supposed to be my home but Marian cannot stand the place because it is small. She would much rather be in the grandeur of Roxburgh Castle and not the less ornate halls of Halliden. I like the place, however. It is quiet and beautiful and it suits me. I will send you there and we shall raise Maxwell together."

Isabeth didn't say anything right away. She pondered his intentions before averting her gaze, clearly deep in thought.

When the silence grew oppressive, Ronan looked at her.

"What are you thinking?" he asked quietly. "Does this not appeal to you? We could be together, Esa. Shouldn't that be the most important thing?"

She didn't answer right away. Dropping the coverlet, she stood up and went to find her shift, affording Ronan an unobstructed view of her delicious, nude body. Her breasts were full, her belly rounded, and everything else was beautifully proportioned. It was enough to turn his thoughts dirty again but that view was cut off when she found her shift and pulled it over her head.

"You do not seem to have the same dilemma as I do," she said. "It has been like this from the start."

"What dilemma?"

She picked her surcoat off the ground. "Simple," she said. "I am a woman. If I allow myself to become your mistress, then my reputation is ruined. Do you think that will make it easy for Maxwell when it comes time to foster or even marry?"

"But I…"

She stopped him with a raised hand. "Please let me finish," she said. "I realize you are a de Wolfe. Your father is the great Blayth de Wolfe and your grandfather is the legendary William de Wolfe. The House of de Wolfe is one of the most distinguished houses in all of England, if not the world. You can get by with having a mistress and it will do nothing to harm your reputation. In fact, men will applaud you for it. But me… I will be ruined. Soiled. Reduced to being a man's whore. Do you think that is all I am worthy of?"

He sighed heavily. "Of course not," he said. "You are the most worthy woman I know. You deserve to be treated like a queen and that is what I intend to do. You make this sound as if the situation is cheap and opportunistic. It isn't, Esa. I love you and you love me. Our relationship is built on love."

Isabeth pulled her surcoat over her head and he went to help her, straightening out the back of it, helping her with the ties, all very sweet gestures. He was quite attentive to her, as Dyce was. He'd realized long ago why Dyce had been so solicitous with her, so hovering. She was a sweet, pretty, delicate creature.

He'd turned into a hoverer, too.

"I do love you, Roe," she said softly. "What's not to love? And I know I can never be as happy anywhere else, or with anyone else, as I am with you. Were it only me to be concerned over, it would not matter, but there is Maxwell to consider. Were I to become your mistress, he would have to live with that shame his entire life. It will denigrate him in the eyes of others. I do not think that would make Dyce happy."

Ronan drew in a long, heavy breath, one that was pregnant with thought and contemplation. He turned away from her, going in search of his tunic, which was lying across a table where it had been tossed in the heat of passion. Slowly, he picked it up.

"You do realize that you are already my mistress," he said. "You are already part of me. Dyce asked me to accept responsibility for you and I did, though in a way I had not intended. I do not think he would be displeased to know that I love you and will undoubtedly take care of you for the rest of your life."

Isabeth smoothed her surcoat. No matter what she wore these days, it was clear that she was pregnant. Maxwell was sitting high in her belly, under her ribcage, where he liked to roll and punch and kick. Considering this was the furthest into a pregnancy she had ever gotten, Isabeth was thrilled with her healthy, thriving child. But Ronan consumed so much of her thoughts and heart these days that the babe in her belly seemed to come in second behind Ronan at times. She felt guilty for that, one of the many things she felt guilty for, but she did not regret falling in love with the most handsome, kind man she'd ever known, one who encouraged her to learn and thrive and to be true to herself. That was something Dyce had never done. He was so busy building a glass wall around her that he never stopped to ask her what she wanted.

But Ronan did.

As she had said… *what's not to love?*

But, God… it had all been such a whirlwind.

"You must know how much I appreciate you and everything you wish to do for me," she said after a moment. "But tell me this – if I go with you to Halliden, how will you introduce me to others? How will you introduce me to your father and his wife, and your mother and her husband? Will you introduce me as your mistress, the woman who warms your bed, or will you simply keep me hidden away? Do you think they will respect my position with you and look upon me kindly?"

He looked at her with a somewhat pained expression, desperately trying to keep up the confidence in his decisions. "I will introduce you as the woman I love," he said simply. "Everyone knows I do not love Marian and she certainly does not love me. Esa, I have spent the past ten years being faithful to a woman who has absolutely no loyalty to me. I've had to stand by and watch her bear other men's children, children who bear the de Wolfe name. I have accepted this as the way of my life and have never complained about it because I was instructed not to. My marriage to Marian secures a great alliance and I understand that. But am I not allowed to find happiness on my own?"

Isabeth went to him, reaching out to grasp his enormous arms and force him to look at her. "I do not have the answers you seek because I would be biased," she said. "You are a man of great honor and compassion, and if it were up to me, I would say that you deserve all of the happiness in the world. If I could live with you in love and harmony and raise Maxwell as Dyce's son, and as yours, I would do so happily. But you have a position in life, one that will protect you from judgment. I do not have that luxury. I will be judged, and judged poorly, as your mistress. And so will my son."

Ronan knew she was right but he refused to admit it. Still, her words hurt him. "Then what do you want me to do?" he asked softly. "Do you want me to go away and leave you forever?"

She snorted softly. "I have tried to tell you to do just that, but you will not."

"Nay, I will not."

She grinned. "Then we have a dilemma, you and I."

"I will ask you again – what do you want to do?"

She shrugged. "I do not know," she said honestly. "Much like you, I know I cannot walk away from you."

"You will not leave me?"

"Not ever."

"But you do not want to live at Halliden."

She hesitated a moment before shaking her head. "I do not think it would be a good idea," she said. "If my relationship with you will never be proper, I prefer we not make it obvious for all to see. I prefer to be more… discreet."

He sighed unhappily, but he understood. He pulled her into his arms, gazing down into that magnificent face. "If I were to buy a home elsewhere for you to live, would that be acceptable?" he said. "Mayhap a townhome in Berwick or even Wooler. A small place where you could live as part of the community and I would see you as often as I could."

She smiled wryly. "People would figure it out sooner or later."

"Then I'll build you a castle in the middle of the moors where no one lives," he said with some sarcasm. "You'll be completely alone, but at least you would not be the fodder for gossip."

"I will consider that."

He laughed softly. "Good," he said. "But I want to be clear with you. The most important thing is that we always speak on our feeling and fears so that we can work through them. You will not keep anything from me and I will not keep anything from you. Mayhap… mayhap this isn't the most proper and desirable of circumstances, but nothing can take away from the fact that we love one another. What has happened between us was meant to happen. I do not take it lightly and I know you do not, either."

Isabeth nodded, accepting his sweet kiss and then falling against him when she lost all self-control. The man had the ability to suck that right out of her. Ronan's kiss was powerful yet passionate and Isabeth finally had to pull away so she could catch her breath. When he grabbed at her again, she pulled away completely, out of his reach.

He frowned.

"Why are you over there?" he asked. "You should be *here*."

He had his arms in a circle, as he did when he was embracing her, but she giggled. "Because if I am *there* and not over here, I shall never get any work done," she said. "Truthfully, I only came up here to rest for a few minutes before returning to my task, so I think I have rested long enough. If I stay here any longer, I will rest all afternoon, if you get my meaning."

He grinned wolfishly. "I get your meaning all too clearly," he said. "I am willing if you are."

She laughed softly as she moved for the door. "Tonight, my love," she said. "And mind you be careful next time. The maids almost saw you last night on the stairs. They no sooner left than you were at my door."

He shrugged as he sat down to pull on the boots he'd yanked off and tossed aside. "I am always eager to see you," he said. "I will not apologize for that."

She lifted the latch. "Be careful next time," she said again, lifting her eyebrows for emphasis. "I will see you tonight at sup."

He had one boot on but paused to blow her a kiss. "Until tonight."

She smiled at him, giving him a wink as she quit the chamber.

Leaving Ronan to finish dressing, Isabeth made her way down the stairs, a smile on her lips as she thought on the powerful, handsome knight she'd fallen so madly in love with. She'd wrestled with it since she realized her feelings for him, but more and more, she was overcoming the guilt in lieu of being completely selfish. Selfish that she was feeling something she'd never felt for Dyce. She was still fond of the man, as she had always been, and her feelings for Ronan did not affect that. What she felt for Ronan was entirely something of its own, delight and adoration so powerful that she could no longer resist it.

Every day that passed proved that.

Emerging from the manse, Isabeth crossed the courtyard,

now busy with men and women going about their duties. It was just after midday on this warm summer day, but to Isabeth, it seemed like the most beautiful day in the history of the world. She'd never seen the sky so blue or the sun so bright. Clouds skittered across the sky, pushed by the sea breeze, and every cloud had Ronan's name on it.

But as she was watching the clouds, someone else was watching her.

❧

"THERE SHE GOES. He's not come out of the keep yet."

"He will. He always does."

Two soldiers stood over near the postern gate that led towards the path down to the sandy beach below. They were older men, one with a milky right eye and the other with a scar that ran from the corner of his mouth down his chin. They were seasoned soldiers, having come from the House of de Grey ten years ago when Marian de Grey married Ronan de Wolfe. They may have worn de Wolfe tunics, but their loyalties were purely de Grey.

"She's with child," the man with the milky eye said. "Anyone can see that, though she tries to hide it."

The man with the scar nodded. "I know," he said. "The men know. Soldiers gossip like a gaggle of fishwives, so everyone knows. It's all they can speak of."

The milky-eyed soldier watched Lady de Brito cross the courtyard. He may have been blind in one eye, but his remaining eye was quite good. He watched the lady make her way to the kitchens next to the great hall until she disappeared from sight.

He grunted ironically.

"How many years have we been in service of de Wolfe?" he asked.

The scar-faced man cocked his head in thought. "Ten years," he said. "Ever since he married de Grey's daughter."

The man with the milky eye shook his head. "A marriage that should have never happened," he muttered. "I remember de Grey's daughter bedding the squires when she was young. She liked men before she met de Wolfe and she liked them after. A man deserves a faithful wife."

The man with the scar looked at him. "What do you want to do about this?" he said. "De Grey told us when we came with his daughter that we were to watch de Wolfe. We were to tell him if anything was amiss. We've served the man for ten years and nothing has been amiss until now."

The milky-eyed solider nodded slowly. "But this will get around," he said. "Men will say that the child she carries is a de Wolfe. Her husband has been dead these few months and only now she is showing signs of a pregnancy? Of course de Wolfe is the father. He sent his wife away and bedded the widow."

"You think so?"

"I do," the milky-eyed one said. "That's what I told de Grey in the missive I sent him."

The soldier with the scar looked at him sharply. "You've already sent the man word?"

The man with the white eye nodded slowly. "Back when we realized the de Brito woman was with child," he said. "We've not had anything to tell de Grey in all these years, but now… now, we do. He'll not think us useless now."

The soldier with the scar scratched his chin. "And the daughter?" he said. "She told us to keep an eye on him, too. We've never had anything to tell her, either."

"She wants to know if her husband is doing exactly as she has been doing all of these years," the milky-eyed man said. "That's all she cares about – catching him at what she has been doing so she can hold it over him."

"Do we send word to her, too?"

"I did when I sent word to her father." He looked at his companion, the remaining eye glittering dully. "We've done our duty, Euan. Let de Grey do as he pleases with the information. Let his whore of a daughter choke when she is told what her husband is doing. It matters not to me what she does."

Euan leaned against the wall that separated the courtyard from the troop yard to the north, a contemplative gesture.

"'Tis a pity you had to tell her at all," he said. "De Wolfe is a good man."

The milky-eyed soldier slapped him on the shoulder. "Good man or not, Edmund de Grey would hunt us down and punish us if he heard about de Wolfe's bastard from someone else," he said. Then he waved an arm to him as he headed back towards the troop yard. "Come along. Sir Christian will make an example of us if he sees us standing around. Let's see the sergeant and find something to do."

Euan pushed himself off the wall and followed. In truth, they had a fairly easy job of it with Ronan de Wolfe these days, far from the Scottish border and Roxburgh Castle where something was always happening. Ever since they were gifted to the House of de Wolfe as part of Marian's dowry, they'd seen quite a bit of action. It was good, for once, to know a little peace. But he secretly wondered how much peace Ronan was going to have once Edmund de Grey caught wind of his affair.

He had a feeling that life, for them all, was going to change in the near future.

CHAPTER ELEVEN

Portepool Manor, London
Three weeks later

H IS BODY WAS creating a raging fire within her loins.

Marian could feel Gaspard's manroot moving in and out, a primal rhythm that she eagerly mimicked. Her hips began to grind against his, lightning bursting every time their bodies would come together. The bursts of lightning grew stronger and brighter. Marian cried out in passion, living for the stroke that finally brought about the roll of thunder and ecstasy rippled through her body. Gaspard thrust into her a few more times, his strokes so hard that her teeth rattled, before spilling himself deep into her beautiful body.

The roll of thunder eventually faded but did not die completely. Marian lay beneath her lover, feeling his sweaty body atop her with great satisfaction. But her body was still so highly aroused that when he stroked her gently one last time, out of the sheer pleasure of being inside her, the thunder clapped again and she experienced the thrill of another climax. Gaspard felt her tremor bursts and he clutched her buttocks against him, thrusting in and out of her sensually and feeling at least two more releases until they faded away completely.

When the panting died down and the only sound filling the room was the soft crackle of the fire, Gaspard just lay there and stared at her. Marian's eyes were closed, her lips softly parted as she dozed in exhausted bliss. This was a peaceful moment, something that was few and far between for the both of them. Ever since they arrived in London, it seemed like all they did was rush about. But at this moment… it was still.

Until her eyes flew open.

"Go," Marian hissed, slapping his bare arse. "Go before my cousin sees you. You know she comes around at the most inopportune times before supper and I do not want her to find you in my bed."

Gaspard frowned as he propped himself up on one elbow. "She would have to be a fool not to already realize I am in your bed nightly," he said. "Somehow, I think she knows."

It was Marian's turn to frown. "That does not mean I have to be obvious about it," she said, displeased that he had the audacity to speak his mind. "Go back to your quarters and I will send for you later."

Gaspard sighed heavily, running a hand over his dark locks before pushing himself up and climbing out of the bed. He collected his breeches from the end of the bed, turning to look at Marian as she lay there with the coverlet down around her ankles. Her full, ripe body and gently rounded belly was softly illuminated in the firelight.

He looked back to his breeches as he pulled them on.

"Has she asked about the child yet?" he said. "Surely she knows."

Marian's hand immediately moved to her swollen belly. "Of

course it is my husband's child," she said. "Why should she care?"

"Because the child is mine."

Marian glared at him. "You will never speak those words again," she said. "I have told you that this child, male or female, will be born a de Wolfe, which is a far better family than yours. You should be pleased that your child will have such advantages. Rather than being the offspring of a lowly knight, the child will be part of a great empire. That's much better than anything you could ever do for it."

She'd said those words before, something that stabbed right into the heart of Gaspard's pride. Over the past three months, Marian had become more and more condescending with him, treating him no better than a servant at times, but he hung on because of the coinage she gave him when her mood was good. He tried to keep it good on a daily basis, bedding the woman whenever there was opportunity and catering to her every whim.

As far as her cousin knew, Gaspard was simply another de Wolfe knight who was Lady de Wolfe's protector, but the rumor mill at Portepool Manor knew the truth. As in any big house, there was gossip – and much of it – but no one was willing to tell Millicent de Haydon that her young cousin was a married woman carrying on an affair.

But the truth was much more than that.

Now, Marian was pregnant with her lover's child.

Sadly enough, Gaspard had been pleased with the pregnancy. He didn't have any children and he had been delighted with Marian's news, but this was her fourth illegitimate child, from four different lovers, and she had no intention of letting Gaspard claim the child in any fashion. It was a de Wolfe and it belonged to her husband and she laughed bitterly at any sentiment from Gaspard about it. So, he suffered in silence.

But the money was good.

Still...

"Marian," he said, focusing on the ties of his breeches. "I must ask you something."

She grunted as she pulled the coverlet over her and rolled onto her side. "What is it?"

He finished with his breeches. "Have you thought any further on what we discussed when you were sent away from Ravenscar?"

"What do you mean?"

"About your husband."

Marian's eyes opened when she realized what he meant. "About ridding me of him?"

"Aye."

She fell silent for a moment. "I have," she said. "And I am not entirely sure what advantage it would be to do that."

"You could do whatever you want. His wealth would be yours."

"I already do what I want and his wealth *is* mine."

Gaspard looked at her. "Then listen to what I have to say," he said somewhat pleadingly. "If he is gone, you will marry me. We shall raise this child as our son and we shall live the life you wish to live. We can travel and drink and feast and do anything you wish to do, only we will do it with each other. I will be at your side, always. Is that not better than being married to a man who is cruel to you?"

Marian rolled away from him. "He *is* cruel to me," she said. "But our marriage forms an alliance between two powerful families, Gaspard. Ronan is an important man in his family and he is an elite knight. You make it sound as if doing away with him will be an easy thing but I can assure you it will not be. The man isn't going to stand still while you drive your sword through his belly."

Gaspard's reaction was to become frustrated and walk away, but he couldn't walk away from what Marian could offer him. At least not yet. That bachelor knight at the Middlesbrough tournament had found a gold mine and he wasn't about to let it go.

Not yet, anyway.

He backed down.

"There are many ways to kill a man and not all of them involve a sword," he said quietly. Bending over her, he kissed her on the head. "Think about it. I will wait for you to summon me later, *ma douce.*"

Marian didn't say anything. She simply lay there, listening to him quit the room and trying to decide if a dead Ronan was attractive to her. She wasn't a fool; she knew what Gaspard was after and the fact that she was pregnant with his child complicated things a bit. She knew the man was a fortune hunter. She'd known that from the start. If Ronan had one value to her it was the fact that he was her excuse for not marrying the fortune hunters she'd run into during her lifetime. As long as she had a husband, she couldn't marry any of them. A fling with no responsibility.

But Gaspard… she was growing rather fond of him.

Perhaps she really would think on it.

With thoughts of Gaspard and Ronan on her mind, she began to drift off to sleep until a series of sharp raps on her door jarred her awake. Clutching the coverlet over her naked body, she sat up.

"Who comes?" she demanded.

"'Tis me," came the muffled reply. "Millie. May I enter?"

The door wasn't locked. She hadn't locked it after Gaspard left. "Enter," she said.

Millicent de Haydon entered the chamber. An older woman, handsome and well-groomed, she was the daughter of Marian's father's sister. The woman had married into the House of de Haydon, a very wealthy house, but she had only given birth to a daughter in all her years of marriage. Millicent had therefore inherited all of the de Haydon wealth and she had never married, although rumor had it that she was in love with her housekeeper, a woman who had been with the family since Millicent was young. Millicent was a good woman and her housekeeper was an excellent servant and the two enjoyed each other's company greatly.

Whether or not they were lovers was immaterial.

Marian certainly didn't care.

"Good eve, Millie," she said. "What brings you here?"

Millicent had something in her hand as she came to the bed, but she paused and looked her cousin over.

"Are you sleeping in the nude these days?" she asked. "What is wrong? Don't you feel well?"

Marian pulled the coverlet up to her neck. "I feel well enough," she said. "I… I was simply weary and came to nap before sup. I pulled my clothes off and was too weary to find a shift."

Millicent accepted the excuse. She had no reason not to. Coming around the side of the bed, she extended what looked like a vellum envelope.

"This came for you a short time ago," she said.

Marian had to let go of the coverlet with one hand in order

to accept the envelope. She peered at it closely, front and back.

"Who is this from?" she said. "I do not recognize the seal."

"The only way you will know is if you open it," Millicent said, moving away from the bed and sitting in a chair near the windows that overlooked the street. "The messenger came from Yorkshire."

Marian's eyebrows lifted even as she looked at the seal. "Ronan?" she said. "He is at Ravenscar, in Yorkshire."

"Is it a de Wolfe seal?"

Marian shook her head. "There is no signet."

She finally broke the seal and opened it, flipping it around because it was upside down. In the weak light of the bank of tapers that was lit to stave off the coming darkness, she peered closely at the writing, which she did not recognize. She was halfway through the missive when she began to catch on to the message it bore. As Millicent watched, Marian's jaw went slack and her eyes widened.

Then, she read it again.

"What does it say, Marian?" Millicent asked, curious. "Who is it from?"

"I *knew* it!" she exploded, tossing off the coverlet in her rage. "I knew he sent me away from Ravenscar so that he could… could *fornicate* with that woman! I knew he sent me away just so he could shame me!"

She leapt out of bed, completely unmindful of the fact that she was now exposing her pregnant body to her cousin, who expressed some shock when she saw Marian's rounded belly.

"Marian!" she gasped. "Are you with child?"

Marian had just collected her shift from a stool where Gaspard had tossed it when he tore it off her body, but her cousin's words had her coming to a confused halt. Puzzled, she took a moment to process what Millicent had said before suddenly realizing what she had done. Her cheeks flamed as she quickly turned away and pulled the shift over her head.

"Aye," she finally said, struggling to get control of her composure. "Aye, I am, but now… now I am shamed by my own husband!"

She was trying to turn the subject away from her, back to the source of her rage, but Millicent was on her feet, making her way towards her.

"Calm yourself," Millicent said, taking her by the hands and bringing her back over to the bed where the missive lay upon the linens. "Calm yourself and tell me what has happened. Excitement is not good for the child. What does the missive say?"

Marian was quite agitated. "Read it for yourself," she said. As Millicent reached for it, she began to blurt it all out. "I told you that Ronan is in Yorkshire to see to the affairs of a friend who was killed, but the friend has a beautiful wife whom my husband has apparently taken up with. Read the missive! And she is with child! *His* child!"

Millicent looked at her with concern as she picked up the missive and read the contents. As she did so, however, Marian was back on her feet again.

"Ronan has impregnated another woman!" she nearly shouted. "How can he do this to me? How can he shame me and my family like that? I cannot believe he would do such a thing!"

Millicent finished reading the missive and set it back on the bed. She watched her cousin stomp around, shouting threats and curses at her husband, but Millicent had known her cousin all of her life. She had been present at the marriage between

Marian and Ronan, so she had seen from the start of the marriage how little affection there was between them. Edmund de Grey and Blayth de Wolfe had orchestrated a miserable marriage for their children for the sake of an alliance, so Millicent knew enough to know that Marian's posturing was all for show. Perhaps there was some wounded pride there but, mostly, it was all for show.

Millicent wasn't fooled.

She had also heard, from her servants, about the de Wolfe knight that went to Marian every night and bedded the woman until dawn. Portepool Manor was a tight community of servants, people who had served de Haydon for many years, and they were extremely observant. Millicent hadn't missed the rumors of her cousin whoring around, but then again, it wasn't the first time it had happened when Marian had come for a visit. She was fairly adept at finding men to fill her bed. Men who weren't her husband. It was a shame because Millicent genuinely liked Ronan and they shared a good relationship.

She just happened to hate her own cousin.

"This is the first time he has done such a thing?" she asked calmly.

Marian threw up her hands. "Probably not," she snapped. "He is gone so often and I never know where he is. There are probably a dozen de Wolfe bastards that I do not know of."

"Including your own children?"

Marian's raging came to an unsteady halt. "What do you mean?"

Millicent's dark eyes lingered on her. "I mean the children you gave birth to," she said. "I have seen them, Marian. Your husband is not the father and I would wager to say he is not the father of the one in your belly, either, as you would more than likely wish me to believe. Shall we be completely honest with one another now? Lies do not become you, though you have been telling them all your life, so mayhap they do. But no more lies between us, please."

Marian's eyes were wide with shock and perhaps chagrin. "How can you…?"

Millicent cut her off. "Because everyone knows the children you have given birth to are not Ronan's," she said. "You may as well stop pretending they are because everyone knows the truth. I also know that the knight you brought to Portepool Manor has been warming your bed nightly. Do you carry his child now?"

Marian stared at her for quite some time. Simply stared at her. Then, she went to collect a robe, all the while moving slowly and thoughtfully. Pulling the robe around her body, she went to sit in a chair near the hearth.

"I will answer your question if you answer mine," she finally said.

"What question is that?" Millicent said.

"Do you love your housekeeper, as a wife would love a husband?"

"We are not speaking of me, Marian."

Marian cocked an eyebrow. "Mayhap not," she said. "But if I were you, I would not throw stones at others when you yourself have many secrets to hide."

Millicent sat back in her chair, eyeing her cousin for a moment. "Mayhap I have misjudged you," she said. "You are more cunning than I gave you credit for, but that does not change the fact that I know the de Wolfe knight has been in your bed every night since you arrived."

"And if he has been?"

"Then I would say your outrage at Ronan is misplaced."

"Since you have never been married, you are not in a position to give me advice about my husband."

Millicent smiled thinly. "I may not have been married, but I know disloyalty when I see it," she said. "Marian, you have not fooled anyone. Even your father knows what you do. Do you think he would not? Do you think your activities have not reached his ears? You would be wrong. He knows you for what you are."

"And he knows you for what *you* are."

"At least I am not bearing bastards and trying to tell the world they are my husband's children."

"At least I have children."

Millicent grinned. Then, she laughed softly. "You are a defiant, bitter woman," she said. "But I respect you for the sheer fact that you do whatever you please, no matter what others think about you. That is commendable."

Marian smiled thinly. "I could say the same thing about you."

"I am not defiant and bitter."

"Mayhap not," Marian said, still smiling. "But I am happy with my life. Are you happy with yours?"

"Delightfully so," Millicent said. "Do you trust me not to speak of this conversation, Marian?"

Marian thought a moment before nodding. "I do," she said. "You are many things, but you are not a gossip."

"True enough," Millicent said. Then she quickly sobered. "Do you trust me?"

"Strangely enough, I do."

"Then listen to me well," Millicent said. "Leave Ronan alone. No matter what he is doing, it is far less than what you have been doing all your life. Remember what Jesus said – let he who is without sin cast the first stone. And you, my darling, are full of sin so unless you want your sins to find you, I would suggest you not confront Ronan about this dalliance. Fingers may start pointing to you and you could not explain away all of the affairs you have had. Right now, it is a well-known secret that no one speaks of, but should you press Ronan for his infidelity, he has more than enough evidence against you to charge you with the same. I would wager to say the church would grant him a divorce in that case, which would ruin you. Is that what you want?"

Marian was pale by the time she finished. The smile from her lips was gone and her features were taut with distress. "He would never get a divorce," she said firmly. "I would never allow it."

"You may not have a choice, my darling."

"I will kill him first!"

Millicent tipped her head back as if something had just occurred to her. "Ah," she said. "So it comes. You want to kill the man, do you?"

Marian backed down. "I did not say that I want to," she said. "I only said that I can. And I will if he tries to divorce me. I may kill him because of his disloyalty and no one would blame me."

A smile played on Millicent's lips. "If you were to do that, I am sure his father would have something to say about it," she said. "The House of de Wolfe can crush the House of de Grey. Would you be willing to risk that?"

Marian sighed sharply. "You are putting words in my mouth," she said. "You are trying to force me into confessing that I want to kill Ronan, but that is not what I wish."

"That is *not* what you just said."

Marian stood up, turning her back on her cousin as she pulled the robe about her body more tightly. As if to protect herself from Millicent's sharp gaze.

"I will not be lectured to by someone who has never had a husband," she said. "And how I live my life is my own affair. I will not be judged by you. Now you twist my words when it comes to Ronan and I'll not let you do it. My marriage is my own affair, Millie. It does not involve you."

She was right and Millicent knew it, but she was old enough and rich enough to speak her opinions and not worry about backlash. But she didn't want to fight with Marian about it, mostly because she knew she was right about Marian and her torrid life. She was also certain that Marian knew she was right and simply refused to acknowledge it. With a sigh, she stood up.

"Very well," she said. "We will not speak on it any longer, but know my opinion about it. What do you intend to do now? Will you return to Yorkshire?"

The thought of the long journey north again didn't appeal to Marian, but scolding Ronan about his affair with the de Brito widow would make that journey well worth it. It wasn't often she had the opportunity to berate her husband and certainly not for something she did every day. Ronan had never, in all the time she'd been married to him, been caught breaking his vows. Not that Marian thought he ever had, but when she did it, it was different. When he did it…

She didn't like it.

"I think so," she said. "I will return to Ravenscar and demand he return to Roxburgh Castle with me. If he does not, I will go straight to my father and tell him about it. My father will have something to say."

"When will you leave?"

"Immediately," Marian said. "I see no reason to remain here when I have business to attend to in the north."

Millicent simply nodded. "As you wish," she said. Then she cocked her head thoughtfully. "Marian, will you allow me to travel with you? I've not been north in quite some time and could do with a little adventure. Besides… it would make the time pass more quickly if you had someone to talk to."

Marian turned to her, frowning. "You cannot come if you are going to argue with me all the time."

Millicent shook her head. "I promise I shall behave," she said. "Now, may I go? I might continue north to see your father for a time. Edmund and I were always companionable."

Marian shrugged. "Come if you wish," she said. "But behave yourself."

"There is no fun in that."

"Then I shall make you walk all the way. You cannot ride with me."

Millicent laughed softly and went to her. She put her hands on Marian's shoulders and kissed her on the cheek. "Do not fret," she said. "We will enjoy ourselves. I will send my maids up to help you pack your things and I will make sure the escort is prepared. Do you wish to leave tomorrow or the next day?"

Marian turned back towards her bed. "The next day," she said. "Tomorrow, we will prepare."

"As you wish."

Millicent quit the chamber and Marian locked the door behind her this time. She could hear Millicent's footfalls as they faded away, down the stairs. She couldn't decide if it had been a mistake to let Millicent come with her or not, but she settled on indifference. Millicent would insist on paying for everything, which was fine with her. If Millicent wanted to come with her and pay all expenses, then Marian would let her.

Maybe she'd have Gaspard kill her, too.

Aye… that's what she was considering.

Now that Ronan had humiliated her, Marian was wondering if she shouldn't take Gaspard up on his offer. With no Ronan, all obstacles would be removed. Millicent hadn't been wrong when she said that everyone knew of Marian's activities. Everyone knew what kind of a wife she was. Marian lived her life pretending to be so discreet in everything but the truth was that people were smarter than she gave them credit for.

Especially Millicent.

And perhaps that would be her undoing.

CHAPTER TWELVE

Roxburgh Castle

"**P**APA! RIDERS!"

Sir Blayth de Wolfe, born James de Wolfe, turned to see his youngest son running towards him. Garreth, known as Garr, was turning twelve years of age later that month and had yet to grow into the gangly arms and legs he'd sprouted earlier in the year during a growth spurt. All Blayth could see were those arms and legs flying towards him as the boy nearly lost his footing. Blayth stepped out of the way to avoid being crashed into and grabbed his son by the arm at the same time.

"If you keep running like that, one of these days I will not be here to stop you," he said. "I am going to find you smashed against a stone wall like vermin when it is stepped on. Your innards will be everywhere. That is an undignified way to die, Garr."

Garr grinned. He had his father's toothy smile and his quick wit. "A wall cannot stop me," he said cheekily. "Neither can you!"

With that, he pulled away, snorting, leaving Blayth to shake his head at his feisty son. "Would you care to test that declaration?" he asked.

Garr shook his head. Though his father was older, with an enormous and muscular body, he had slowed down over the years a little. Not much, but a little. His slow and deliberate speech was the result of a head injury he'd sustained many years ago, a massive scar on the left side of his head now covered with graying blond hair. Though Blayth's speech might have been slower than most, his mind most certainly was not. He was as cunning as ever. Even if he was physically slower these days, Garr was smart enough to know not to tangle with his father.

He may have been young, but he wasn't stupid.

"Not now," he said, eyeing his father. "I am too tired from running and it would not be fair to me. I came to tell you that standards have been sighted."

He was diverting his father's challenge, which wasn't missed by Blayth. He fought off a grin as he allowed the boy to change the focus. "Colors?" he asked.

"Blue and white stripes."

Blayth thought on that for a moment. "Blue and white stripes," he repeated. Then, it occurred to him who it might be. "De Grey?"

"That is what the sentries are saying."

Blayth didn't know whether he should be pleased or concerned. He settled for curious. Edmund de Grey was the only de Grey he knew that he ever had any business or dealings with, a man with a big castle near Lancaster and a grip on most of northern Cheshire. That's why Blayth had wanted an alliance with the man. The House of de Wolfe was already allied with nearly everyone in Northumberland and North Yorkshire, so the de Grey alliance brought in new and powerful blood. It was something that benefitted every de Wolfe castle, ally, and friend.

But he tried to ignore the cost of that alliance.

He had for years.

"I will meet him at the gate," he told his son. "You will go inside and inform your mother. She will want to make preparations for our honored guest."

Garr took off running again, nearly tripping as he did so. Blayth watched his boy run off, all arms and legs, before turning his attention to the massive gatehouse of Roxburgh.

Curiosity was turning to apprehension.

There was no real reason he could think of behind a visit from Edmund de Grey and most certainly the man would not have traveled over one hundred miles for a social visit. Blayth was coming to think that perhaps the man had come to ask him for support, which would have been the most logical reason. Or mayhap he had another daughter he wanted to marry off into the de Wolfe clan. In any case, Blayth was ready for him. The answer would be no.

And he waited.

It was a clear day over the Scottish Lowlands, the sky overhead a brilliant blue. Visibility was for miles in any direction and as Blayth stood at the gatehouse, he could see the de Grey party approaching quite clearly. Edmund hadn't brought an army with him, but he had about three hundred men. It was a big escort for a man who had come to ask for support.

So maybe it wasn't support he needed.

As preparations in the keep and great hall of Roxburgh were in full swing, Blayth watched the de Grey party cross the river and come to the first of two enormous gatehouses. At the first gatehouse, they could only pass through about three abreast but by the time they reached the second gatehouse, where Blayth was, they were nearly single file. That was a design element that prevented an enemy from rushing into the castle grounds too quickly should the gatehouses be breached. Edmund de Grey, a pale man with graying hair and a hook nose, was riding at the front astride a fine stallion that was worth more than some castles.

He headed straight for Blayth.

"Greetings," he called out.

Blayth smiled at the man, lifting a hand. "My lord," he said. "We are honored by your visit. Why did you not send word ahead? We would have met you on the road."

Edmund waved him off. "No need," he said. "I did not want to create a big fanfare."

"I hope your trip was pleasant."

Edmund reined his horse to a halt, stiffly dismounting as he handed the animal over to a soldier. "Pleasant enough," he said. "At least the weather held."

"It has been good weather for several days, at least."

Edmund looked around at the massive structure of Roxburgh as he pulled off his heavy leather gloves. "I'd forgotten how big this place is," he muttered. "Magnificent."

"Thank you."

Edmund looked at him. "Why do you say that?" he said. "You did not build it."

Blayth started laughing. "True enough, but it belongs to me," he said. "Will you come inside and refresh yourself? And then you can tell me why you've traveled over one hundred miles, without sending word ahead, just to see me."

Edmund seemed to demure a little. "I will tell you," he said. "But give me your best wine first."

"It shall be done."

Together, they headed to the great hall, an enormous building that was attached to the keep. Since Roxburgh was built on an island in the middle of the River Tweed, it followed the slender shape of the island. The keep was built with the great hall behind it and other buildings behind that, all in a line. Blayth led the man along the rather slender strip of a bailey flanking the buildings until they arrived at the stone hall.

He ushered him inside.

Blayth's wife, Asmara, was in the vast hall. Tall, lovely, and brunette, she greeted Edmund politely. Asmara was Welsh, a descendant of kings, and was grace and power personified. She made small talk about the weather and Edmund's health before making sure there was plenty of food and drink for their guest. She departed the hall to leave the men to their conversation and Edmund sat down, followed by Blayth, who poured a measure of wine for the both of them.

Edmund drank deeply.

"God," he muttered. "I'd forgotten just how much I hate travel. I've not traveled in years, you know. And that stallion of mine has the worst gait of any horse in the land. It is like riding atop a pile of rocks that is constantly in motion."

Blayth grinned. "I am sorry to hear that," he said. "He is a beautiful horse."

"Beautiful and stupid."

"Would you take a fair price for him?"

Edmund eyed him before breaking down into snorts of humor. "I would not," he said. "He is too pretty for you and your war machine up here in the wilds of the north. The Scots would want to steal him."

"That is more than likely true," Blayth said. He watched

Edmund take another drink of wine before speaking. "But you did not come here to speak of stallions or Scots."

Edmund shook his head. "Nay," he said. "I hope you realize that only something very important would cause me to travel like this."

"How may I be of service, Edmund?"

Edmund cleared his throat softly as they came to the point of his visit. "You can punish your son before I do."

Blayth's brow furrowed. "Punish my son?" he said, surprised. "I'm assuming you are speaking of Ronan?"

"I am."

"Why? What has he done?"

"He has impregnated another woman."

Blayth tried desperately not to let his shock show but he only managed to make himself look angry. "What in the world are you talking about?" he said, incredulous. "My son has never conducted a relationship with anyone other than his wife since the day he married Marian."

Edmund held up a hand. "Mayhap that was true in the past," he said. "He has been a faithful husband. But I received word that your son has been carrying on with the widow of Ravenscar and that the woman is pregnant with a de Wolfe offspring."

Blayth couldn't believe what he was hearing. "Who told you this?"

"Men loyal to me."

"*What* men, Edmund?"

It was clear that Edmund was reluctant to elaborate but he knew that he had little choice. "De Grey soldiers within the de Wolfe ranks," he said. "And before you lecture me about their loyalties, I know you have men that serve others that still report to you, too, so you will not condemn me."

That was true of most great warlords to a certain extent so Blayth didn't comment. He was more focused on what Edmund had been told than men spying on his son.

"I know that Ronan went to the manse at Ravenscar to bury his good friend, Dyce de Brito," he said evenly. "The men who accompanied Ronan to the Middlesbrough tournament, including several nephews, returned several months ago to tell me that. I assumed Ronan was still at Ravenscar administering the lands until a suitable replacement could be found."

"Did you know about the widow?"

Blayth nodded. "I was told about her," he said. "But only that there was a widow as the result of Ronan's friend being killed. From what I was told by my nephews, Ronan promised to take care of the woman and Ravenscar. The promise was made on the man's deathbed, Edmund. What was he supposed to do?"

Edmund waved him off, irritated. "Did he also promise to bed the woman?" he snapped. "Did you know that Marian accompanied him to Ravenscar for propriety's sake but that he sent her away shortly after their arrival? Marian has been in London with her cousin for the past few months while Ronan and the widow of his friend are carrying on. Now the widow is pregnant and I demand justice for this slanderous behavior against my daughter."

Blayth just stared at the man for a moment. In truth, he didn't trust himself to answer. It was true that he was shocked by the allegations but he was more shocked by Edmund's self-righteous attitude. Blayth knew the history of Ronan and Marian's marriage better than anyone, so the more he thought about Edmund's demand, the more offended he became. He stood up and paced away from the table, contemplating what his reply would be.

"Edmund," he said slowly, turning to face the man. "May I ask a question?"

Edmund was impatient with the lack of immediate response. "Ask anything."

Blayth folded his enormous arms across his chest. "When Ronan and Marian's first daughter was born and she looked nothing like my son and everything like a de Grey knight who had been rather solicitous towards Marian, did I demand satisfaction that your daughter had given birth to another man's child?"

Edmund's jaw popped open in outrage. "What do you mean by that?"

Blayth wasn't going to let the man bully him. "You know exactly what I mean," he growled. "Marian has given birth to three children, all from different fathers, and everyone in the north knows it. Your daughter was a whore when she seduced my son and she has been a whore ever since. Have I ever demanded satisfaction? Have I ever demanded that you punish her for shaming the de Wolfe name every hour of every day since she took her vows of marriage? I've not said a word because I was concerned for our alliance, but if you've come here to slander my son with these foolish accusations, I will tell you plainly now that I am no longer concerned for our alliance. If I were you, I would be concerned for the very welfare of my properties. You will not like it if I turn the de Wolfe armies on you. You will not survive."

Edmund was on his feet by now, shock and fear and outrage rippling across his face. "You dare say such things about my daughter?"

"Deny them. I dare you. I can find a hundred men who would tell you differently."

Edmund opened his mouth to reply but he knew, as Blayth did, that he couldn't refute anything that was said for it was all true. It was simply something they never spoke of. Edmund pretended it was a family secret and Blayth never said anything because he was concerned for the alliance, as he had said.

But now… now, no one was concerned for such things any longer.

The situation was deteriorating quickly.

"I will not stand here and let you insult my daughter, de Wolfe," Edmund said, moving away from the table. "Your son has…"

"My son, if the allegations are proven true, has done nothing your daughter hasn't done a hundred times over."

Edmund was starting to turn red in the face. "Then you will do nothing?"

Blayth was tracking the man as he moved near the entry door. "I will not punish him if that is what you are asking," he said. "I will, however, go to Ravenscar and discover the truth for myself. But I will not let you level threats against Ronan. If he did what you say he did, then he was only following his wife's example."

Edmund was so angry that he was twitching. "Speak ill of her one more time and our alliance is finished."

Blayth cocked an eyebrow. "I want you to listen to me carefully, Edmund, because it is important," he said with thinly held patience. "I am going to Ravenscar to discover the truth of what you have said. If it turns out to be false, I will march on your home of Borwick Castle and raze it to the ground in punishment for speaking ill against my son. If the rumors prove to be true, however, I will not punish him. I will encourage him to divorce Marian, which he has more than enough grounds to do. I have advised him against it all of these years because I wanted to keep our alliance, but if you say it is finished, then there is no reason for him to remain married to her. I will encourage him to divorce her and it will ruin her. No decent man will ever marry her again."

Edmund was breathing heavily with pent-up emotion. He wanted to explode at Blayth, but he didn't want to find himself in a sword fight because he knew he couldn't win. He'd been able to bully Blayth de Wolfe for ten years, but that domination was ended. Blayth was taking a stand when it came to his son's reputation and Edmund understood that completely. Frankly, he wondered what had taken the man so long to do it, for Marian had indeed been shaming the de Wolfe name for many years.

Now, it seemed that de Wolfe would have the last laugh.

His stomach began to churn.

"I am her father," he said, starting to feel some desperation as the tables were turned on him. "Marian was always a… difficult child. Do I know those children she has given birth to are not de Wolfe offspring? Of course I know. But she is my daughter. I am not supposed to see the bad in her. I am only supposed to love her because she is my child."

Blayth wasn't in a forgiving mood. "Yet you attack my son based on a rumor," he said. "I am not sure I can forgive that, Edmund. Ronan… he is special to me. He is my first born. He does not deserve what Marian has done to him."

Edmund sighed heavily, struggling to gain control of his emotions. "I know," he said. "He is a good lad. But Marian behaves as she does and he says nothing."

"Because I told him not to out of respect for the de Wolfe and de Grey names," Blayth said quietly. "You know this. Sometimes it is better not to say anything at all. That would be giving attention to the situation and sometimes that makes it worse. We all have demons that we struggle with and Marian happens to be Ronan's."

Those were wise words. Edmund hung his head. "Then what will you do now?"

"I told you," Blayth said. "I will go to Ravenscar and discover the truth for myself. But until I do, you will say nothing of the rumors. Keep them to yourself, as I have done with Marian all these years. When I discover the truth, I will send you word."

Edmund nodded and slowly, wearily, returned to his seat at the table. It seemed that the situation was over, for now, and the dull apprehension of what the future would bring settled. Edmund really didn't want to break the alliance.

He was starting to feel like a fool.

"Please," he said quietly. "Please do not seek a divorce. Please do not shame my family like that, Blayth. Although you have every right, I beg you not to do it. It will ruin Marian and her sisters, her nieces… something like that has far-reaching implications. Not just with my family, but with yours as well. It would be a stain we could never recover from."

Blayth knew that. It was the worst possible social and religious curse for the family of the woman at fault, but it would also disparage the House of de Wolfe, too, for bringing it about. His angry stance began to waver.

"If I do not, then you must speak to your daughter about it," he said. "I know you have not interfered with Marian's behavior in the past but know that I will advise Ronan to divorce her if she continues along her present path. If she gives up her wild ways and becomes a good wife, I will not consider it, but if she does not…"

Edmund understood. "Say no more," he said. "I know what I must do."

"Then make sure you do it."

Edmund nodded wearily. "I will," he said. Then he looked at the table before him. "May I at least rest for the night before going home?"

He sounded utterly defeated. Blayth went back to the table as well, standing opposite of Edmund now rather than next to him, as a friend would. "You may stay as long as you wish," he said. "But we will not speak of Ronan or Marian anymore."

"Agreed."

"Would you like to see Priscilla?"

Edmund's tired face lit up, just a little. "How is my youngest grandchild?"

Blayth nodded. "She is well," he said. "I will send for her."

While Edmund drowned himself in more wine, Blayth headed out of the hall through a servants' entrance that would take him into the keep. He found that he needed to get clear of Edmund and calm his anger. He was no sooner through it and heading into a dark, stone-lined passage than someone grasped his arm from behind. Startled, he turned to see his wife behind him.

"Christ," he muttered. "You nearly scared the wits from me. I was about to unsheathe a dagger and start slashing."

Asmara grinned. "And I would defend myself and you would be in a world of pain," she said. But she quickly sobered. "I heard what was said, that terrible man."

Blayth grunted with disapproval. "You know better than to eavesdrop on my conversations."

Asmara shrugged. "Not when the conversation is with Edmund de Grey and he comes to Roxburgh unannounced," she said. "I am inclined to cut out that man's tongue for what he said about Ronan. You know it is not true."

Blayth nodded. "It would be out of character for him, I agree," he said. "But Titus told me that the de Brito widow is quite beautiful. A beautiful, vulnerable widow and Ronan never knowing any comfort from his own wife... I am not saying he did what de Grey said he did, but the truth is that he is human. In a moment of weakness, he could have..."

He didn't need to finish. They both knew that he was right, though Asmara didn't want to admit it. She had not given birth to Ronan – he was a product of Blayth's first marriage in the days when he was James de Wolfe, before a severe head injury in battle had robbed him of his memory of his previous life – but she loved the man as if she'd given birth to him. She was fiercely protective of him.

But as her husband said, he was only human.

"He does not need the temptation," she said after a moment. "What if the de Brito widow is using grief to her advantage and playing upon his sympathies? Ronan has a good heart. He would want to comfort her and if it became more, surely it is not his fault."

Blayth could only shake his head. "He is a grown man," he said. "He can make his own decisions. But you are right when you say that he does not need the temptation, nor does he need the burden of being responsible for another man's property and family. He has been there for several months. When will he decide that he has done enough for his friend and the man's widow? And if she is keeping him there with emotional guilt and grief, does he plan to stay forever?"

Asmara was unhappy at the thought of an opportunistic widow. "What she needs is another husband," she said. "One to fill the void that Ronan now fills."

Blayth cocked his head thoughtfully. "What do you mean?"

"I mean that we should find her one," Asmara said pointedly. "She needs a husband and it cannot be Ronan. If this situation is not changed, it will ruin his life and his reputation, all because he was honorable in helping his friend."

Blayth thought on that. "I fear you may be right," he said. "I will go to Ravenscar, find her a new husband, and bring Ronan back with me to Roxburgh. No more gossip, no more problems."

"But where will you find her a husband?"

Blayth scratched his head. "Good question," he said. "Any ideas?"

Asmara thought quickly. "It is not as if you can go from town to town, looking for one," she said. "It must be someone we know, someone who we can convince."

"You mean coerce."

She cocked an eyebrow at him. "Convince or coerce, it is all the same thing," she said. "But *who* do we know?"

Blayth sighed. "I cannot think of anyone," he said. "Mayhap by tomorrow I will… wait. I think I may know of someone."

"Who?"

"De Litton."

Asmara's eyes widened. "Of course!" she gasped. "Randolph de Litton is perfect! He was only just turned down by the Wakefield lass over at Chillingham Castle. His heart was broken from what Garr told us. What better way to heal a broken heart than with a new and willing wife?"

They were speaking of an older knight, big and rather clumsy but quite kind and likable, who had been unlucky in securing a wife during his adult lifetime. It wasn't for lack of trying. He was simply big and awkward, with no real wealth or prestige, and women tended not to notice him because of it. He had been vying for the hand of one of the Wakefield daughters from Chillingham Castle, about twenty miles south of Roxburgh, until the woman decided on another, more handsome knight from Nottingham. Yet again, Randolph was jilted for someone else, so the truth was that he'd be perfect for a young widow whose prospects weren't all that good.

And Ronan would be free of whatever pledge he'd given the widow, and her husband.

"It is the best possible solution," Blayth said. "Let me see if I can convince Randolph that being lord of his own manse is more appealing than remaining at Roxburgh and fighting Scots."

"I think it is a brilliant idea."

"As do I," Blayth said. "I will find him tonight. Meanwhile, you will bring Priscilla to Edmund. He'd like to see his granddaughter."

Asmara wasn't thrilled with having to have contact with Edmund, but she obeyed. As Blayth went in search of someone to save his son from a preying widow, Asmara collected Marian's youngest daughter, who lived with them, and took her to see her grandfather. What she didn't expect was for Edmund to burst into tears when he saw her.

That told Asmara that Edmund was more heartbroken about Marian than he let on.

Heartbroken about his wayward daughter.

CHAPTER THIRTEEN

September

"WHERE DID YOU get this?" Isabeth gasped. "Ronan, it must have been frightfully expensive. Whyever did you do it?"

There was delight in her tone. She was holding up a necklace that Ronan had just given her, a spectacular five-point star that was set with pearls and a big sapphire to represent the moon and the stars. Hanging from the bottom of it on the end of slender, gold chains were three large pearls. In all, it was a spectacular piece.

But Ronan simply grinned.

"Do you always ask such questions when someone gives you a gift?" he said. "That is very rude. Just put it on your neck and wear it like a good girl. Stop asking questions."

Isabeth obeyed, putting it on her neck and looking into the polished bronze mirror that had a surprisingly true reflection. She was wearing a simple yellow garment this day, which made a perfect backdrop for the spectacular necklace. She fingered it as she looked at herself in the mirror.

"It's magnificent," she said sincerely. "It is the most beautiful thing I have ever owned."

Ronan smiled as he watched her marvel at it. "I'm not sure that's true," he said. "I've seen some of the pieces Dyce bought you. This is not a competition, of course. I simply thought of you when I saw this in Scarborough. I wanted to give it to you, as a token of my feelings for you. It wasn't meant to outshine anything Dyce ever bought you."

She smiled at him in the reflection. "I know," she said. "You have always been very respectful of Dyce's memory. He would have been very grateful."

Ronan's smile faded. "Do you think so?"

She nodded, turning around to look at him. "I do," she said. "I truly do. You have never tried to push him from my memory. You've always kept him very much alive, which has been a delicate balance. But you have handled it splendidly."

His smile returned, weakly. "I hope so," he said. "I have tried."

Isabeth reached out, touching his cheek fondly. "Your heart is true, my love," she said, kissing him sweetly. "And I shall cherish this always."

He wrapped his enormous arms around her, kissing her again, but she was more interested in inspecting the pendant. He was still holding her as she held it up between them, watching it glitter in the light, when she suddenly noticed something on it.

"There is writing on this," she said, trying to get a good look at it. "Did you have it inscribed?"

He grinned. "I was wondering how long it would take you to notice."

"What does it say?"

He released her as she went over to the bank of tapers to get a better look. "It says *'Tis thee, my dear, that I adore and will, my darling, forever more,*" he said. "I had the goldsmith inscribe it on the back."

Isabeth looked at him with astonishment. "That's so beautiful," she said. "Did you think of it yourself?"

He nodded. "Me and the goldsmith," he said with a twinkle in his eyes. "I wanted him to inscribe *'Tis thee, my dear, that I adore.* He liked it so much that he added the rest. I think it describes my love for you perfectly."

She sighed dreamily and clutched it against her breast. "How wonderful," she said. "You are quite the poet, Roe."

He shrugged modestly. "You seem to bring it out in me."

"Say more beautiful things to me."

He frowned. "I cannot do it on command," he said. "I am not *that* clever."

Isabeth giggled. "I think you are," she said. "I think you are perfect."

She went back over to her dressing table and carefully hung the necklace on a peg that was built into the mirror for just such an item. Ronan pointed.

"Why do you put it there?" he said. "You must wear it and never take it off."

She smiled at him as she picked up a kerchief neatly folded on the table. "Sup approaches and I will be in and out of the kitchens," she said. "I do not want to risk damaging it. It is a magnificent piece, but I do not think I should wear it when I am tending to my chores."

He frowned. "Then I shall buy you another one that is less elaborate, one that you can wear every day," he said. "I cannot buy you a ring, but I can buy you a necklace. It is still a circle that never ends, like my love for you."

Her eyes twinkled as she looked at him. "You see? You are a poet on command. That was very lyrical."

"It is the truth."

Isabeth smiled at him as she tied the kerchief around her hair. "I would rather have the poetry from your lips than all the glittering necklaces in the world. But I thank you for it just the same."

He watched her as she finished with her hair. "I simply wanted to give you something that would remind you of me every time you looked at it," he said. "But I have a confession to make – I also gave it to you to lighten your mood. You and I must have a discussion."

She glanced at him as she fussed with the kerchief. "What about?"

"Ravenscar," he said.

She paused a moment. "I see," she said. "What about it?"

He sighed. "I have been here for several months," he said. "You know, and I know, that it is not my home. I cannot remain here forever. My life is in Northumberland and as much as I would like to remain here with you, eventually, I must return home."

Isabeth nodded. "I know," she said. "I have been thinking on our discussion from a month ago when we spoke of my possibly going to the foundling home or to the small outpost that belongs to you. You even offered to purchase a home in a town near Roxburgh."

"I remember."

"I have thought about it quite a bit."

"And what conclusion did you come to?"

She stopped fussing with her hair and put her hand on her

belly, which had grown quite large. There was no denying her pregnancy these days.

"I want Maxwell to be born at Ravenscar," she said quietly. "He is Dyce's son and it is important to me that he be born in his father's home."

"Agreed," Ronan said. "But after he is born? What then?"

She turned towards him. "Have you notified my cousin yet of Dyce's death?"

Ronan shook his head. "I have not," he said. "I cannot hold out indefinitely on that, either. Sooner or later, your cousin will hear of it and I would like to inform him firsthand before he does."

"Then why haven't you done it?"

"Because I wanted to give you time," he said. "If what you say is correct, then your cousin will want to find another knight to man this property and you will be removed. I did not want to see that happen before you were ready."

She smiled at his thoughtfulness. The man, as always, was trying desperately to take care of her. "And I appreciate that very much," she said. "But the truth is that I shall be forced to leave at some point and when I am, I've been thinking about the foundling home. Since I must be useful, as I cannot simply sit around day after day with nothing to do, I was thinking... there are many children in need of love and care. What if I were to have my own foundling home with your patronage? I realize it is a lot to ask, but I could tend to less fortunate children and raise my son with other children around him, like a family. I could take care of all of them and teach them to read. Mayhap even teach them a trade or a skill. I would be productive and useful, not simply a kept de Wolfe woman."

He sobered greatly. "You make it sound as if I am caging

you."

She shook her head. "Nay, my love, you are not caging me," she said. "But the truth is that I shall be your mistress – the kept woman of a married man. I am not complaining – it is simply a statement of fact. But I fear that I've been a kept woman all my life, Roe. Dyce did that to me and I did not realize how wrong it was until I met you. You've made me realize that I am more than just a woman to be kept like a cherished pet. I want to be useful. I know I can do good if given the chance."

A smile flickered on his lips. "I think it is a very noble intention," he said. "You have a generous heart, my darling, and I know you would do an excellent job with less fortunate children. They would be lucky to have you."

Her face lit up when she realized he wasn't going to discourage her. "Do you think so?" she said. "I have wanted to talk to you about it but I have been afraid."

He scowled. "Of what?" he demanded softly. "As if I could deny you, silly wench. If this is what you wish, then I will speak to my uncle and his wife. They know much about foundling homes and they would be able to help us establish one if that is what you truly want."

Isabeth nodded eagerly. "It is," she insisted. "It truly is. Thank you, my love. I am overwhelmed with gratitude."

She rushed to him, throwing her arms around him as he embraced her tightly. "Anything for you," he whispered, kissing her cheek. "I will send the necessary missives on the morrow. We have time before Maxwell is born and, certainly, you will not want to do anything right after he is born, so there will be plenty of time to find the right location for this. Somewhere close to Roxburgh, although my aunt's foundling home is in Kelso. It is called Edenside. We can see it from the castle."

She cocked her head curiously. "So far from the earl's seat?"

"It was my aunt's foundling home before she married my uncle."

Isabeth understood. "I look forward to meeting her and learning all I can to be successful at it," she said. But almost immediately, she sobered. "But how do you intend to introduce me to her?"

Ronan cleared his throat softly. "You wanted to be discreet," he reminded her. "I was not planning on telling her that you are the woman that I love. I was only planning on telling her that you are the widow of my dear friend and I am sworn to help you."

Isabeth watched his face for a moment, sensing his reluctance. "And you feel that is being dishonest."

He nodded. "I do," he said truthfully. "They will figure out my attachment to you sooner or later. I would rather be truthful from the beginning. This is my family and I have no secrets from them."

Isabeth could see that perhaps he thought his honor might be at stake again if he wasn't entirely truthful with his family. She wrapped her soft hands around his big mitts.

"The truth is that I am a widow of your dear friend," she said. "You would not be dishonest to say that. I feel that the way may be easier for me if you introduce me that way and not as your lover. Mayhap with time we will be forthcoming about the extent of our relationship, but I feel that if you tell them who I am to you right away, they will always look down upon me. A mistress is not respectable. A widow is."

He knew she was right and he was just being stubborn, but it was difficult for him to admit that. He wanted to shout to the world that he was in love, but he knew that, ultimately, it would make things more difficult for her than for him.

He had to face that reality.

"As you wish," he said quietly. "I do not want to make you uncomfortable in your new life. But know I will be with you, every step of the journey, and proud for it."

She could see that he was a bit dejected about not being able to tell anyone about their relationship but she truly thought it was for the best. She went to him and put her arms around him.

"Sometimes God's will is not always perfect," she said. "I did not expect to lose Dyce and you did not expect your marriage to be as unsavory as it is, but we cannot change the situation. So we must make the best of it. As long as you are with me, I am happy knowing I am being productive in life and knowing you will always be with me. Truly, Roe, we must be grateful for what we have, not lament what we do not have."

He forced a smile and kissed her on the nose. "You are right, of course."

She grinned and patted him on the cheek, pulling away. "I know," she said. "Now, I must get down to the kitchens. I will see you later."

He followed her to the door. "Aye, you will," he said. "I will check the posts for the night and find Christian. We will see you in the hall."

They headed out of the chamber and down the steep stairs that led to the levels below. Ronan got in front of her, making sure to keep her steady so she would not slip down the steps. He was very careful with her until they reached the bottom and she blew him a kiss in thanks before she headed off towards the kitchens. Ronan watched her go before heading out into the courtyard beyond.

The mist had rolled in this night and he could see the torches on the walls, giving an eerie glow against the darkness. He could hear men shouting to each other and it seemed to him that there was quite a bit of commotion going on, though he had no idea what it was until he drew closer to the gatehouse and realized it was open. Men were entering on horseback and it looked to him as if a small army had arrived. The closer he drew, the more he could see that the men bore de Wolfe tunics.

That brought him to a halt.

"There you are," Christian said as he came up behind him. "I was about to hunt you down myself."

Ronan gestured to the gatehouse. "Who has arrived?"

He heard Christian sigh. "Your father, Roe," he muttered. "He is in the hall. And he does not look pleased."

Ronan didn't even have to ask what had his father upset.

Somehow, he already knew.

CHAPTER FOURTEEN

BLAYTH COULDN'T SEEM to stop hugging his son. Ronan was close to being strangled as the man clung to him, his big arms around Ronan's neck.

Maybe there was a threat in that, too.

Knowing his father as he did, he couldn't discount anything.

"It is a surprise to see you here, Papa," Ronan said, coughing when Blayth's arm smacked his Adam's apple. "Why did you not send word that you were coming?"

"You are looking well," Blayth said, avoiding the question. "I was sorry to hear about your friend. Titus told me what happened at Middlesbrough."

Ronan nodded, indicating for his father to sit. Blayth settled his big body down onto the seat and Odo immediately provided him with a drink. The majordomo was making sure everything was running smoothly for the unexpected guests.

"It was devastating, to be sure," Ronan said as he sat down next to his father. "Dyce and I have been friends for many years. He was a good man, Papa."

Blayth took a drink of the rich, red wine. "I remember this

man, I think," he said. "He came to Roxburgh once or twice."

Ronan nodded. "He came more than that," he said. "A big man with a black beard."

"I do remember him."

Ronan went to collect his own cup. "His death was vicious," he said, lowering his voice. "A de la Londe knight impaled him on a lance. A slow and terrible way to die."

Blayth frowned. "I heard," he said. "Titus said the de la Londe knight was beaten to death."

Ronan simply lifted his eyebrows in response. "The punishment fit the crime," he said. "In any case, Dyce lived long enough to ask me to take care of his wife after he was gone. So here I am."

Blayth took another drink of his wine. "Here you are, indeed," he said, toying with his cup once he set it down. "Tell me what your plans are, Ronan."

"What plans?"

"With Ravenscar and the widow of your friend," Blayth clarified. "Surely you have plans for the future. Or will you simply remain indefinitely?"

Ronan shrugged. "I will return to Roxburgh eventually," he said. "Ravenscar belongs to Lady de Brito's cousin, whom she does not share a good relationship with. She is certain he will ask her to leave now that Dyce is gone so I have offered to bring her north where she may find a position with Aunt Mae at her foundling home."

Aunt Mae was the Countess of Northumbria, his aunt by marriage, who was a very good and true lady. "When does Lady de Brito's cousin want her to leave?" Blayth asked.

"I do not know. He does not yet know of Dyce's death."

Blayth frowned. "Why not?"

"Because Lady de Brito is with child and she wants it born here," he said. "This was Dyce's home and she wants the child born at the home of his father. I'm afraid if we notify the cousin too early, he would want her out before the babe is born."

Blayth looked at him curiously for several long moments, enough so that Ronan wondered what his father was thinking. He lifted his eyebrows.

"What?" he asked. "Why do you look at me like that?"

Blayth sighed. "Lady de Brito's child," he said. "It is her husband's?"

Ronan nodded. "Aye," he said. "Why? That is a strange question."

Blayth shook his head. "It is not when you hear what I have to say," he said. "You want to know why I am here, Ronan? I shall tell you. It is because I had a visit from Edmund de Grey. He was informed by men within your ranks, former de Grey men, that you are carrying on an affair with Lady de Brito and that the child she carries is yours. Edmund is demanding that I punish you. Though I did not believe the child to be yours, I cannot be sure that you are not carrying on with a vulnerable widow. Tell me what is happening here, Ronan. Tell me the truth."

It was Ronan's turn to stare at his father in surprise before letting out a hissing sigh. He took a deep swallow of his wine before answering.

"I understand now," he said. "You are here based on gossip."

"Gossip or not, tell me the truth."

"You want the truth?" Ronan said. "I will always tell you the truth, Papa. I have never lied to you and I do not plan to start now. The truth is that I am in love with Lady de Brito but the child is not mine. It is Dyce's."

There it was. The verity of the situation that Blayth had come all the way from Roxburgh to hear. He nodded faintly, accepting what he'd been told, before finishing off the contents of his cup.

"I see," he said. "So you have remained at Ravenscar to be with her."

"Aye."

"It is not like you to have dalliances, Roe."

"This is not a dalliance, Papa," Ronan said seriously. "I love Isabeth and she loves me. She is fine and sweet and compassionate, everything a woman should be. She makes me feel loved and respected. She is a wonderful woman and I am not ashamed that I love her."

It was a rather passionate speech, one that had Blayth believing every word. Ronan was usually the silent type, so the eloquent statement had Blayth taking notice. It was also the least bit heartbreaking to realize what his son had gotten himself into.

"Then bringing her north was really so she could be near you," he said, watching Ronan nod. "Do you really intend to ask Mae if Lady de Brito can help her in her foundling home?"

"Aye," Ronan said. "Wait… that's not exactly true. Isabeth wants to have her own foundling home and I was going to ask Mae for assistance and advice. Isabeth is very good with children, Papa. She would do good work."

Blayth thought on that. "There is more to the situation if you bring her north," he said. "She comes north as your mistress, Ronan. That is not a respectable position for any woman. Is that the life you truly want for her?"

Ronan averted his gaze, unable to look his father in the eyes.

"You were fortunate, Papa," he said. "You were able to marry the woman you loved, both times that you were married. I will never have that chance. Therefore, I want her with me."

But Blayth shook his head. "It is not a good idea," he said. "Roe, I know you do not want to hear this, but Edmund and I had a very long discussion about the situation. He begged me not to permit you to divorce Marian and, after considering all of the implications of such a thing, I have agreed. Furthermore, he has agreed to speak to Marian about her… ways. He assures me that she will settle down and become a fine wife to you. How can you expect her to stop her parade of men when you will have a mistress nearby?"

Ronan didn't like what he was hearing, so much so that he rudely waved a hand at his father. "Marian will never stop her parade of men no matter what Edmund says," he said. "If Edmund has convinced you that he has the power to force Marian to behave, then he is mistaken. It cannot be done and most certainly not by him. More than that, I do not want her to be a fine wife to me. I do not even like the woman. I never have."

"She is your wife, Roe."

"She is the wife *you* picked, not me!"

His voice was growing louder and Blayth could see just how much the de Brito widow meant to him. Or at least, what he thought she meant to him. Asmara's words came floating back to him… *she needs a husband and it cannot be Ronan.* Having not met the de Brito widow he couldn't be sure that she wasn't emotionally coercing his soft-hearted son, but Ronan was definitely in love with her.

That was a problem.

"Whether or not I selected her is immaterial," he said calmly. "She is your wife and you are bound to her by God and the church. Your wife is a whore because she carries on with other men. What does that make you if you carry on with another woman?"

"This is different."

"Is it?" Blayth shot back softly. "Just because you say you love her does not make it acceptable. I've never known you to make a bad decision in your life, Roe, but I'm seeing it now. You don't understand that this affair is damaging."

"To whom?"

"To you," Blayth said firmly. "Most importantly, to Lady de Brito. She's no better than a whore herself if she allows herself to become your mistress."

That was it for Ronan. He was on his feet, standing several feet away from his father because he was genuinely concerned that he might lash out at the man. As it was, he glared at him from more than an arm's length away.

"I will never hear you call her that again," he growled. "I would have run any other man through who said what you just said. Isabeth is the finest woman in the world and far more worthy than you allow."

Blayth was watching his son's body language, wondering if he was going to have to dodge a flying dagger at some point.

"And you would allow the finest woman in the world to become your mistress?" he asked quietly. "*Think*, Ronan. Lady de Brito deserves a husband and a home of her own. She deserves that dignity. She does not deserve the life of being a mistress to a married man."

"It is far more than that."

"If you do this to her, you are ruining her life," Blayth said flatly. "Is that what you want? Better still, is that what your friend would have wanted for her? Being another man's courtesan? You vowed to take care of her but this is not taking care of her. This is making her your property, like a horse or a sword. Is she no better than that?"

Ronan wanted to argue with him but he couldn't. Unfortunately, his father was making perfect sense and he was feeling despair and desolation.

God, is he right? Is that what I am doing to her?

He began feeling sick in the pit of his stomach.

"I love her, Papa," he said hoarsely. "Were it not for you and your manipulation, I would not have married Marian. I would have had a chance to be happy but because of you, I am not. Isabeth offers me what you did not – joy. And now you want to take that away from me, too."

With that, he turned away and headed out of the hall. Blayth watched him go with tears stinging his eyes, feeling Ronan's pain but knowing that they both knew he was right.

It was a horrific realization.

With a heavy heart, Blayth sat down and collected the pitcher of wine, pouring himself a full measure. He could see from the corners of his eyes that some servants had entered the hall in preparation for the coming meal and when he glanced up, he saw a beautiful pregnant woman directing them. She was dressed in a garment far nicer than what a servant would wear and gave her commands softly but firmly. When she conversed with the majordomo and gave that man direction as well, Blayth took notice.

Lady de Brito, he thought. In his mind, it couldn't be anyone else.

He stood up and went to her.

"My lady?" he said evenly. "Lady de Brito?"

The woman looked at him with luminous green eyes and a smile on her lips. "I am," she said. "Are you part of the de Wolfe party that just arrived?"

Blayth nodded. "I am Blayth de Wolfe," he said. "Ronan is my son."

Her face lit up with delight. "It is an honor, my lord," she said. "I am very sorry that we are not prepared for your visit, but we shall have a warm bed ready for you in a few short minutes. Surely you wish to rest."

She had a sweet, delicate way of speaking and, in those few words, Blayth could see what had his son so enamored. The woman was all shades of lovely, fine-featured and fair. She had an aura about her that was difficult to describe, but it was a likable one. Already, it was a likable one.

He was deeply curious about her.

"Please do not rush overly," he said. "I came quite unannounced and I do not expect that you would be prepared, so I will gladly wait in the hall."

She smiled. "You are very kind, my lord," she said. "I promise it will not be much longer and we shall make you comfortable. Your chamber will be one with a view of the sea, though on a night like tonight, I do not expect that you can see very much."

Blayth nodded. "It is quite misty," he said. "Is it like this often?"

She shrugged. "Often enough," she said. "But when it is clear, the views are brilliant."

Blayth simply nodded, visually inspecting this woman who had Ronan's heart. He didn't blame the man a bit, but he wanted to speak with her more and come to know her better. Any woman who had his son's full attention, love even, deserved his notice.

He indicated the table he'd been sitting at.

"Will you sit with me a while, my lady?" he asked. "I heard what happened to your husband. May I offer my condolences?"

Isabeth's smile faded a little, but she graciously complied and moved with him towards the table. "Thank you," she said. "And may I say that Ronan has been the greatest help I could hope for? He has been, you know. My husband was so very fond of Ronan and when everything… happened, he asked Ronan to ensure that I, and Ravenscar, would be taken care of. He has upheld that promise."

They had reached the table and Blayth pulled out a chair for her. He waited until she sat down before claiming his own chair. "My son has a great sense of honor," he said. "I am glad he was able to help you when you needed it. I know that he was quite fond of your husband."

"The feeling was mutual," Isabeth said, her eyes glimmering. "Have you seen Ronan yet? I was sure he would be here in the hall with you."

Blayth nodded. "He was here but left to tend to something," he lied. "I am certain he will return but, meanwhile, I am glad to have the time with you. He speaks highly of you."

"And I of him," Isabeth said sincerely. "Ronan has made all things possible at Ravenscar. Were it not for him, I do not know what we would have done."

Blayth had to admit that he was swept up in her charm, but he also had to admit that he wanted to engage her in conversation for his own purposes. Asmara had mentioned that the woman might be using guilt to keep Ronan at Ravenscar but, so far, Blayth hadn't seen any hint of that.

"Who is Ravenscar's liege?" he asked.

"My cousin," she replied promptly. "Oston de Royans of Briarfield Castle. I am from the Netherghyll branch of the de Royans family."

Blayth recognized that. "I know the family," he said. "Heston de Royans is lord of Netherghyll, is he not?"

Isabeth nodded. "My father was his cousin," she said. "There are many of us, spread out all over North Yorkshire."

"Where were you born?"

"Briarfield."

"Is that where you met your husband?"

"Aye," she said. "Dyce served my father."

"I see," Blayth said. "I am sorry to say that I never knew your father, I don't think. What was his name?"

"Merton de Royans."

Blayth shook his head. "I did not know him," he said. "But I take it your cousin knows of your husband's passing and being generous to allow you to remain?"

He was trying to see if she would tell a different story from Ronan. Not that he thought his son would lie to him, but it was possible he had left out some details.

"My cousin does not know of his death yet," she said. "You see, he and his wife do not like me very much for reasons unknown to me, so Ronan thought it would be better to tell him after my son was born. I very much want the baby to be born here where his father lived."

"And after he is born?"

"Ronan has offered to help me find a position," she said without elaborating. "He is a great friend."

That was as far as she would go and Blayth knew if he asked her any further questions that she might become suspicious, so he changed his approach.

"He is well loved by all, to be sure," he said. "Tell me about Ravenscar. I've never been here before. I think I saw a small village to the north, through the mist."

Isabeth nodded. "There is," she said. "We are a fishing community, so there are many fishermen who work these shores. Truthfully, I never much liked fish before I came to Ravenscar. That has been a... challenge."

She giggled and Blayth grinned. "I sympathize," he said. "I cannot stand the smell or taste of it, either."

"Then you share my aversion."

"Very much so."

"I promise I will not serve you any during your stay at Ravenscar."

"That would be much appreciated, my lady."

A servant was evidently trying to get Isabeth's attention and she looked over, realizing she was needed.

"I am very sorry to leave you, my lord," she said. "I have duties that require my attention, but please sit and refresh yourself. Fresh bread should be out shortly."

Blayth waved her on. "Thank you for taking the time to speak with me," he said. "I enjoyed it very much."

She stood up, smiling at him. "As did I," she said. Then, she hesitated before continuing. "My lord... I want you to know how grateful I am for Ronan's assistance. You should be very proud of him. He is a rare man."

Blayth simply smiled, nodding his head to acknowledge the compliment. He watched her scurry back towards the servants' entrance, taking servants with her as she went. His smile faded, realizing very clearly why Ronan was so enamored with the woman. She was positively magnificent, which made his task more difficult. Ronan was in love with her and he didn't want to disappoint his son, but he also couldn't let it go on.

It would only end up hurting him in the end.

"Uncle Blayth?"

Shaken from his train of thought, Blayth turned to see Christian coming up behind him. Grinning, he stood up and hugged his nephew, the son of his twin, Katheryn.

"God's Blood," he muttered. "What are you doing here?"

Christian was quite fond of his Uncle Blayth, happily taking a seat beside him. "I was with Ronan in Middlesbrough," he said. "You saw me leave with him."

Blayth conceded the point. "But I did not hear that you hadn't returned to Berwick Castle where your mother and father are," he said. "So you remained here with Ronan?"

"Aye."

"But why?"

Christian's smile faded. "Because he needed me," he said simply. "He was very upset over Dyce's death so I came to help."

"But you are still here."

Christian's smile vanished completely. "Because he is still here," he said. "Uncle Blayth… I do not want to betray Ronan in any fashion, but much is happening here. Have you spoken to Ronan at all?"

Blayth nodded. "Enough for him to tell me that he is in love with Lady de Brito," he said quietly. "I only just spoke to her. She is a lovely woman. But I want you to tell me truthfully what is happening here, Christian. That is why I have come – rumors of Ronan and a pregnant widow have reached my ears."

"The child is not his," Christian said quickly. "Lady de Brito was newly with child when her husband was killed, so you can rest assured that the child is not his."

"But my son is carrying on an affair with her."

"A love affair," Christian said quietly. "He is happy, Uncle Blayth. I've never seen the man this happy in my life. She is very good to him and he is good to her. You know I cannot stand Marian and I have never made a secret of that, so I cannot condemn Ronan for being happy for the first time in his life. If you would only let him…"

He trailed off, unwilling to continue. "If I would only let him… *what*?" Blayth said.

Christian sighed heavily. "I meant that Marian has mistreated him so badly for all of these years," he said. "She does not deserve him. Ronan has enough cause for a divorce but he will not because you have insisted he must remain with her."

Blayth could see that Christian was hurting on behalf of Ronan and that touched him. Christian and Ronan had always been close. But it did not change facts.

"Christian," he said patiently. "I know you think that I am being cruel to my son, but the truth is that his marriage is vital to us. The House of de Grey is an important one and brings power with it. Edmund de Grey has heard the rumors of Ronan and Lady de Brito and he is understandably concerned. He begged me not to end our alliance and I have agreed, so no matter what you feel or what Ronan feels, it is important to the entire de Wolfe family that he remain married to Marian. Do you understand?"

Christian nodded unhappily. "I do."

"Then you will not tell him how terrible his wife is and how sorry you feel for him. I know you tell him those things and it does not help the situation, so you will kindly stop."

Christian made a face and looked away. "Then what are you going to do?" he asked. "Have you come to take him back to

Roxburgh?"

Blayth wasn't going to tell Christian his intentions before he told Ronan so he simply shrugged. "I have come to discuss many things with him," he said. "Go and fetch him for me. Tell him I wish to speak with him."

Begrudgingly, Christian left the table and wandered off to find his cousin. Blayth turned back to his wine and hot loaves of bread that were being put upon the table. His mind went from Ronan to Christian to Isabeth and finally to the knight he'd brought with him as a husband for Lady de Brito. The man was out settling the escort that had come all the way from Roxburgh and, certainly, Ronan wouldn't think anything strange of Randolph de Litton's presence. He was a Roxburgh knight and it was perfectly natural for him to accompany his commander.

What Ronan didn't know was that de Litton was prepared to marry the woman he loved.

Blayth, quite truthfully, wasn't sure how to tell him.

CHAPTER FIFTEEN

MARIAN AWOKE TO Gaspard making love to her from behind.

She was lying on her side, sleeping peacefully, when she began to have dreams of a man touching her in her most sensitive places. By the time she opened her eyes, Gaspard was taking his pleasure with her, his hands on her breasts and rounded belly. Marian was too tired to actively participate, so she simply let him have his way with her. It didn't even bother her that Millicent was in the other bed because she never woke up when things were going on around her. The woman could sleep through the Second Coming. The entire trip had been like this – Gaspard slipping into the room Marian shared with Millicent and then slipping out at dawn again and Millicent was never the wiser. When Gaspard was finally finished, he tried to hold Marian close but she pushed him away.

"Nay," she muttered. "You are too hot. This room is too hot."

Even though she'd pushed him aside, Gaspard was still running his hand down her torso. "The fire is banked," he said. "It is cold in the chamber. I was simply trying to warm you."

Marian rolled onto her back. The dawn was breaking outside her rented room, which was the same room she'd stayed in the night Ronan had exiled her from Ravenscar. They were very close and would be at Ravenscar this morning, something that would have normally made her quite eager but she couldn't seem to manage it. It had been a long journey from London and she was exhausted.

But she was determined to come.

Just a few more hours and she'd be at her destination.

As she lay there and gazed at the ceiling, Gaspard leaned over and began sucking on her nipples. Marian imagined how shocked Ronan would be when she showed up at Ravenscar, unannounced. She began to smile when she thought of berating the man and how that would crush his spirit. She greatly anticipated the look on his face that told her he was defeated and crumbled, that she had the upper hand on him and forever would.

She'd lived for that moment since receiving that missive in London informing her of her husband's activities. But more than that, she'd been contemplating what Gaspard had suggested those weeks ago, how he could do away with Ronan and they could live on the man's wealth as they traveled the known world. At first, she'd been resistant to the idea because Ronan represented safety when it came to her affairs – she could have all the flings she wanted to have but couldn't marry any of them so long as she was already married.

But with Gaspard, that opinion had slowly changed. More and more, she was coming around to his way of thinking. Perhaps a world with no Ronan would be best for her. It would guarantee her the status of a respected widow without the encumbrance of a husband.

Maybe that's what she wanted, after all.

"Gaspard," she muttered. "I have been thinking on your offer."

"What offer?" he asked, his mouth still on her nipple.

She put her hand on his head, pulling him up by the hair and forcing him to look at her. "Your offer to kill Ronan."

He looked surprised. "You are thinking about that *now*?"

He was a little miffed that he hadn't been able to arouse her, but Marian wasn't concerned with that. "We will be at Ravenscar today and we must have a plan," she said quietly. "Just *how* do you propose to kill him?"

Gaspard propped himself up on an elbow and looked at her. The change of subject didn't please him but, on the other hand, perhaps it did. This was what he'd wanted all along – Marian and her husband's money without the interference of the husband himself. Therefore, he struggled to focus on her question and not on his semi-aroused state.

"I do not know," he said honestly. "I will have to decide that when the time is right. When do you want me to do it?"

Marian scratched her head, pondering the question. "As I recall, there are cliffs all around Ravenscar," she said. "There is a drop down to the rocks and the sea. Mayhap you can catch him on the wall walk, unaware, and push him over the side. That would be the swift way to do it."

Gaspard appeared thoughtful. "I would have to be very clever," he said. "If he saw me coming, I would not have the advantage of surprise."

"Mayhap I will be on the wall walk to distract him and you can sneak up behind him."

Gaspard nodded. "That would work," he said. "Are you willing to do it?"

Marian nodded. "I was not in favor of it at first, as you know, but the more I think on it, the more I have come to the conclusion that it is the only thing to do," she said. "The man has shamed me with the de Brito widow and I will not stand for it. I am better off without him."

"And better off with me," Gaspard said, a smile on his lips.

For now, Marian almost said, but she held her tongue. She wasn't sure she wanted to marry Gaspard although she had no hesitation in traveling with him and doing whatever she pleased. Only she didn't want Ronan around any longer, reminding her that she was married, reminding her of that terrible choice she'd made when she'd seduced the man. She should have never done it but he'd been hung like a bull and that had intrigued her. Truth be told, it still did.

But now the de Brito widow was getting that part of the bull.

Speaking of bull…

Somehow, discussing a murder put her in the mood for love, so she wrapped her arms around Gaspard's neck as her mouth slanted over his. Gaspard responded immediately and strongly. Soon, Marian was on her back with her legs spread as Gaspard thrust into her. She tried to keep quiet because Millicent was still sleeping. Or, so she thought.

Little did she know that Millicent was wide awake and had been for quite some time.

And she'd heard every word.

CHAPTER SIXTEEN

"I SENT CHRISTIAN to find you last night," Blayth said. "You did not come."

It was early morning. Blayth had found Ronan on the battlements overlooking the sea as the fog lifted. Rays of sunlight were piercing the mist, illuminating the land below. Ronan was wrapped up against the cold in a heavy cloak, his nose pinched red as he turned to his father.

He sighed faintly when he realized who it was.

"I had the night watch," he said. "And I did not want to argue with you, so it was best to let me cool my temper."

Blayth knew that and he respected the fact that Ronan knew his limitations, but it didn't change the situation. "I did not mean to make you angry, lad," he said. "But this is not something you can run from."

"I know."

"We must discuss this now, I'm afraid. There is little time and much you should know."

Ronan grunted unhappily and turned away, looking out over the sea again. "Now? The sun is barely up."

"As I said, there is little time."

Ronan looked at him. "Why?" he said. "What is so pressing that I must know immediately, Papa?"

Blayth had been awake most of the night trying to figure out how to carefully couch what he had to tell his son. He'd come to the conclusion that honesty was the best policy and Ronan, being an obedient knight and a dutiful son, would have to accept it.

Whether or not it was easy.

Today would be the test of that faith.

"Ronan," he finally said. "If I told you my heart was not breaking for you, I would be lying. I want you to know I am not unsympathetic to your plight."

"That does not make me feel better."

"Nay, I would expect that it shouldn't," Blayth said. "But I have the unhappy duty of seeing you miserable with a decision I must make. I came here to discuss this situation with you and running from me will not stop what I must say. It will not stop anything. You are a knight and knights obey orders. I am here as your father as well as your liege. Do you understand this?"

"I do."

"Good," Blayth said. "Then I will continue. Although I admire your sense of honor in helping your friend's widow, the truth is that this is not a good situation for you. I fear your emotions for the lady have clouded your judgment. Would you say that is a fair statement?"

Ronan shrugged. "Possibly."

"Do you trust me to see the situation clearly?"

Ronan didn't hesitate. "I trust you with my life, Papa."

Blayth moved closer to him, forcing his son to look him in the eyes. "Then hear me now," he said. "The situation is this – you are a married man. I know you do not like to acknowledge that, but it is the truth. You are also a de Wolfe and a de Wolfe husband does not take a lover. Am I making myself clear? If this gets out, you will shame the entire family. Every unmarried de Wolfe male will be looked upon as a lesser marriage prospect because of your behavior. It will damage men's trust in our vows, from marriage to warfare. It will damage everything. You are jeopardizing the future of your brothers and cousins with this behavior. Do you understand this?"

Ronan stiffened as his father painted a picture of the broader implications of his love for Isabeth. "I am not jeopardizing anything."

"You are blind, Ronan," Blayth said, unable to back down. "If this was happening to Markus or Tor or Andreas, or any of your other married cousins, what would you tell them?"

"I would want them to be happy.

"By breaking their word of honor?" Blayth fired back softly. "Lad, you gave your word of honor when you spoke your marriage vows. For a man so concerned with honor, I am shocked that you do not realize you have broken your word. It does not matter if it is to Marian – you have broken your bond. As a knight, this diminishes you."

Ronan stared at him. It was clear that hadn't occurred to him. As much as he hated to admit it, his father was right – he was quite honor-bound in anything he did, so with his father breaking down his violation of his marriage vows, he was coming to see that he had, indeed, broken his bond regardless of who he had made the promise to.

That was a terrible thing to realize.

"Mayhap," he finally said. "But Marian broke hers many times over before I ever considered such a thing."

"It does not matter what she did," Blayth said. "What matters is what *you* did. You are a knight. A knight does not break his word, to anyone."

It was a harsh statement, but a true one. He didn't want to see this situation through his father's eyes but that's what was happening. Blayth was giving him another perspective he hadn't considered. He resisted it; God knows, he did. He was trying to come up with some logic that the marital bond didn't apply to him but he couldn't. He was using Marian's actions to justify his own.

His father's words began to sink in.

Closing his eyes, he looked away.

"I love her, Papa," he said, feeling a lump in his throat. "I did not mean to fall in love with her, but I did. I love her more than anything and, if it comes down to it, I love her more than my honor. I cannot lose her."

Blayth could see that he was breaking down. Ronan had always been the emotional type but never the unreasonable type. Blayth went to his son and put his arm around the man's shoulders in a show of support.

"I know what love is," he said softly. "I have been fortunate enough to experience it. Now, you have, too. But she was never yours to begin with, lad. If you love her as much as you say you do, then you must love her enough to let her go. You must love her enough to want what is best for her even if that means *you* are not best for her. Do you understand that?"

Tears filled Ronan's eyes. "I do," he said. "I may not agree with it, but I understand it."

"Do you understand that keeping the woman as your mistress is completely selfish?"

Ronan sighed heavily. "I suppose," he said. "But she loves me, too."

"And she has not expressed concern that being your mistress will ruin her?"

Ronan thought about it, realizing he couldn't lie to his father. "She has expressed it several times," he admitted. "She does not want our relationship to be public to the family. She feels as if she would be looked down upon."

Blayth gave his boy a squeeze. "And still, you would force her to be your mistress?" he said softly, incredulously. "Ronan, you cannot do this to her. If you love her as much as you have declared, then you must love her enough to want what is best for her. *Not* what is best for you."

Ronan knew that. His father was absolutely right. He closed his eyes and hung his head, tears streaming down his face. Blayth hugged him tightly, feeling his pain, knowing how difficult it was for him. He knew what it was to love a woman and, in truth, couldn't fathom his life without Asmara. But what Ronan was doing...

It simply wasn't right.

"I still want to help her, Papa," Ronan said hoarsely. "I cannot leave and consign her to her fate."

"I know," Blayth said softly. "I believe I have a solution, if you will let me."

Ronan wiped his face. "What solution."

"A new husband."

Ronan stiffened in surprise, standing tall to look at his father as Blayth was forced to release him.

"A new *husband*?" he blurted. "How could you –?"

Blayth cut him off. "The only way for Lady de Brito to survive in a respectable manner is for her to marry a man of good standing," he said. "That is what your friend would have wanted for her. That is what you want for her if you think hard enough about it. Don't be stubborn, Ronan – *listen* to me. If you truly want her to thrive, then you must accept the fact that she must marry again. It is the only way, lad."

Ronan was quickly becoming distraught. "But… but a *husband*?"

"What else is there?"

Ronan threw up his arms. "The church," he said. "She can become a beguine, a woman dedicated to the church who does charitable things."

"What about her son?" Blayth said. "You want your friend's son to be raised in a church?"

That brought Ronan pause. "Nay," he said after a moment. "The nuns would more than likely not allow it. But the boy can come to foster at Roxburgh. I can watch over him."

Blayth crossed his arms. "And you would rather have Lady de Brito commit herself to a church rather than enjoy a full life and possibly have more children?" he said. "Ronan, listen to yourself. That's incredibly selfish of you."

Ronan knew that but he couldn't stand the thought of another man having the woman he loved. He couldn't admit that, but Blayth knew. They both knew. As Ronan realized that fully, the bitterness began to come.

"So I must find her a husband," he said. "Is that what you are telling me? That I must find a husband for the woman I love?"

Blayth wasn't without sympathy. "It would be your greatest gift of love, Ronan," he said gently. "Don't you see that? You would be ensuring her happiness. Isn't that what you want? Her happiness, even if it is not with you?"

God, it was so difficult for Ronan to accept that. Harder than anything he'd had to accept in his life. Somehow, he was beginning to see clearly for the first time, clearly enough to realize that his father was trying to help him. Trying to help him *help* Isabeth. Ronan thought that loving her and taking care of her was enough, but for a woman like Isabeth… she deserved so much more. He had always known that, but not as much as he knew it at that very moment.

"Aye," he finally said. "I want her to be happy even if it is not with… me. She deserves the very best life can bring her, a husband who will love her and appreciate her. Someone with whom she can keep her self-respect."

Blayth felt as bad as he possibly could. "Even if that is not you."

"Even if that is not me."

Blayth didn't reply for a moment. He let it sink in. He wanted Ronan to understand everything, to digest it, to realize that the life he wanted was not the best life for him or Lady de Brito. It was something he would have to reconcile in his own mind. It wasn't something Blayth could force on him. He could see, however, that Ronan was starting to understand it.

His pale-faced son leaned against the wall of the battlements.

"What do I do now?" he asked dully. "Do I find her a husband? Where do I go?"

Blayth shook his head. "It would be asking you to engage in a monumental task," he said. "No one would expect you to do such a thing, so I have assumed the duty in your stead. I will be truthful with you, Roe – when I came to Ravenscar, it was with a husband in mind for Lady de Brito. I simply needed you to understand the logic of it. I have already made the arrangements."

Ronan's eyes lifted to his father. Then he frowned. "You've

already selected a husband for her?" he said suspiciously. "So all of this talk was simply to have me justify a decision you've already made?"

Blayth nodded. "Before you become enraged, I want you to listen carefully to me," he said. "Since Lady de Brito means so much to you, it would be better if she had a husband we both know and trust."

"*Who*, damnation?"

"Would you rather see her married off to someone you don't know? Would that be easier?"

That question doused Ronan's building rage. "Of course not," he said, cooling but still unsteady. "But who did you select?"

"Someone who would be very good to her, Ronan," Blayth said. "I hope you trust me enough to know I would only select the finest husband for her, someone who is kind and gentle. Isn't that who you would want?"

Ronan was struggling not to bark at his father. "*Who*?"

"Me."

The voice came from the mist. Ronan and Blayth turned towards the southern portion of the battlements only to see a big figure emerging from the mist.

Ronan's eyes widened.

"De Litton?" he gasped. "Randolph?"

Sir Randolph de Litton came into full view. A big man with angular features, dark hair and dark eyes, there was a faint resemblance between him and Dyce. They both had the dark, flashing eyes, dark beard, and big smile. Ronan had known Randolph for many years and there was no finer man in battle. De Wolfe knights were always the elite of the elite. Randolph was also a little quieter, perhaps a little less witty than some, but he was deeply loyal and had an excellent sense of judgment. As Ronan's shock wore off, he realized why his father had chosen Randolph.

Truly, he was an excellent candidate.

"I apologize for interrupting," Randolph said. "In the mist, voices carry. I could hear you down below so I thought I should present myself. Ronan, your father has told me what has happened. What I did not realize is how much you love her. While your father has asked me to marry Lady de Brito and provide her with a good life and I have agreed, I will not do it without your permission. Clearly, this is a lady you value greatly and I would not assume the role of her husband without your consent. I could not, in good conscience, do this."

That was typical of Randolph. He was obedient to a fault, perhaps even too obedient and considerate, but even as Ronan looked at the man, he knew that was exactly what Isabeth needed. Someone to be kind to her, to defer to her, to hold her in high esteem as her husband.

That was something Ronan could never give her.

Marriage.

He felt more defeated than he ever had because Randolph was a truly good candidate. Blayth had known what he was doing when he selected the man because he was someone that Ronan couldn't truly protest.

No matter how much he wanted to.

"You and I have been colleagues for many years, de Litton," Ronan finally said. "I have fought next to you and supped next to you and I consider you a friend. That being said, I know you are a man of character. You are a good man. I do not know how much you have heard, but I know you will keep it in the strictest confidence."

Randolph nodded. "Of course, my lord," he said. "You may trust me."

"I know," Ronan said. "I suspect my father told you that there was a woman who had me in her clutches, a woman who needed a husband in order to free me, but the truth is much different. Lady de Brito and I are very much in love."

Randolph nodded rather sadly. "I know, my lord. I heard."

"I am not in her clutches. Rather, she is in mine and I do not want to let her go."

"I understand, my lord."

"Have you met Lady de Brito yet?"

Randolph shook his head. "Not formally," he said. "I saw her in the hall last night, but we were not introduced."

Ronan stepped away from the wall, moving in Randolph's direction. He wanted to look the man in the eyes when he next spoke.

"This is not a simple thing for me, as you can well imagine," he said. "But I want to explain to you very clearly what is happening. I was asked, by Lady de Brito's dying husband, to look out for his wife. I have done that. What I did not anticipate was falling in love with her and she with me. We love each other very much, but as my father pointed out, her only hope of a respectable life is another marriage. A woman of her charm and grace does not deserve what I want her to be – my mistress. Do you understand me so far?"

Randolph nodded sharply. "I do, my lord."

Ronan's eyes were glittering. "I hope you do," he said. "Because I will tell you now that she deserves all of your respect and affection and if you show her anything less, if I hear you have mistreated her in any way, I will ride down here to Ravenscar and cut your heart out. Is this in any way unclear?"

Randolph didn't hesitate. "It is clear, my lord."

"Good," Ronan said, gazing at him intently. "Because I am surrendering my happiness to you. You had better treat that woman with all due respect."

"Until the day I die, my lord," Randolph said. "If it makes any difference, know how grateful I am. Truly and deeply grateful. I will do everything in my power to ensure she and the lad are safe and happy. But now it is my turn to make something abundantly clear."

"What is that?"

"If you try to carry on this affair after I have married her, I will not tolerate it," he said, his voice like cold steel. "Once she becomes my wife, she becomes mine, body and soul, and I will not abide any interference from you. If you do not feel that you can adhere to this and stay away from her, then I will not marry her at all."

Ronan knew that nothing he said was untrue or unreasonable. Could he stay away? He would have to. For the sake of his honor, he would have to.

"You will not have any trouble from me," he finally said in the final surrender. "I will stay away from Ravenscar forever. But don't ever bring her north, Randolph. I do not want to see her."

"I will not return to Roxburgh, I swear it."

The understanding was made. Lines were drawn and rules were established. Ronan had an astonishing sense of hollowness filling him at the moment, threatening to throw him off balance. He'd never felt so sick or desolate in his life. Lowering his gaze, he backed away.

"Then I must find Lady de Brito and tell her what her future holds," he said. "Randolph, go to the hall and wait for me. I shall bring her to you and you can come to know her. And, Papa?"

Blayth, who had been listening to everything with a broken heart, stepped forward. "I am here," he said.

Ronan turned to look over his shoulder. "When did you plan for this marriage to take place?"

Blayth sighed faintly. "I see no reason to wait," he said. "Today, if Lady de Brito is feeling well enough for it."

Ronan's shoulders slumped; they both saw it. "She will be," he said. "I will tell her that she must. And I... I must leave today."

Blayth put his hand on the man's arm. "You do not have to rush out of..."

"I do," Ronan snapped softly. "Papa, I am agreeing with you on this matter. I am letting you take control because I am unable to see beyond my emotions. But if you think I am going to stay here and witness the wedding mass, you are wrong. I am not staying. I will be leaving as soon as I can."

With that, he pushed past his father and headed to the tower where stairs led down to the courtyard. Blayth and Randolph watched him go, both with sadness. When Ronan finally disappeared into the mist, Blayth turned to Randolph.

"I apologize that you are in the middle of this situation, de Litton, but I believe you are the best man for this," he said. "My son is in turmoil. Please take that into account when witnessing less than pleasant actions or words. He does not mean anything personally."

Randolph lifted his eyebrows. "I cannot say my actions or words would be any less dramatic were I in the same situation," he said. "I have been, in fact. It is not a happy thing to lose the woman you love to another man. That is why I will be very respectful of Lady de Brito's feelings as well. It seems that we shall be married first and conduct a courtship afterwards. I hope you understand that it will be my goal that I should make her forget Ronan. If the marriage has any hope of succeeding, I must."

Blayth knew that. "Do what you will," he said. "I will not judge you for it, for I understand your point. But please… whatever you do, be kind to Ronan's memory. If Lady de Brito has difficulty forgetting him, do not be angry. Do not paint my son as a villain. He is a man in love and that is something he may never get over, I fear."

"He has my sympathies, my lord," Randolph said. "Truly, he does. But I have a new life and a new marriage to establish and you must let me do it in a manner which I feel is best."

Blayth didn't argue with him, mostly because he was right. With a heavy heart, he followed Ronan's path through the mist, thinking about the son he condemned to a loveless marriage and feeling that guilt to his bones.

CHAPTER SEVENTEEN

"**M**ARIAN?" MILLICENT SAID. "Do you have a plan once you reach Ravenscar?"

The mist was heavy as Lady de Wolfe's party plodded along towards the coastal manse of Ravenscar. The salt in the air was so heavy that it was coating everything with a damp, gritty crust. Marian and Millicent were riding at the front of the escort with Marian's brutish ladies several feet behind them and Gaspard several yards ahead, scouting for any threat in the mist.

He couldn't hear the conversation going on behind him.

"Of course I have a plan," Marian said. "I intend to find my errant husband and punish him. And then I intend to find Lady de Brito and punish her as well. She'll not get away with this and neither will he."

Millicent was asking for a purpose. Back in London, they'd touched on the subject of killing Ronan. Millicent had been positive she was serious at the time, or trying to cover up her ultimate goal, but having heard Marian and Gaspard's plans for Ronan yet again, she knew Marian to be quite serious about it now.

She wanted Ronan dead.

Millicent had known Marian all her life and she'd never been afraid of her until this moment. She knew her cousin to be shallow and immoral, but now the woman was intending to add murder to that collection of sins. That was something she'd never done before. Millicent was genuinely concerned that she might be included in those murder plans because she and Marian had discussed killing Ronan, once, so the truth was that she'd come north for a very good reason.

To save her own life by warning Ronan.

That was the one and only reason she'd come. If she hadn't, and Marian was successful in her scheme, it was quite possible that her own life would be in jeopardy for what she may or may not know. With Marian, it was difficult to anticipate which direction she would take, but she knew that above all Marian was a survivor. She'd been proving that all her life.

Therefore, Millicent proceeded carefully.

She had to get to Ronan before Marian did.

"I would recommend caution," she said after a moment. "Remember that you are acting on hearsay. Those who sent you the missive could very well be mistaken."

Marian looked at her cousin incredulously. "Do you take his side, then?"

Millicent shook her head. "I am not taking any sides, as I have assured you repeatedly during this entire journey," she said. "We have discussed this situation multiple times, have we not?"

"We have."

"I have only ever tried to advise you to be cautious," Millicent said. "You do not want to stir up a hornet's nest unless you have good reason."

Marian shot her a withering look. "I *have* good reason," she said. "He is betraying me!"

Millicent sighed faintly. Marian didn't have a reasonable bone in her body and all the admonition in the world wasn't going to force her to take a calmer approach to the situation. This entire trip north had proven that. Now, they were nearly at their destination, so Millicent knew it was time to shut her mouth lest Marian become suspicious of her true motives.

"I've come to support you, whatever you choose," she lied. "Would you like me to speak to Ronan first? He and I have always gotten on well enough. Mayhap I could send a repentant man to you."

Marian actually pondered the suggestion. "Nay," she finally said. "I will tell him myself. I want to see his face when I tell him what I know. I want to see him cower."

Millicent was fairly certain Ronan de Wolfe would never cower, but she didn't say anything to that regard. She remained neutral. "What would you have me do?" she asked.

Marian shook her head. "For now, do nothing," she said. Then she looked down at herself. "How do I look? Can you see my belly?"

Millicent looked at her cousin. Astride her palfrey, she was dressed in many different silk layers, bound up under the breast and all of them covering her bulging belly. She didn't want her husband to see that she was pregnant, knowing it was not his, since she had come to scold him for his infidelities. Somehow, a pregnant belly would make her position far less effective when she was trying very hard to gain the upper hand.

Millicent was quite aware of this.

"Nay," she lied again. "One cannot tell for certain but be cautious. Make sure the fabric flows loosely around your middle."

Marian pulled at it to ensure it was loosely draped, as Millicent suggested. The conversation died at that point because, truthfully, there was nothing more to say. They'd both made their positions clear from the beginning of the receipt of the missive in London to this very moment, so all there was to do now was confront Ronan and let the situation play out as it should.

That time would come, soon enough.

CB

THIS MIST HAD lifted by the time Marian and Millicent reached Ravenscar.

Marian was ready. She thought she would be charging into a peaceful courtyard only to stir it up with her particular brand of mayhem, but as she rode into the ward after yelling at the gatehouse sentries to admit her, an entire de Wolfe escort was laid out before her. Clearly, some de Wolfe uncle or relative had come to Ravenscar but as Marian looked more closely at the standards on the horses, she could see that the usual green and black de Wolfe standard was outlined with red.

That meant Roxburgh.

Her ladies were right behind her as she rode in, including Millicent, but truth be told, Marian was the slightest bit confused at Blayth de Wolfe being at Ravenscar. He was Roxburgh and the red-lined colors were only used when he was in transit or when Ronan was in transit, and since Ronan was already at Ravenscar, that could only mean one thing – Blayth had arrived.

That forced Marian to regroup a little. She was, if nothing else, a fast thinker. Dismounting her palfrey with the help of The Bull, she ordered her women into the hall to locate Ronan and announce her arrival but they were called off by Millicent. She volunteered to do it herself in spite of the fact that Marian told her not to, but she darted off before Marian could stop her, so Marian's women simply clustered at the front of the escort in a confused little bunch while Marian herself walked back through the troop to where Gaspard was positioned. He was to the rear now, trying to stay inconspicuous, but he dismounted when he saw Marian approach.

He met her halfway.

"My lady?" he asked, gesturing to the escort. "Who is here?"

"Roxburgh," Marian muttered, eyeing their surroundings to ensure she wasn't being overheard. "Millie has gone inside to summon Ronan. Blayth de Wolfe is here, somewhere. But I am glad he is here."

"Why?"

Her eyes glittered. "So I do not have to tell him of his son's death," she said frankly. "He will be here to know of it firsthand."

Gaspard was trying not to appear the slightest bit nervous with the fact that the legendary knight known as Blayth de Wolfe was at Ravenscar. "Roxburgh," he mumbled. "The man is a fearsome warrior. Our plans to be rid of your husband may not be so simple with him about. He could prevent it."

Marian knew that but she wasn't going to back out now. "He will not have the chance," she said quietly. "This evening when it grows dark and before sup, I will lure Ronan out to the battlements against the sea. Be on those battlements, do you understand? I will tell him I wish to speak with him privately so we will be away from any sentries."

"But what of his father?"

"He will not be on the battlements, you fool," she snapped.

"Stop being so cowardly. This was *your* idea!"

Gaspard held up a hand to quiet her. "Ease yourself, *ma douce*," he said softly, glancing around to make sure no one had heard her. "I will be waiting on the battlements tonight before sup. I will not fail."

She eyed him. "You'd better not," she said. "You will only have one chance, so do not ruin it."

With that, she turned her back on him, heading towards the great hall while the men of Ravenscar tried to figure out where to settle Lady de Wolfe's escort. The small courtyard of the manse was already full.

Logistics, however, didn't concern Marian. She was only concerned with finding her husband when she caught sight of Lady de Brito and her majordomo heading towards the hall also. When the majordomo suddenly rushed in another direction, that left Lady de Brito alone. The sight of a solitary woman fed Marian's bravery and she practically ran in the woman's direction. As she drew closer, she could see the woman's large belly and she shouted, catching Isabeth's startled attention.

"It is true!" she cried, pointing to Isabeth. "You are with child! My *husband's* child! How can you be so shameless flaunting yourself about for all to see?"

Caught off-guard, Isabeth could hardly believe what she was seeing. Marian was rushing towards her, shouting and pointing fingers, and Isabeth quickly moved away from the woman, fearful that she would attack her. She had no idea what Marian was doing here but, already, she could feel the anxiety and trepidation that she associated with Ronan's shrew of a wife. It was all quite shocking on this cold morning. But as she moved away and Marian ran forward, Isabeth noticed something else –

she could clearly see that Marian was pregnant, too.

Wildly confused, she continued to back away.

"You are spouting like a madwoman," she said. "What do you mean by saying such things to me? And what are you doing here? You were sent away and told not to return."

Marian was still advancing on her but she was no longer running. She was simply stalking her, pointing fingers. "Look at you," she hissed. "All the time you spoke of friendship, you were seducing my husband behind my back. And when I think of how you accused me of infidelity! You were bedding my very own husband!"

Isabeth was backing into the wall of the great hall and Marian came too close. She was crowding her, threateningly. Terrified she was about to be hurt, Isabeth lashed out and slapped Marian across the face as hard as she could. As Marian staggered, Isabeth slipped towards the hall entry.

"Leave me alone, you vile creature," she said. "Go away and leave me alone!"

Marian was still reeling with the slap but she managed to regain her balance and pursue Isabeth into the hall. Unfortunately for her, Isabeth had time to grab an iron fire poker and, for the second time in her relationship with Marian, was forced to defend herself. Wisely, Marian came to a halt when she saw the poker.

She remembered what had happened the last time.

"Do you deny it is my husband's child?" she said. "You accused me of being a whore, but *you* are the whore!"

Isabeth was more in control now that she had something to defend herself with. "Though it is none of your affair, I will tell you so that you cease your mad accusations," she said steadily. "This is my dead husband's child. It is not Ronan's. But I know the child in your belly is not his, either, so I would assume that, yet again, you carry another man's child?"

Marian's eyes widened. "You *dare* accuse me of such things?"

"I am not accusing you of anything," Isabeth said. "I am stating a fact. That child you carry is not your husband's."

Marian's indignance grew. "I will have you severely punished for saying such things."

Isabeth had had enough. She had no idea why Marian was here, or why she had even come, but she knew she wanted her out of Ravenscar. She jabbed the poker in Marian's direction.

"Get out," she hissed. "Get out before I bash your brains all over the floor. You come into my home, threaten and accuse me, and expect that I will not respond? You are quite wrong, Marian. Get out before I kill you."

Marian let out a shout of outrage. "Now you are threatening *me*!" she cried. "I have witnesses! You have threatened to kill me!"

"Marian! Isabeth!"

Ronan was suddenly in the doorway, followed by Millicent, his father, Randolph, Christian, Odo, and several servants. When Marian saw him, she shrieked and ran towards him.

"She is trying to kill me!" she said. "Save me!"

She came too close and Ronan put up a hand to keep her at arm's length but he ended up accidentally pushing her into Blayth, who caught her to keep her from stumbling. Marian began to wail as Ronan went to Isabeth.

"Are you well?" he asked, greatly concerned. "Did she hurt you?"

Isabeth shook her head, tossing aside the poker with trembling hands. "She did not," she said. "But she came running towards me in the courtyard, screaming that I was carrying your child. I believe she was going to hurt me."

Ronan shook his head in exasperation, holding up a hand to both calm her and beg her patience as he turned to Marian.

"What on earth are you doing here?" he asked, not at all happy to see her. "You were told never to return, Marian. Why have you come?"

Marian was indignant and distressed. "I came because you and that… that *woman* are carrying on behind my back," she said. "You sent me away and now I know why. Because you wanted to fornicate with your friend's widow!"

Ronan could see, in that brief statement, that Marian had been told what her father had been told. Spies within the de Wolfe ranks, spies loyal to de Grey, had told the same tale to both father and daughter. Realizing that, he sighed heavily with disgust.

"So you come all the way to Ravenscar to make accusations?" he said. "Marian, you have had dozens of lovers since we were married and I've never once accused you of anything. Therefore, your outrage is greatly misplaced. You have no right to accuse anyone of anything when it comes to infidelity. You have set a perfect example of it."

"She's pregnant, Roe," Isabeth said softly. "Is it your child?"

Shocked, Ronan looked at Marian as if the woman had completely lost her mind. "Is this true?" he said, incredulous. "Are you pregnant *again*?"

With the focus on Marian now, she began to cower. As she struggled to answer what was not a difficult question, soldiers were gathering at the entry to the great hall to see what the commotion was about and Gaspard picked that moment to wander into the crowd. He moved up towards the front, trying to stay inconspicuous, but Millicent, who was on the fringe of the group, caught sight of him.

And he was armed.

"Ronan," Millicent called out. "Watch out for de Maurienne. He plans to kill you. He is the father of the child in Marian's belly and they want you dead so they may take your fortune."

Surprised, Ronan whirled around to see Gaspard standing in the entryway. He was indeed armed, though the sword remained in its sheath. Blayth and Randolph and Christian were closer to Gaspard, but Blayth didn't have his sword. Randolph did because he never went anywhere unarmed and Christian, being young and ready for any fight, was armed as well.

When their attention suddenly turned to Gaspard, the man realized he was in trouble. Those quiet plans of murder were now in the open for all to hear and everything he feared was coming to pass. In a panic, he unsheathed his sword, catching Blayth in the arm and as Blayth quickly moved aside, Randolph and Christian unsheathed their weapons and everyone began to scatter.

Marian began to scream.

"Nay!" she cried. "Nay, do not hurt him! Gaspard, run! Run away!"

For a woman who had accused him of being a coward only minutes earlier, she had quickly changed her tune. But Gaspard didn't run. Startled, like everyone else was by Millicent's loud allegations, he surprisingly held his ground as Randolph and Christian circled him. It was a sudden standoff at the entry to the great hall as all of Ravenscar came to a halt with the drama unfolding before them.

The quiet morning was now verging on a knight fight.

Ronan seemed to be the only one not moving towards Gaspard with a weapon drawn. He gazed at the man with genuine puzzlement before looking to Marian, who was weeping with fear. Reaching out, he grabbed her by the arm and moved towards Gaspard, pulling his sobbing wife along behind him.

"Millie," he said, his focus on Gaspard. "Tell me what you know."

"Millie, if you say anything more, I shall never forgive you," Marian wept. "You are my cousin. You are loyal to *me!*"

Millicent gazed quite unemotionally at Marian before looking to Ronan. "I heard them speaking of their plans for you when they thought I was asleep," she said. "They had hoped to push you over the battlements into the sea and make it look like an accident. Ronan, I'm very sorry to tell you that Marian has been carrying on with this man since her arrival in London and, I'm sure, well before that. She is pregnant with what I am sure is his child, although with Marian, it is difficult to know. She has so many lovers. I've always been fond of you and although I've never approved of Marian's behavior, it was none of my affair. But when she started speaking of killing you, I could no longer remain silent. You must know of their plot."

Truth be told, Ronan wasn't surprised to hear any of it. Perhaps in the back of his mind, he'd always wondered when Marian would try to do away with him and steal his money because the woman's immorality knew no bounds, so this wasn't any great shock when he thought on it. But Marian began to shriek angrily.

"It is *not* true," she said. "Millie is lying. How can you do that to me, Millie? Why would you say such things?"

Ronan didn't believe her for a moment. He looked at his

father, who took the hint and moved closer to Marian, taking her away from Ronan. That left Ronan free to face Gaspard alone.

And face him he did.

The French knight was taut with anticipation and perhaps a little fear as he met Ronan's gaze steadily. He still had his sword leveled, with Randolph and Christian nearby, but his focus was on Ronan. In fact, it was strange for Ronan to finally be confronting one of his wife's many lovers. She'd had so many, men he'd never even met, that to actually confront one of them was something quite odd.

He took a couple of steps in the man's direction.

"You do realize she will grow tired of you, don't you?" he said. "Marian has never kept a lover for more than a year. She grows bored too easily. And the child she carries? It is her fourth. You are the fourth father. I knew the father of her eldest daughter, as he was the son of a de Wolfe ally, but I never met the father of her second child. I was told that he was a priest who was sent to France after the affair was discovered. The third child is the offspring of a stableboy and now, there is you. If you truly thought that Marian would let you spend any of my money after I was gone, you are sorely mistaken. She will discard you quickly and find someone else to entertain her."

Gaspard didn't lower the sword. "Mayhap that was true in the past," he said. "But Marian and I love one another."

"She has never loved anyone in her life but herself."

"You will not speak so coldly of her."

"Why not? I am her husband. I know her better than any-one."

"Not me," Gaspard insisted. "She is humorous and her generosity is grand. She would never leave me."

"You are a fool, de Maurienne."

Gaspard studied him for a moment before lifting his sword. "Would you care to test that accusation?" he said. "Fight me. If you die, I will marry Marian. If I die… well, I shall not die, so that is not a possibility. But first you will call off your de Wolfe dogs. Unless you are so weak that you need them."

A smile flickered across Ronan's lips. "Are you sure you want to do battle against me?"

"I challenge you for Marian. If you are not too cowardly."

That was the second time he'd insulted Ronan, trying to provoke a response, and he received one. Without a word, Ronan unsheathed the sword against his right thigh. He was still armed from having taken the night watch, not in full armor as he usually was when he went to battle, but he was protected enough. Certainly enough in a battle against a lone knight. Gaspard's challenge had him taking the offensive immediately.

After that, the fight was on.

CHAPTER EIGHTEEN

UNFORTUNATELY FOR GASPARD, the little boy William de Wolfe once called The Shield came to life.

All of the angst and turmoil Ronan had been feeling about giving up Isabeth found an outlet against a French knight who was quite good, but not good enough. He was no match for a de Wolfe of Ronan's size and training. That was something evident from the outset when Ronan charged him with his sword leveled and Gaspard was driven back into the courtyard, so fast and so brutally that he tripped on the uneven surface. Only terror and sheer agility had him on his feet again as Ronan brought down a blow that nearly knocked the sword from Gaspard's hands.

Somewhere, someone was screaming as Ronan went after Gaspard with a vengeance. Ronan could hear the sound, knowing it was Marian, but he didn't care. In fact, the sound fed him. It was music of unimaginable beauty to his ears as Gaspard continued to back away from him, now on the defensive as Ronan continued to strike and strike hard. Every time Gaspard tried to fight back, Ronan beat him down and then some. Swords were clashing and sparks were flying as Ronan let his emotions run away with him.

Perhaps every blow was for one man Marian had given her attention to. Perhaps every blow had Marian's name on it, for the shame she'd put Ronan and his family through. But then, the thrusts and blows began to come harder and faster – those were meant for Isabeth and those who were trying to take her away from him. They were meant for his father, for the pain Ronan felt for the decisions made on his behalf. Certainly, he'd never hurt his father, but that didn't mean he couldn't physically express his angst.

And he did.

Repeatedly.

Somehow, they ended up over in the stable yard. Ronan kicked Gaspard through a fence, collapsing part of it as goats bleated in fear. Gaspard got to his feet, beaten and winded and with bloodied arms where Ronan's sword had made contact, and desperately tried to fight back, to drive Ronan back so he could gain the upper hand. But the entire battle had been Ronan intent on beating him down and, in the end, killing him. Gaspard knew that.

He began to fight dirty.

In the stable yard, he grabbed a handful of dirt and dung, throwing it into Ronan's face in an attempt to blind him. The sea breeze blew most of it aside but some of it made contact, which only managed to make Ronan angrier. That had him slashing at Gaspard in measured thrusts, but in a surprising show of strategy, Gaspard had managed to back into the side of the corral and when Ronan lunged at him, his sword became embedded in the wood. Before he could pull it free, Gaspard used the opportunity to thrust his sword at Ronan's head. Ronan had to release his sword and duck the strike or risk getting his head cut off, so he relinquished the blade that was stuck in the wood, fell low under Gaspard's strike, and came up with an enormous fist to Gaspard's face.

The man, and the sword, went down.

Now, Ronan was on top of Gaspard, who had blood flowing from his nose. Reaching down, he yanked the man to his feet and began battering him.

Now, it was a fist fight.

Blood and other bodily fluids were flying through the air as Ronan and Gaspard went at it with hands and feet. Ronan had the size and strength advantage and easily tore Gaspard down in a short amount of time, but Gaspard was taller with longer arms. That meant he could get in a blow now and again, but it wasn't enough. Ronan backed Gaspard into the postern gate, which wasn't secured because of the time of day. It was always open in the morning to allow servants and those doing business with the kitchens to pass through, so Gaspard fell out of the gate onto a narrow strip of ground overlooking the sea.

Now, there were no walls to contain them.

The path to the sandy beach was directly in front of them while the steeper cliffs were to the right, overlooking the pounding ocean with the rocks below. Gaspard was dazed and exhausted, struggling to his feet as Ronan loomed over him. Ronan grabbed him by the arm and the hair and began dragging him towards the cliff.

"So you were going to throw me off the cliff, were you?" he snarled, winded. "That is a terrible way to die, de Maurienne. It is unfortunate that you selected that death for me because I am going to do the same for you."

Realizing where they were going, Gaspard began to fight. His exhausted body began to twist and kick and he managed to dislodge himself from Ronan's grip. When Ronan went to grab him again, Gaspard kicked him as hard as he could in the right thigh. Ronan staggered back, giving Gaspard the opportunity to lurch to his feet.

"I'll not let you kill me," he said, blood and spittle flying from his lips. "You may think I've made an easy target, but I assure you that you will be the one going over the cliff. Not I!"

Ronan went at the man. "And you think you will survive such a thing?" he said, now grappling with him close to the edge. "My father is here. He will ensure your death is as painful as possible if anything happens to me, so I would rethink that strategy."

The punches were no longer being thrown as Ronan and Gaspard wrestled and twisted their way right to the edge of the cliff. There was a one hundred-foot drop to the jagged rocks below. Ronan knew he was too close so he tried to switch his position, forcing Gaspard right up to the edge of the cliff. When Gaspard realized what Ronan had done, he made a swipe for the man, trying to grab his neck and force him over the side. But Ronan ducked low, throwing himself to the ground and kicking at Gaspard's knees in the same motion.

Losing his balance, Gaspard went over the edge but as he did, he grabbed for anything to keep him from falling, which happened to be Ronan's right foot. Ronan lost his balance and went down on his right side, heavily, but he quickly realized that he was being dragged over the side. There was nothing for him to grab hold of in order to stop his descent. He was beginning to think that this might truly be the end when he was suddenly grabbed from behind.

Blayth had his son, trying to keep him from falling as Christian and Randolph rushed forward to help. They'd all been watching, vowing not to interfere, until they realized Ronan was in serious danger. That was all it took for Blayth to break his stance and the knights along with him.

As Blayth and Randolph pulled, keeping Ronan from going over the side, Christian used his dagger to slash Gaspard in the hand that was holding Ronan's foot. Gaspard screamed and released his hold and as the four men watched, the French knight went spiraling down the cliffs, crashing into the rocks below. A massive wave arched up over the rocks at that moment, dragging his broken body out to sea.

As quickly as the fight had started, it was over.

Winded, and realizing it could have very easily been him on those rocks, Ronan collapsed against his father, breathing heavily and struggling to recover. Blayth and Randolph managed to pull him well away from the edge as Christian simply stood there, looking below and watching Gaspard's body being tossed around by the surf. But Blayth hadn't let go of his son, even with all of the tugging and moving they'd done with him.

He held him tightly, absolutely terrified at what he'd just witnessed.

"Are you well, Roe?" he asked, a hint of panic in his tone. "Did he hurt you?"

Ronan could hear the terror in his father's voice and he patted the old man's arms. "He did not, Papa," he said. "I am well, thanks to you and Randolph and Christian."

Hearing his name, Christian turned to him. "You know we wouldn't have interfered unless we thought you were in real danger," he said. "I hope you are not angry."

Ronan smiled wearily. "On the contrary," he said. "I am very grateful."

Christian grinned and held out a hand to him, offering to help pull him to his feet, but Ronan quickly realized he couldn't move. Blayth had such a tight grip on him that he couldn't move at all. Ronan patted his father's hands, clenched around his chest.

"Papa, release me," he said gently. "I'm well enough. You can release me now."

But Blayth didn't budge. He simply held on with a death grip. "I will in good time," he said. When Christian and Randolph peered closely at him, they could see that his eyes were clenched shut. "My father lost a son once, right before his very eyes. It affected him for the rest of his life, so he told me. I never completely understood my father's terror until this very moment. I almost lost you, Ronan. I do not know what I would do if that happened. It would be a nightmare without end."

Ronan felt rather sorry that his father was so traumatized, but he understood what he was saying. He also understood the context of Blayth's comment – Blayth, in fact, had been thought to have died in battle in Wales many years ago. Badly wounded in an ambush, William de Wolfe had been unable to retrieve what he thought was his son's body and it was something that haunted him for five years until James de Wolfe returned from the dead as Blayth. As it had turned out, James hadn't been killed – William got him back – but Ronan knew there would be no coming back from falling over a jagged cliff.

His father knew it, too.

"I'm well, Papa," he said, holding the man's hand. "I promise, I'm well. Let us retreat into the hall and recover from this."

Blayth reluctantly loosened his grip and Christian pulled Ronan to his feet. The man was battered and sore, with a huge bruise on his jaw. But he was alive. Randolph helped Blayth to his feet, seeing him as an old man for the first time in his life. Ronan's brush with death had greatly affected him. Ronan took his father's arm as they headed back for the postern gate.

A crowd was waiting for them, including several armed soldiers along with Odo, Isabeth, Millicent, and Marian, who was weeping dramatically. Ronan noticed that Odo had put himself between Isabeth and Marian, a touching protective move, but Millicent had a grip on Marian so she couldn't run away or attack anyone in her grief. As they approached the group, Christian muttered to his cousin.

"What are you going to do with her?" he asked. "She plotted to murder you. You cannot let that go unanswered."

Ronan's gaze was lingering on the woman who was an utter mess of weeping and hysteria. His gaze also drifted over to Isabeth, who was standing several feet away. He could see that she'd been crying, though she was trying to be very brave. His heart just about broke as he saw here there, wanting to run to her and take her in his arms but knowing he couldn't. He couldn't go back on all of those things he'd reconciled with his father because he would only have to go through it all again.

But God, it was killing him.

"I know," he said after a moment. "Papa, what say you?"

Blayth grunted. "Lock the wench in a chamber until my rage towards her has cooled," he said. "After that, I am not certain. I will discuss it with her father. Mayhap we shall send her back to her father for good. Let him deal with the animal he has raised."

Perhaps that was the best that could be done at the moment. Ronan was too tired to argue but his heartbreak was starting to overwhelm his senses. He was coming closer to the women, seeing the one he wanted and the one he was saddled with. It all seemed too ridiculously unfair to him, but it only reinforced what he already knew – if he remained at Ravenscar, he wouldn't be able to stay away from Isabeth. His heart cried out for her, his soul longed for her, and there was nothing more powerful on earth than what he felt for her.

But he couldn't take her in his arms.

That was the worst defeat of all.

"Murderer!" Marian screamed at him. "You killed Gaspard, you murderer! God will punish you, Ronan de Wolfe. He will make you pay with your blood and sweat and immortal spirit!"

Ronan looked at her. "He already has," he said. "I am married to you, aren't I?"

Marian's face twisted in outrage. "You contemptable bastard!"

Ronan chuckled, though it was without humor. "Marian, there is no need to send me to hell because I live it every day with you," he said. "God forgive you for what you've done to me, because I can't."

Marian shrieked angrily, managing to yank her arm from Millicent's grip. "It is not forgiveness I seek but vengeance," she snarled. "Vengeance against you is all I shall live for all the days of my life. With every breath I take, I hate you more. With every second that passes, I wish you a thousand painful deaths and the deaths of those you love. I curse you, Ronan. I shall curse you until I die!"

Ronan simply didn't have the strength to argue with her. Truthfully, he didn't care what she thought or said or did any longer. For all intents and purposes, she was dead to him.

Gone.

But there was someone who wasn't.

His gaze fell on Isabeth, standing next to the open gate.

Their eyes met and, for a moment, he was back with her, loving her and cherishing her. The pain and exhaustion he felt was instantly gone, replaced by a powerful sense of peace. The mere sight of her did that to him. But then he caught sight of his father and it all came crashing down again.

The anguish.

The grief.

Lowering his gaze, he moved through the open gate, but not before Isabeth reached out and touched his arm. It was a simple touch and an innocent one, perhaps one of comfort, but that small touch meant the world to him. It was the last touch he'd ever have from her and tears came to his eyes as he moved through the postern gate without a word to Isabeth.

His *Esa.*

But he did glance back at her, one more time, which was a mistake. It wasn't missed by Marian, in the midst of her throes of grief, and she saw in that moment how to hurt Ronan as he had hurt her. She was free of Millicent even though the woman was standing behind her, but she was free enough to grab a dagger from one of the soldiers who happened to be standing within arm's length. Before Millicent could stop her, she lifted the blade and charged straight at Isabeth.

"My lady!" Millicent shouted.

It was such a panicked cry that everyone looked in Millicent's direction only to see Marian about three feet from Isabeth with a wicked-looking blade in her hand. Odo was between them but Marian slashed at him, stabling him in the shoulder. He fell to his knees even as he grabbed for her legs, but Marian was too fast.

That's when Isabeth saw her.

She caught the flash of a dagger in Marian's grip and immediately fell back, tripping over the hem of her garment and ending up on the ground. It was a vulnerable position but Marian was running too fast and too recklessly to take advantage of it. She had been aiming for Isabeth but when the woman fell to the ground, there wasn't time to change course. Marian ran straight into the gate itself, bending her right arm towards her, the same arm that was holding the dagger. The blade, sharp and long, pushed straight into Marian's chest and Marian collapsed on the ground with the hilt of the dagger sticking out of her breastbone.

By this time, Ronan and his father and the knights had pushed back through the postern gate to break up the attack. Without hesitation, Ronan picked Isabeth off the ground, scooping her up and moving her away from the threat of Marian's madness. He paused just long enough to turn to see what was happening, noting that Randolph was tending Odo as his father and Christian bent over Marian, who was lying quite still.

"Papa?" Ronan said, his voice trembling.

Blayth's gaze lingered on Marian for a moment before looking up at his son. "She's dead," he said simply.

Shocked, Ronan gently set Isabeth to her feet, making sure she wasn't injured before going to stand over his wife's body.

He simply couldn't believe it.

"Are you certain?" he said, kneeling down and feeling for a pulse. "She's gone?"

Blayth was on his feet now, standing over Marian with an unsympathetic gaze. "She is," he said. "I'm not sure how I am going to explain this to Edmund, but Marian's evil finally caught up with her. In trying to kill Lady de Brito, she ended up killing herself. I should not like to think that God had a hand in this, but it seems to me that this was divine justice."

Ronan was so stunned that he ended up sitting on his buttocks next to Marian's body. His head was whirling with the surprise, the suddenness, and the completeness of what had just happened. Marian had been shouting curses and then she was on the ground with a dagger in her chest.

God… did this really happen?

He was still trying to grasp it.

"Millie," he finally said. "Take Lady de Brito inside. Get her out of here, please."

Millicent didn't know Lady de Brito personally, but she didn't have to. All she could see was a lovely, delicate woman with a big belly, someone that Ronan was clearly quite fond of. That was enough for her. She went to Isabeth and helped the woman through the gate even though she was reluctant to go. In fact, she called out.

"Ronan?" she said anxiously.

Ronan looked up from Marian, his gaze meeting with Isabeth's frightened one. Millicent had her arm around Isabeth's shoulders and he suspected that was the problem – the woman who had arrived with Marian was now trying to take charge of her and Isabeth was understandably wary.

But Ronan wasn't.

"'Tis okay," he assured her. "You are safe. That is Millie and she will take you inside."

That put Isabeth at ease, but only a little. "But I want to remain with you."

Ronan shook his head. "You must rest," he said. "Please. Go now and take Odo with you. He can use your help. I will come to you later."

With Millicent's coaxing and a bleeding Odo walking under

his own power, Isabeth finally headed towards the manse. Christian cleared out the soldiers, but not before ordering them to corral Lady de Wolfe's escort until they could decide what was to be done. That also meant her brutal ladies, who were still with the escort. All of them grouped and guarded until some decisions could be made.

As the soldiers faded away, Ronan was still looking at Marian's body.

He was still trying to grasp what had happened.

"Why?" he finally asked. "Why would she try something like that when she knew it could not end well? Why be so foolish?"

Blayth shook his head. "Who is to say?" he said. "She has never been the most rational creature, Roe."

Ronan's gaze trailed down her body, at the pregnancy. It wasn't very large, but it was obvious. "The child," he said. "Should we try and save the child? There may be a chance."

Blayth was looking at it, too. "The child would be too small to survive, lad," he said quietly. "While I share your noble sentiment, to remove it from the mother right now would be to see it die a lingering death with no way to help it. This way… it is probably already dead. It is a sad thing to see an innocent life ended, but there is nothing we can do."

Ronan knew that but the compassionate man in him, even with a child from his wife that was not of his loins, had to ask the question. "You are more than likely right," he said. "But if she had been any further along, I would have taken the chance."

Blayth looked at him. "Something Marian never gave you," he said. "She never even gave you a chance, in any aspect. But you mustn't blame yourself."

Ronan took one last look and stood up. "I do not," he said.

"I never have. But this… this is beyond what I thought she was capable of. I suppose I should not be surprised and, in a sense, I am not. But I am bewildered."

"Revenge," Christian finally said. "She was trying to take revenge. You killed her lover and she was going to kill yours."

Given the sequence of events, they couldn't argue the point and Ronan nodded. "It is as good an explanation as any," he said. "She was most definitely the vengeful kind. I've seen it before. But now we must contend with Edmund de Grey, who will think I was responsible for this somehow. Mayhap in her last action on this earth, Marian has sealed my fate. I will forever have an enemy in Edmund de Grey."

Blayth shook his head. "He will not blame you," he said. "He only has himself to blame in the way he raised his daughter, so I will make sure he understands what happened. He will know that she was plotting to kill you and Millicent can attest to it. All of this is her doing, Ronan. Marian's wickedness has finally come full circle."

Ronan wasn't so sure, but he wasn't going to linger on it. Marian was dead and that was all that mattered. By her hand or any other, the result was still the same but his conscience was completely free.

He was free.

The thought suddenly occurred to him and his head shot up, his gaze finding Randolph. *Marriage.* He was free to marry Isabeth now, in a wild stroke of fate, something he never thought he'd see in his lifetime. Perhaps it was distasteful for him to think of that at this moment, but he was thinking of it nonetheless.

A chance to be happy.

He never thought he'd have the opportunity. It was a new

life, all laid out before him, and he struggled not to become too excited about it. With a dead woman laying at his feet, that would have been terribly disrespectful, but the truth was that it was Marian laying at his feet. The woman who had caused him ten years of misery, the woman he thought he'd be anchored to for the rest of his life, never to know peace or love or joy.

But all of that had changed in the blink of an eye.

He simply couldn't keep silent.

"Papa," he said slowly. "What we were speaking of earlier… about Lady de Brito… it is no longer necessary, is it?"

Blayth had been looking at Marian but when he heard the hopeful tone in Ronan's voice, he flicked his eyes up, looking at his son. The son he'd nearly lost. The son he adored more than anything. He had other sons, younger sons, and he loved them all desperately. But Ronan… he was his firstborn, his shining star, the man he expected such great things from. A man who had endured unspeakable shame and misery at the hands of an adulterous wife, something that Blayth himself had a hand in. Aye, there was guilt in his heart. There always had been.

Now, he knew what Ronan wanted. He knew *exactly* what he wanted.

Blayth couldn't, in good conscience, deny him.

But it wasn't up to him.

"You must ask Randolph," he said quietly, looking to the big, dark knight. "By all rights, the decision belongs to him. Randolph? Do you understand what Ronan is asking?"

Randolph had been standing to the side, taking a horse blanket from one of the soldiers who had brought it to cover Marian up. He shook it out, watching the dust fly, before laying it over Marian's body.

"I do," he said simply.

"And?" Blayth said. "You are within your rights to deny him. No one would blame you."

Randolph brushed off his dusty hands. "Does the lady know why I am here?"

"She does not."

"Then do not tell her," Randolph said, looking at Ronan. "Do you truly think I could marry the woman you love, Ronan? I may long for a wife, but I could not marry a woman you were in love with, a woman who was in love with you. That would not be right and I would spend my entire life dealing with the guilt of it. When I marry, I want it to be to a woman who will be at least fond of me and not pining after a de Wolfe stallion."

Ronan was so overwhelmed by Randolph's response that he was starting to feel weak. It was too good to hope for.

"Are you certain?" he said. "It is a terrible thing we have done to you – asked you to take a bride and now asking you not to take her. I hope you know that my father asked you in the first place because he respected you, not because he was trying to manipulate you."

"I know," Randolph said. "But this is not the right bride. She is yours, Ronan."

Ronan smiled, tears stinging his eyes. "My God," he muttered. "Are you sincere? Truly sincere?"

"I have never been more sincere," Randolph said. "Be happy, my friend."

Ronan put a hand to his heart, a show of gratitude, of joy. "I intend to be," he whispered tightly. "I truly intend to be."

With that, he took off in the direction of the manse, as fast as his beaten body would take him. Randolph, Blayth, and Christian watched him go, with Christian turning to grin at his uncle before departing in the direction of the stables in order to give Blayth and Randolph a moment alone.

Intuitively, he knew they needed it.

"That was a very noble thing you did," Blayth said. "You have my undying gratitude."

Randolph shrugged. "There was nothing else I could do, my lord," he said. "I am not willing to fight the ghost of Ronan for the rest of my life if I marry a woman who loves him. That would put me in a worse position than he was in with Lady de Wolfe."

Blayth nodded faintly. "That is astute of you," he said. "But you have my gratitude, nonetheless. You have made him very happy. I would like to reward you for that."

"No reward necessary, my lord."

"There is nothing you want?"

Randolph almost denied him but a thought occurred to him. He cocked his head thoughtfully. "There may be something, if you are willing, my lord."

"All you need do is ask."

Randolph cocked an eyebrow. "Your brother, Patrick, has a daughter named Thora," he said. "She is a beautiful and vivacious woman and, as far as I know, unspoken for. Would you be willing to propose me as a suitor?"

Blayth's eyes widened. "You want to marry Atty's daughter?" he said, referring to Patrick de Wolfe, Earl of Berwick, by his family nickname. "Good lord, man, have you lost your mind?"

Randolph shook his head. "Not at all," he said. "She is lovely and eligible. She is a de Wolfe bride. If you truly think to reward me for my noble action, a de Wolfe daughter would be suitable."

Blayth's eyes were still wide at the mere thought. "Randolph," he said steadily. "Thora is the most sought-after bride in all of Northumberland, but do you know why she has not yet been spoken for? Because her father is as tall as a tree and so are her four older brothers, who are fearsome warriors that strike fear into the hearts of all men. And you want to court her with those five beasts breathing down your neck?"

Randolph grinned. "It would be an honor."

"It would be your death!"

"Mayhap you think I am unworthy and do not have the courage to tell me?"

Blayth quickly shook his head. "Nay, lad, you are quite worthy," he said. Then he pushed his shock aside and shrugged. "Very well. If you think you can go up against Atty and his male offspring, that is your affair. Do not say I didn't warn you."

"I won't."

"I can only put in a good word for you and nothing more."

"I understand."

Blayth wasn't sure he did, but he let the subject drop. The mere thought of taking de Litton to his brother as a potential husband for his eldest daughter was giving him hives. Patrick was a mountain of a man, the best warrior in the de Wolfe arsenal, and he was terribly protective of his daughters. Blayth was fairly certain that de Litton didn't have a chance, but that would be up to Patrick.

A battle for another day.

Meanwhile, they had some clean-up of their own to do.

"Please find a place to put Marian until we can have a casket built for her," he said. "Surely Ravenscar has a vault we can put her in for now. As for de Maurienne – his body will undoubtedly wash ashore and we should dispose of it. You will want to notify the priests in town of this so when the body comes ashore, they know what to do."

Randolph nodded. "It will be done, my lord."

With orders set and the drama of the morning passed, men around them were returning to their duties and that included Blayth and Randolph. Blayth left Randolph tightly wrapping Marian in the old horse blanket as he headed to the manse, to his borrowed chamber where his writing kit awaited. He had some missives to send about Marian's death, to his brother, Scott, as well as to Edmund de Grey, but most of all, he had a missive to send to Asmara about the turn of events and a wedding on the horizon.

Finally, Ronan will be happy.

That's really all he had to tell her.

Sometimes, the most unexpected days brought about the greatest changes.

EPILOGUE

Roxburgh Castle
Six months later

"Good heavens," Isabeth said with some chagrin. "Are they *always* like this?"

"Like what?" Ronan asked.

"Like.. *loud*," Isabeth said. "Are they always this loud?"

Ronan grinned as he listened to his father, his uncles, and several cousins indulge in a few stanzas of what was known in the de Wolfe family as the *Naughty Wedding Song*. It wasn't even a wedding song, but something that was first sung at his Uncle Edward's wedding years ago by none other than Blayth himself and, for some reason, it had been sung at every single wedding since. But it wasn't just the male de Wolfe contingent singing it – he could clearly see Millicent in the middle of it, belting it out and drinking wine as if she'd been born to it.

He was very glad he'd invited her.

"There once was a lady fair,
With silver bells in her hair.

I knew her to have,

A luscious kiss… it drove me mad!

But she denied me… and I was so terribly sad.

Lily, my girl,

Your flower, I will unfurl

With my cock and a bit of good luck!

Your kiss divine,

I'll make you mine,

And keep you a-bed for a fuck!"

Gales of raucous laughter arose from the crowd in the vast and imposing great hall of Roxburgh Castle. More laughter and cheers arose when Millicent drained a cup of wine before several de Wolfe men did. It was a wedding of great proportions, the union of Blayth de Wolfe's son, Ronan, and the widow formerly known as Lady de Brito.

Now, she was Lady de Wolfe.

"You have no idea what a tradition this is," Ronan said. "It's more than just the song."

"Why?" Isabeth asked.

Ronan leaned over, his arm around her shoulders, his lips near her ear. "Because when my father first sang it many years ago, my grandmother became furious," she said. "She would chase my father all around the hall and threaten to beat him. My Aunt Jemma became furious also. You remember Jemma? My Uncle Kieran's wife?"

Isabeth nodded. "You have told me of her," she said. "But it has been quite a task remembering your family lineage. There are so many of you."

Ronan laughed softly. "There are, indeed," he said. Then,

something caught his eye at the end of the able and he sat back, smiling. "Ah. We are to be honored."

Three little girls were heading in his direction. The eldest one was around nine years of age, with bright red hair and brown eyes, while the middle lass was seven years of age with black hair and blue eyes. The third child, a little girl of four years, had curly dark hair and very dark eyes.

Anne, Esther, and Priscilla de Wolfe had come to bid their father and new stepmother a good night.

Ronan drew the girls into his embrace.

"It is late," he told them. "You should already be in bed. Where is Aunt Mae?"

Esther, the most vocal of the three, pointed to the edge of the hall where Mae de Wolfe, Countess of Northumbria, was waiting. Whenever children were involved, Mae was always the first to volunteer to watch over them or assist. But another woman was standing with her, tall and strawberry-blonde, cradling an infant. The moment Isabeth saw the woman and the child, she was on her feet.

"I must bid Maxwell a good eve," she said.

Because she was up, Ronan was up. Anne had one of his hands while Priscilla had the other. Esther grasped Isabeth, pulling her along until they reached the edge of the hall.

"I told them to bid you a good night, not to bring you away from your celebration," Mae said. "I am sorry they took you away."

Isabeth smiled at the woman she was coming to like a great deal. In fact, she liked all of Ronan's aunts and mother and stepmother a great deal. Each de Wolfe wife had great virtues and kindness of their own and she was very much coming to appreciate them.

"And how is our strong lad tonight?" Isabeth said, leaning over the baby that the strawberry-blonde was holding. "Has he been a good boy?"

Cassiopeia de Wolfe, wife of Edward de Wolfe, aunt and uncle to Ronan, smiled as she looked at the black-haired infant. "He is a very good baby," she said. "I wish mine had been so peaceful and content."

Isabeth couldn't help but scoop the child out of Cassiopeia's arms. He stirred a little but she crooned to him softly, rocking him. She could feel Ronan leaning over her, his big hand on the baby's head.

"He will lead the next generation of strong de Wolfe knights," he said firmly. "Of course he is a good lad. With you as his mother, he could be nothing else."

He kissed her on the cheek and Isabeth smiled at him gratefully as Priscilla tugged on him. "Papa," she said. "I want to see Maxie."

Ronan grunted as he lifted her up so she could see the baby. "His name is Maxwell," he said flatly. "Max if one is so inclined, but not Maxie."

Priscilla was a truly adorable child and she was dearly loved. All of Marian's girls were, in fact, even if Ronan wasn't their father. He had never treated them any differently, nor had anyone else. They were part of the House of de Wolfe, loved for who they were and not shunned because of who their mother was. Ronan had set that example long ago in yet another show of his good character. As he held Priscilla, she leaned over to kiss the baby but then squirmed until Ronan was forced to set her down.

"Come!" she told her sisters. "Let's play!"

They ran off squealing as Mae headed out after them, calling for them to stop running. Cassiopeia remained behind so she could take the baby, but Isabeth didn't seem inclined to give up her son.

At least, not yet.

"I cannot thank you enough for minding him," she said to Cassiopeia. "You have so many children and grandchildren of your own, so I hope one more was not a burden."

Cassiopeia smiled at her. "Not at all," she said. "If I thought I could get away with it, I would steal him from you, although your maid, Gerta, is quite possessive of him."

"Has she been a help to you?"

"A great help," Cassiopeia said. "All of the children seem to like her and she has been a tremendous help minding them. But little Maxwell has her full attention. He is a wonderful baby."

Isabeth smiled gratefully. "Thank you," she said. "I have waited a long time for him. I am enjoying him very much."

Cassiopeia smiled in return but something over Isabeth's head caught her attention. She elbowed Ronan.

"Look," she said. "Here they come. They're going to make demands for your wedding night so if I were you, I would quickly leave."

Ronan looked over to see his uncles and cousins heading in his direction. It was quite a group of knights, without Millicent this time, who seemed more content to sing with some of the other guests. Cousins close to his age, including Titus, Edward, and Christian were grinning at him and Ronan knew they were in for it.

"Take the baby, Aunt Cassie," he said, urging Isabeth to give her the child. When the baby was safely transferred, he took Isabeth by the hand. "Come with me. Quickly."

Isabeth had no idea what was wrong but she did as she was

told. Roxburgh was an enormous castle with towers and rooms and she still wasn't exactly clear where all of them were, or even where she was half the time, so she simply followed her husband up the stairs and through some dark passages. They finally made their way to their wedding chamber in a room that overlooked the town of Kelso in the distance. The views were quite astonishing but once they reached the room, they were greeted by familiar faces inside.

Blayth and Rose, Ronan's mother by birth, were waiting for them.

"Christ," Ronan said as he entered the door and staggered. "You startled me. I thought you were that horde behind us, having beaten us to the chamber."

Blayth grinned. "Nay," he said. "But they will be here shortly. Shut the door and bolt it."

Ronan did as he was told. Isabeth gravitated towards Rose because she was a little nervous about the situation, while Blayth and Ronan seemed on alert, and Rose smiled as she took Isabeth's hand.

"Not to worry," she said. "We will protect you."

"Protect me from what?" Isabeth asked, concerned.

Rose laughed softly. She was a lovely woman, petite, with dark hair and pale skin. She and Blayth had known each other all their lives and back when Blayth had been known as James, they had fallen in love. They had married but when James had been declared dead, Rose had grieved and eventually married another man. But the friendship, the long-standing affection, for James – now Blayth – was still there, as the pair got along splendidly.

This moment, when their eldest son married for love, was particularly poignant to them both.

"The de Wolfe men tend to be quite boisterous when one of their own is married," Rose said. "They will not tangle with me, so I am here to protect you. But I'm also here because I want to give you something."

Ronan heard her, turning away from the door with interest. "What is it, Mama?"

Rose smiled at her eldest child. "I will try to be brief, but do bear with me," she said. "This goes back to the day your father and I were married. It was a snowy winter's day and our families had been having the best of times. We were playing games, throwing snowballs at each other, and I remember that your Aunt Penelope and I were being particularly brutal with each other. But Penny was always the brutal sort, so that is no surprise."

Blayth grinned. "I do not remember that day," he said, looking at Isabeth when he spoke and gesturing to the big scar on the left side of his head. "I know that Ronan has explained my injury in Wales and, as you can see, it damaged my skull. The result of the damage is the loss of my memory. I do not remember many things that happened before the injury, including the birth of Ronan, but I do remember small things sometimes. Like a dream, they come to me fleetingly. I remember that snowy day because of the conversation I had with my father, when I told him that he was the man I most wished to emulate. With everything that happened to me, that is one of the few things I do remember."

"It was a grand day," Rose said, for Blayth's benefit as well as Isabeth's and Ronan's. "My father was as I will always remember him – big, strong, and healthy. He had no sickness as he did in his later years. It was a glorious day for all of us, but more glorious because we knew that we were expecting you,

Ronan. Blayth does not remember, but he was more than thrilled. He knew you would be a son and he knew you would do great things."

Isabeth was smiling. "That is a sweet story," she said. "I do not have a big family, so I can only imagine the happy chaos such a family must create."

Rose laughed softly. "Chaos, indeed," she said. "Like the chaos that is now approaching your door. Do not be afraid of them or think ill of them. They are all simply part of that happiness, of a family who truly loves one another and who celebrates the great moments like this. We are very happy to welcome you into our family and now you, too, are part of the happy chaos."

Isabeth rather liked the sound of that. She smiled at Ronan, who winked at her, but even as that was going on they could hear the noise from the approaching gang of uncles and cousins. Laughter and shouts were echoing off the walls. Someone was calling to Ronan and explaining what he needed to do with his manhood, which was ridiculous considering he had been married before.

But that wasn't something anyone spoke of, ever.

Marian was a thing of the past.

Edmund never did question what had happened when Blayth brought her body home to Lancaster. He was crushed, of course, and he wept appropriately, but he never questioned Blayth. He never even questioned the alliance except to insist it remained intact. It had been a strange reaction from a man who had been so eager to for a marital alliance that he had forced it on Ronan but, in the end, he let that marital link go rather easily even if the alliance remained in force. Blayth wasn't quite sure why except to think that perhaps guilt motivated Edmund's reaction.

Guilt in the daughter he had raised.

In any case, Ronan had married the woman he loved six months after she gave birth to Dyce de Brito's son and, truly, a child had never looked so much like his father. Ronan was enamored with the lad, who was big and healthy, and he knew that Dyce would have been thrilled. In fact, everyone was thrilled, for so many reasons.

Finally, Ronan was to know a little happiness.

It was something not lost on Rose. She'd never agreed with Blayth and the de Grey marriage, so it was a relief to see her son finally happy. The best part of it was that she liked Isabeth, a lovely and gentle creature who treated Ronan with the greatest of respect. That did her mother's heart good.

And that's what brought her to this moment.

"I want to give you something and then Blayth and I will leave, but we both wanted you to have this," she said, pulling forth a small gold ring. Holding it up to the light, she showed them the simple band with two distinct stones – one was blue and the other was brown. "Blayth gave this to me after we married. Ronan, I had always wanted to give you this for your wife but I am sorry to say that I did not want Marian to have it, so I saved it for your eldest child. But now… now, I would like to give it to Isabeth. The blue stone represents your father, because his eyes are blue, and the brown stone represents my brown eyes. The inscription on the inside reads *avec tout mon coeur*."

"With all my heart," Isabeth murmured in translation. "What a beautiful sentiment."

Rose took Isabeth's hand and put the ring in her palm. "I give it to you," she said. "Blayth and I were very much in love when we married. This ring was a symbol of that love and I pray it brings you good fortune."

Ronan went to his mother, kissing her on the cheek. "It already has," he said softly. "Thank you, Mama. We shall cherish it always."

He'd already purchased a plain gold ring for Isabeth, but his mother's ring went against it. As Ronan and Isabeth were admiring the rings, someone pounded loudly on the door and demanded entry. Isabeth jumped, startled, while Ronan chuckled and shook his head.

"I will admit that I have been part of those groups from time to time," he said. "They only do this if they love you. As I recall, they did not do it when I married Marian."

Blayth put his hand on Ronan's shoulder. "Then this is already a good omen," he said, looking between the pair. "We will mind the baby tonight. You two enjoy your evening."

With that, he dropped his hand and looked at Rose, who moved towards the door. "Ready?" she asked him.

Blayth nodded. "Ready."

What the men outside the door forgot was the fact that Rose was Jemma Scott Hage's daughter. A more fearsome, loud, and courageous woman had never lived, so Rose threw open the door and began bellowing at them to clear the corridor in a manner that would have made her mother very proud. Rose had that aura of intimidation about her, so as she cleared out a gang of drunk and happy men twice her size, Blayth fell in behind her, laughing all the way.

That was the Rosie he, in fact, remembered.

Ronan shut the door when they were gone, laughing at his mother's antics. He could still hear her shouting, chuckling when he threw the bolt and turned to his wife.

"What did you call my family?" he said. "Happy chaos? Sometimes it is *simply* chaos. But it is a good deal of fun."

Isabeth went to him, falling into his embrace as the setting sun cast golden rays through the lancet windows. She kissed him sweetly, her hands in his blond hair, savoring the moment.

A moment she thought would never come.

"Tell me it will be like this forever," she murmured. "You and I, happy and content, forever."

Ronan was quickly losing himself in her sweetness. "It will be like this forever," he whispered. "What does the necklace say that I gave you those months ago?"

"The one I never take off?"

"That is because I told you never to take it off."

Isabeth chuckled as she wrapped her arms around his neck and he lifted her up easily, carrying her towards the bed. "It says *'Tis thee, my dear, that I adore, and will, my darling, forever more,*" she said, fingering the pendant that had been front and center on her wedding dress. "I've memorized those words."

Ronan glanced down at the beautiful pearl and gold necklace in her hand. "As have I," he said. "My parents had a great love, once. Now, it is time for ours. You *are* my forever, my darling."

Isabeth smiled. "And you are mine."

In the light of the setting sun, Ronan and Isabeth found something they had both been looking for – that measure of peace that comes only with loving someone and being loved in return. A sense of bliss that comes full circle only once in a lifetime. A sense of peace that is only known by the few who have loved too deeply for words.

'Tis thee, my dear, that I adore, and will, my darling, forever more.

For the first time in her life, Isabeth knew what those words meant.

And so did Ronan.

ॐ THE END ॐ

De Wolfe Pack Generations:
WolfeHeart
WolfeStrike
WolfeSword
WolfeBlade
WolfeLord
WolfeShield

Children of Ronan and Isabeth
Maxwell "Max" de Brito
James
Rhori
Breton "Brett"

Ronan's daughters with Marian:
Anne
Esther
Priscilla

THE PARENTS, CHILDREN, AND GRANDCHILDREN OF DE WOLFE

(Note: Don't be intimidated by these family trees – refer to them if you need clarification on a relationship)

<u>William (deceased 1296 A.D.) and Jordan Scott de Wolfe (deceased)</u>

Total children: 10

Total grandchildren: 75 (including 4 deceased, 7 adopted, 3 stepgrandchildren)

Scott (Troy's twin) – (Wife #1 Lady Athena de Norville, has issue. Wife #2 Lady Avrielle Huntley du Rennic, has issue)

With Athena

- William "Will"
- Thomas "Tor"
- Andrew (deceased)
- Beatrice (deceased)

With Avrielle

- Sophia (with Nathaniel du Rennic)
- Stephen (with Nathaniel du Rennic)
- Sorcha (with Nathaniel du Rennic)
- Jeremy
- Nathaniel

- Alexander
- Seraphina
- Jordan

Troy (Scott's twin) – (Wife #1 Lady Helene de Norville, has issue. Wife #2 Lady Rhoswyn Kerr, has issue)

With Helene

- Andreas
- Acacia (deceased)
- Arista (deceased)

With Rhoswyn

- Gareth
- Corey
- Reed
- Tavin
- Tristan
- Elsbeth
- Madeleine

Patrick – (Married to Lady Brighton de Favereux, has issue)

- Markus
- Cassius
- Magnus
- Titus
- Thora
- Kristiana

James – (Wife #1 Lady Rose Hage, has issue. Wife #2 Asmara ferch Cader, has issue)

With Rose

- Ronan
- Isabella

With Asmara (as Blayth)

- Maddoc
- Bowen
- Caius
- Garreth (known as Garr)

Katheryn (James' twin) – (Married to Sir Alec Hage, has issue)

- Edward
- Axel
- Christoph
- Kieran
- Christian

Evelyn – (Married to Sir Hector de Norville, has issue)

- Atreus
- Hermes
- Lisbet
- Adele
- Aline
- Lesander (goes by Zander)

Baby de Wolfe – (Died same day. Christened Madeleine)

Edward – (Married to Lady Cassiopeia de Norville, has issue)

- Helene

- Phoebe
- Hestia
- Asteria
- Leonidas
- Dorian
- Dayne
- Stephan
- Pallas

Thomas – (Married to Lady Maitland "Mae" de Ryes Bowlin, has issue)

- Artus (adopted)
- Nora (adopted)
- Phin (adopted)
- Marybelle (adopted)
- Renard & Roland (adopted)
- Dyana (adopted)
- Alexander
- Cabot
- Matthew
- Wade
- Tacey
- Morgan

Penelope – (Married to Bhrodi de Shera, Earl of Coventry, hereditary King of Anglesey, has issue)

- William
- Perri

- Bowen
- Dai
- Catrin
- Morgana
- Maddock
- Anthea
- Talan

Kieran and Jemma Scott Hage

- Mary Alys (adopted) – (married, has issue)
- Baby Hage, died same day. Christened Bridget.
- Alec (married to Lady Katheryn de Wolfe, has issue)
- Christian (died in the Holy Land 1269 A.D., no issue)
- Moira (married to Sir Apollo de Norville, has issue)
- Kevin (married to Lady Annavieve de Ferrers, has issue)
- Rose (widow of Sir James de Wolfe, has issue)
- Nathaniel

Paris and Caladora Scott de Norville

- Hector (married to Lady Evelyn de Wolfe, has issue)
- Apollo (married to Lady Moira Hage, has issue)
- Helene (married to Sir Troy de Wolfe, has issue)
- Athena (married to Sir Scott de Wolfe, has issue)
- Adonis
- Cassiopeia (married to Sir Edward de Wolfe, has issue)

HOLDINGS AND TITLES OF THE HOUSE OF DE WOLFE AND CLOSE ALLIES AS OF 1293 A.D.

Scott de Wolfe – Baron Kilham, heir to the Earldom of Warenton (Heir: William "Will" de Wolfe)

Troy de Wolfe – Lord Braemoor (Heir: Andreas de Wolfe)

Patrick de Wolfe – Earl of Berwick (Heir: Markus de Wolfe, Lord Ravensdowne.)

Blayth (James) de Wolfe – Baron Sydenham (Heir: Ronan de Wolfe)

Edward de Wolfe – Baron Kentmere (Heir: Leonidas de Wolfe)

Thomas de Wolfe – Earl of Northumbria (Heir: Alexander de Wolfe, Lord Easington)

Wark Castle (Wolfe's Eye):
Larger outpost for the Earl of Warenton. Literally sits on the border between England and Scotland.

- Titus de Wolfe (son of Patrick de Wolfe), commander

Berwick Castle (Wolfe's Teeth):
Massive border castle, strategically important, de Wolfe holding and seat of the Earl of Berwick, Patrick de Wolfe.

- Alec Hage, commander
- Edward "Eddie" Hage, commander

Castle Questing (Wolfe's Heart):

Massive fortress, seat of the Earl of Warenton, Scott de Wolfe.

- Apollo de Norville, second
- Nathaniel Hage
- Owen le Mon

Rule Water Castle (Wolfe's Lair):

The largest outpost in the de Wolfe empire, known as The Lair. At this time, commanded by Thomas "Tor" de Wolfe.

- Magnus de Wolfe, second
- Adonis de Norville, second
- Perri de Shera, son of the Earl of Coventry and Penelope de Wolfe de Shera (squire)

Monteviot Tower (Wolfe's Shield):

Smaller outpost in Scotland, strategic. Holding of Troy de Wolfe.

- Brodie de Reyne, commander

Kale Water Castle (Wolfe's Den):

Larger outpost on the England side of the border, strategic.

- Troy de Wolfe, Lord Braemoor, commander
- Troy also commands Sibbald's Hold, former home of Red Keith Kerr (his wife's father). A minor property commanded by son, Gareth de Wolfe.

Kyloe Castle (Wolfe's Howl):

Seat of the Earl of Northumbria, Thomas de Wolfe.

- Christoph Hage, second

Roxburgh Castle (Wolfe's Claw – unofficially)*

Large royal-held castle near Kelso, formerly manned by knights from Northwood, but awarded to the House of de Wolfe by royal decree for meritorious service to the crown. Volatile location, often attacked by Scots, and is manned by both royal and de Wolfe troops.

- Blayth (James) de Wolfe, Lord Sydenham, commander
- Axel Hage, second

*Note: Because of the extreme volatile location and nature of this garrison, Blayth (James) de Wolfe was given the title Lord Sydenham and the Sydenham Barony, a small but strategic barony between Wark Castle and the town of Kelso.

Carlisle Castle (Wolfe's Fangs):

Massive and large royal-held castle, perhaps one of the largest castles in the north. Awarded to the House of de Wolfe by royal decree. Very volatile location, often attacked by Scots, and has changed hands many times in its history. The castle is manned by both royal and de Wolfe troops.

- Will de Wolfe, Lord Irthington, commander
- Hermes de Norville

Northwood Castle:

Massive border castle, very important and strategic. Belonging to the Earls of Teviot. Not part of the de Wolfe empire, but strongly allied to de Wolfe by marriage and blood. The Earl of Teviot is John Adrian de Longley, Adam de Longley's eldest son. John's mother is Cayetana Fernanda Teresita Silva y Fausto de Longley, Princess of Aragon.

- Hector de Norville, captain of the guard (also Lord Bowmont)
- Atreus de Norville, second

- Tobias de Bocage, second

Castle Canaan (Wolfe's Bite):
The Earl of Warenton's southernmost holding in Kendal, not directly related to the Scottish border but a source of additional troops if needed. Inherited the property when he married the widow of Castle Canaan.

- Stephan du Rennic, commander

Seven Gates Castle:
Seat of Edward de Wolfe's Barony – Kentmere in Kendal that adjoins brother Scott's lands at Castle Canaan.

- Isleworth House, Surrey

Hell's Guardhouse (The Hermitage):
- Andreas de Wolfe, commander
- Theodis de Velt, second

Ravenscar (fortified manse near Scarborough):
- Ronan de Wolfe
- Christian Hage

KATHRYN LE VEQUE NOVELS

Medieval Romance:

De Wolfe Pack Series:
Warwolfe
The Wolfe
Nighthawk
ShadowWolfe
DarkWolfe
A Joyous de Wolfe Christmas
BlackWolfe
Serpent
A Wolfe Among Dragons
Scorpion
StormWolfe
Dark Destroyer
The Lion of the North
Walls of Babylon
The Best Is Yet To Be

De Wolfe Pack Generations:
WolfeHeart
WolfeStrike
WolfeSword
WolfeBlade
WolfeLord
WolfeShield

The Executioner Knights:
By the Unholy Hand
The Mountain Dark
Starless
The Promise (also Noble Knights of
de Nerra)

A Time of End
Winter of Solace
Lord of the Shadows
Lord of the Sky
Splendid Hour

The de Russe Legacy:
The Falls of Erith
Lord of War: Black Angel
The Iron Knight
Beast
The Dark One: Dark Knight
The White Lord of Wellesbourne
Dark Moon
Dark Steel
A de Russe Christmas Miracle
Dark Warrior

The de Lohr Dynasty:
While Angels Slept
Rise of the Defender
Steelheart
Shadowmoor
Silversword
Spectre of the Sword
Unending Love
Archangel
A Blessed de Lohr Christmas

The Brothers de Lohr:
The Earl in Winter

Lords of East Anglia:
While Angels Slept

Godspeed
Age of Gods and Mortals

Great Lords of le Bec:
Great Protector

House of de Royans:
Lord of Winter
To the Lady Born
The Centurion

Lords of Eire:
Echoes of Ancient Dreams
Blacksword
The Darkland

Ancient Kings of Anglecynn:
The Whispering Night
Netherworld

Battle Lords of de Velt:
The Dark Lord
Devil's Dominion
Bay of Fear
The Dark Lord's First Christmas
The Dark Spawn
The Dark Conqueror
The Dark Angel

Reign of the House of de Winter:
Lespada
Swords and Shields

De Reyne Domination:
Guardian of Darkness
A Cold Wynter's Knight
With Dreams
The Fallen One
Black Storm

House of d'Vant:

Tender is the Knight (House of d'Vant)
The Red Fury (House of d'Vant)

The Dragonblade Series:
Fragments of Grace
Dragonblade
Island of Glass
The Savage Curtain
The Fallen One

Great Marcher Lords of de Lara
Dragonblade

House of St. Hever
Fragments of Grace
Island of Glass
Queen of Lost Stars

Lords of Pembury:
The Savage Curtain

Lords of Thunder: The de Shera Brotherhood Trilogy
The Thunder Lord
The Thunder Warrior
The Thunder Knight

The Great Knights of de Moray:
Shield of Kronos
The Gorgon

The House of De Nerra:
The Promise
The Falls of Erith
Vestiges of Valor
Realm of Angels

Highland Warriors of Munro:
The Red Lion
Deep Into Darkness

The House of de Garr:
Lord of Light
Realm of Angels

Saxon Lords of Hage:
The Crusader
Kingdom Come

High Warriors of Rohan:
High Warrior

The House of Ashbourne:
Upon a Midnight Dream

The House of D'Aurilliac:
Valiant Chaos

The House of De Dere:
Of Love and Legend

St. John and de Gare Clans:
The Warrior Poet

The House of de Bretagne:
The Questing

The House of Summerlin:
The Legend

The Kingdom of Hendocia:
Kingdom by the Sea

Regency Historical Romance:
Sin Like Flynn: A Regency
Historical Romance Duet

Gothic Regency Romance:

Emma

Contemporary Romance:

**Kathlyn Trent/Marcus Burton
Series:**
Valley of the Shadow
The Eden Factor
Canyon of the Sphinx

**The American Heroes Anthology
Series:**
The Lucius Robe
Fires of Autumn
Evenshade
Sea of Dreams
Purgatory

**Other non-connected
Contemporary Romance:**
Lady of Heaven
Darkling, I Listen
In the Dreaming Hour
River's End
The Fountain

Sons of Poseidon:
The Immortal Sea

**Pirates of Britannia Series (with
Eliza Knight):**
Savage of the Sea by Eliza Knight
Leader of Titans by Kathryn Le
Veque
The Sea Devil by Eliza Knight
Sea Wolfe by Kathryn Le Veque

Note: All Kathryn's novels are designed to be read as stand-alones, although many have cross-over characters or cross-over family groups. Novels that are grouped together have related characters or family groups. You will notice that some series have the same books; that is because they are cross-overs. A hero in one book may be the secondary character in another.

There is NO reading order except by chronology, but even in that case, you can still read the books as stand-alones. No novel is connected to another by a cliff hanger, and every book has an HEA.

Series are clearly marked. All series contain the same characters or family groups except the American Heroes Series, which is an anthology with unrelated characters.

For more information, find it in **A Reader's Guide to the Medieval World of Le Veque**.

ABOUT KATHRYN LE VEQUE

Bringing the Medieval to Romance

KATHRYN LE VEQUE is a critically acclaimed, multiple USA TODAY Bestselling author, an Indie Reader bestseller, a charter Amazon All-Star author, and a #1 bestselling, award-winning, multi-published author in Medieval Historical Romance with over 100 published novels.

Kathryn is a multiple award nominee and winner, including the winner of Uncaged Book Reviews Magazine 2017 and 2018 "Raven Award" for Favorite Medieval Romance. Kathryn is also a multiple RONE nominee (InD'Tale Magazine), holding a record for the number of nominations. In 2018, her novel WARWOLFE was the winner in the Romance category of the Book Excellence Award and in 2019, her novel A WOLFE AMONG DRAGONS won the prestigious RONE award for best pre-16th century romance.

Kathryn is considered one of the top Indie authors in the world with over 2M copies in circulation, and her novels have been translated into several languages. Kathryn recently signed with Sourcebooks Casablanca for a Medieval Fight Club series, first published in 2020.

In addition to her own published works, Kathryn is also the President/CEO of Dragonblade Publishing, a boutique publishing house specializing in Historical Romance. Dragonblade's success has seen it rise in the ranks to become Amazon's #1 e-book publisher of Historical Romance (K-Lytics report July 2020).

Kathryn loves to hear from her readers. Please find Kathryn on Facebook at Kathryn Le Veque, Author, or join her on Twitter @kathrynleveque. Sign up for Kathryn's blog at www.kathrynleveque.com for the latest news and sales.